8|12

The Love of Divena

The Love of Divena

Book 3 of the Blessings in India series

Kay Marshall Strom

Nashville, Tennessee

The Love of Divena

ISBN-13: 978-1-4267-0910-4

Published by Abingdon Press, P.O. Box 801, Nashville, TN 37202

www.abingdonpress.com

Published in association with the Books & Such Literary Agency,
Janet Kobobel Grant,
5926 Sunhawk Drive, Santa Rosa, CA 95409
www.booksandsuch.biz.

Library of Congress Cataloging-in-Publication Data

Strom, Kay Marshall, 1943–
The love of Divena / Kay Marshall Strom.
p. cm. — (Blessings in India series ; bk. 3)
ISBN 978-1-4267-0910-4 (book - pbk. / trade pbk.: alk. paper) 1. Caste—India—Fiction. 2. Peonage—India—Fiction. 3. Families—India—Fiction. 4. Christians—India—Fiction. 5. India—History—20th century—Fiction. I. Title.
PS3619.T773L68 2012
813'.6—dc23

2012013132

Printed in the United States of America

1 2 3 4 5 6 7 8 9 10 / 17 16 15 14 13 12

I humbly dedicate this book to the men and women of faith, from all castes and classes, who refuse to give up their fight on behalf of India's poor and oppressed, and to bring the good news of Jesus Christ.

I looked, and there was a great multitude that no one could count, from every nation, from all tribes and peoples and languages, standing before the throne and before the Lamb. . . . They cried out in a loud voice, saying,

"Salvation belongs to our God
who is seated on the
throne, and to the Lamb!"

—Revelation 7:9-10

Acknowledgments

I lovingly acknowledge the many Indian men and women who have encouraged me in my writing of this trilogy, and who have helped me so greatly. I could not have done this without you. Thank you to everyone who opened your home to me, allowed me to share your life and experiences, and invited me to be your sister. We are family, and will be for eternity.

A special thank-you to Dr. James Stewart, who was born in India, for opening his vast library to me. What a gift that was, Jim!

A warm and loving thank-you to Dan Kline, my husband and best editor. How I appreciate you. And once again I thank my faithful reader/editor/friend, Kathy Force. What would I do without you?

The Love of Divena

1

March 1985

A refreshing breeze wafted through the palm fronds and stirred up the fragrance of spring. Taking in a deep breath, the old lady pushed back an unruly lock of gray hair and heaved a sigh of desperate hope. It looked to be a near-perfect market day. The kind of day that lulled her into dreams of selling enough vegetables to afford a whole bag of rice—a small one, of course. Perhaps, if the profits were especially good, she would even buy herself a few pieces of pineapple. What a treat that would be!

Cocking her head to one side, the old lady evaluated her paltry display of vegetables. She artfully repositioned her basket of peppers and pushed the four pitiful cucumbers forward and to one side. A steady stream of shoppers passed by. Men mostly, but a smattering of married women as well. Wives whose husbands had *not* deserted them. Women who need not fear old age, for they had sons to look after them. Many shoppers crowded by, yet few paused to glance at the old lady's vegetables.

"Beautiful hot peppers!" the old lady called in a reedy voice. A forced smile creased her sunken face. "Fresh today! Picked from my own garden this morning."

Still the shoppers hurried past.

Hours later, long after the sun had sucked away every last vestige of the morning breeze, the old lady still had not earned so much as ten *paise*. Not ten pennies.

"Lovely peppers, spicy hot," the old lady sighed.

No, no! She must not allow herself to sound desperate. She brushed a calloused hand across her weathered face and refreshed her smile.

"Cucumbers, fresh from the garden!" The old lady didn't dare call them lovely. Not such small ones, plucked from the vine before they had a chance to finish growing. Still, if someone should have a particular hunger for cucumbers this day, and if hers were the only ones at the market, well, perhaps then . . .

A woman with two whiney children tugging at her green *sari* stopped to pinch the old lady's peppers.

"Fresh and firm," the old lady encouraged.

"We shall see about that," sniffed the woman in the green *sari*. She dug through the old lady's basket and pulled out an especially nice pepper. After giving it a thorough inspection, she laid it aside. As the old lady watched, the woman chose another pepper, then another and another until she had a pile of the best ones. The woman in the green *sari* scowled at her squealing children. "These peppers will do," she announced as she scooped them into her bag. She handed the old lady three ten-*paise* coins. Thirty cents.

"No, no! One *rupee*!" the old lady insisted. Even that was less than she had hoped to get for her nicest vegetables.

"Hah!" laughed the woman in the green *sari*. "Do you think you are the only one selling hot peppers at the market today?"

The old lady tried to protest. She tried to barter. But the loud shouts of the woman in the green *sari* frightened the children and made them cry all the louder. Other shoppers stopped to gawk at the old lady seller who provoked such outrage in her customer. In the end, simply to get rid of the woman and her screaming little ones, the old lady accepted the coins. The woman in the green *sari* pushed her children along ahead of her and hurried away, a triumphant smile on her lips and her bag filled with the finest of the old lady's peppers.

As the sun sank low, a great weariness settled over the old lady. With a sigh of resignation, she hefted her basket of leftover vegetables onto her head and, clutching the three coins in her hand, turned toward home.

Over the years, the dirt road between the marketplace and the old lady's hut had grown so familiar to her feet that she no longer paid it any mind. It used to be that she prayed to the God of the Holy Bible as she walked the road. But that was before her husband deserted her, back when her sons still lived.

As the old lady approached her home, she slowed and stared toward her thatched-roof hut. A few cautious steps, then she stopped and squinted hard into the gathering shadows. Someone sat crumpled against her door. A filthy, muddy someone with wild hair and ragged clothes. A beggar, no doubt. Yes, certainly a beggar, and right in her doorway, too.

"Get away!" the old lady ordered. "This is *my* house!"

The beggar unfolded her small self and lifted her dirty face. A child! Only a skinny little girl. Nine years perhaps, maybe ten. Possibly even a starving eleven-year-old.

The scrawny wisp of a little one stared up with weary eyes. "*Ammama?*" she whispered.

2

Ammama?" the shabby waif said again, but this time more as a soft question immersed in doubt.

The old lady's legs went limp, and the basket slipped from her head. The child stared hungrily at the cucumbers and hot peppers as they tumbled to the ground and rolled through the dirt.

When the old lady recovered herself, she demanded, "Why do you call me Grandmother?" She had not intended her tone to be so sharp. "Who are you? Why are you cowering in my doorway?"

The girl buried her face in her dirty hands and sobbed.

"What is your mother's name?" the old lady asked. For the girl had called her *Ammama*—"mother of my mother," not *Achama*—"mother of my father."

The girl swiped her hand across her dirt-streaked cheeks. "Ritu," she said, choking back tears. "They called my *amma* Ritu." She wiped her eyes with the tail of her tattered shirt. "But I do not have an *amma* anymore."

"Where is she?"

The girl shook her head sadly. "One day she would not wake up. *Appa* said we must leave her on the sidewalk where she lay. My sister and I said goodbye to her because *Appa* said we must. We left that day. For many days we walked, my sister and me with my father . . ." Tears overtook the girl, and she could say no more.

The old lady sank to her knees. Could it be possible? Her daughter. Her sweet Ritu. The old lady's husband had insisted on marrying the girl off at far too young an age to a selfish little man whose name the old lady struggled to remember. Puran. Yes, that's what he was called. Puran. Shortly after the marriage, he had forced her Ritu to leave the village, and the old lady never saw her again.

"Why did you come here?" the old woman demanded.

The child, her black eyes flashing, shot back, "I did not come! My *appa* brought me. He promised a new home for my sister and me, but then he said he had grown tired of taking care of himself and wanted to find a new wife. He left my sister on the steps of an orphanage, and he brought me here to you."

"What am I to do with you?"

"I did not want to come!" The defiance in the child's voice shocked the old lady into silence. She opened her hand and looked at the three thin coins. Thirty *paise*. All she had reaped for an entire day of work at the market. Her earthenware rice container on the shelf in her hut contained, at the most, two handfuls of rice. Enough to last the two of them three days. Maybe four, if they ate only one small meal each day. She would take her peppers back to the market tomorrow, of course, but she could not make shoppers buy them.

"What is your name?" the old lady asked as she walked toward the girl.

"Anjan," the child said.

"Anjan! Why would my daughter call her child such a name? Fear! What kind of name is that for a little one?"

The girl stared at the ground. But the old lady had already seen the waif's face. She recognized the look of terror in the flash of the child's dark eyes. That poor young one was doomed to live out her name.

"Come," the old lady said in a gentled voice. "I will cook us some rice with spicy peppers. Would you like that? We will have cucumbers, too. They are not quite ripe, but they will still be good."

For the first time, the hint of a smile touched the edges of the girl's mouth.

The old lady pulled dried sticks from her small store of firewood and started a blaze in the cook pit. As she bent down to tend it, she took care to position herself in such a way that she could see the girl hunkered in the doorway. The girl watched her pour water into the cooking pot and set it over the fire. From the almost-empty rice container, the old lady took half a handful of rice and stirred it into the pot. Half a handful and not one grain more.

"We shall eat slowly," she told the girl. "That way we will not need much rice in our bowls."

The girl said nothing.

The old lady dropped a handful of chili peppers into the pot, too. And because it was a special occasion, she added a pinch of precious spices.

"Two cucumbers," she said to the girl. "Do you like cucumbers?"

The girl wrinkled her brow and said, "I do not know. I never ate one."

"Good!" said the old lady. "Then you will not know whether these are ripe or not."

When the old lady handed over a bowl of rice and peppers, the child grabbed it and lapped it up like a starving animal. After she licked her bowl clean, she started on her cucumber. She didn't stop until she had eaten the entire thing, even the wilted blossom that clung to the end.

"I am not particularly hungry," the old lady said as casually as she could manage. "Do you suppose you would be able to finish my rice as well?" She reached her bowl out to the girl.

The girl's eyes narrowed suspiciously.

"Please take it. I have had quite enough."

The girl looked straight up into the old lady's faded eyes, but only for a moment. She grabbed the bowl and quickly scooped the rice into her mouth.

"Tomorrow I will take a water pot and fill it at the pond," the old lady said. "Pond water will be fine to wash the mud from your face. And perhaps—"

"No," the girl insisted. "Going for water is my job. I will take the empty pot to the pond and bring it back full."

The dirt-floor hut, small and cramped and almost always too hot, never provided a pleasant place to sleep. Like most everyone else in the village, the old lady pulled her sleeping mat outside at night and slept under the stars.

"I only have one sleeping mat," she told the girl as she spread it out. "Come, lie down beside me."

The girl didn't move.

"You must be very tired. Come and lie down."

Out of the corner of her eye, the old lady watched the girl's small form squeeze over close to the wall.

Anjan. *Fear.* The only name the girl had ever known. A name for one who must forever cower in the shadows.

"My *appa* was called Ashish—Blessing—because from the day he was born his parents knew he would be a blessing to them," the old lady said. "My *appa* and *amma* named me Shridula because they looked on me as their blessing—even though I was nothing but a girl."

The child pulled away from the wall and inched toward the sleeping mat.

"You did not want to be left in my doorway," the old lady said in a soft voice. "I did not want you left here, either, because I have no money to buy food for you. But here you are. We will live together, you and me."

The child crept a bit closer.

"I will not call you Anjan," her grandmother said. "I will call you Divena. I will call you Divine Blessing, because God sent you to be a blessing to me."

3

Five Years Later

March 1990

Divena, still short and thin at the age of sixteen, sat upright on her sleeping mat and blinked into an early-morning gray sky. Something wasn't right. A gentle puff of pre-dawn breeze ruffled the tree branches overhead. She rubbed the sleep from her eyes. Perplexed, she looked over at her grandmother's sleeping mat that should have been empty by now but was not. Her grandmother, face flushed, groaned in restless slumber.

Odd. Usually her grandmother had a cooking fire started before the first traces of morning light. Soon, swaths of pink and orange would split the gray sky, so the cold fire pit should already be glowing. Divena should already be on her way to the well.

"*Ammama?*" the girl whispered. "Are you all right, *Ammama?*"

Shridula moaned as she rolled over onto her back. Her gray hair, damp and stringy, clung to her perspiration-drenched face.

Gently, Divena caressed her grandmother's hot face. "Wake up, *Ammama*!" she pleaded. If only her grandmother would rouse herself and wipe the sleep from her eyes. She wanted her to pull herself up and lay the morning fire the way she always did. Divena wanted her to grumble about her stiff old bones and scowl at the near-empty food pots the way she did every other morning. But Shridula didn't open her eyes.

Uncertain and shaken, Divena stood up and raked her fingers through the tangles in her thick black hair. She smoothed her dingy *sari* and did her best to tug out the worst of the wrinkles. For a moment she hesitated, but the edges of the sky had already started to turn pink. So the girl grabbed up the empty water pots and set off for the well.

Before Divena had gone far, a voice called from behind, "Wait for me!" Young Neela hurried up, a water pot balanced on her head and another riding on her hip.

Divena sighed. She had no desire to listen to Neela's childish chatter. Not this day, when she had so many worries running through her mind.

"Why do you walk so fast?" Neela demanded. "You have time. The sun is not even up yet."

"My *Ammama*. She is not well."

"Oh." Neela shrugged. "Well, she is old."

An overwhelming urge to run all the way to the well swept over Divena. A longing to leave foolish Neela standing alone in the dust of the road. What did that girl know about *Ammama?* What did she know about anything?

"Yesterday I saw a fine woman walking on our road," Neela said. "She had on a new *sari*—silk, I think. It had pleats in the front."

Pleats? A high caste woman, then. Only high caste ladies wore pleats in the front of their *saris*. It used to be a law. Now it was only a caste rule that everyone obeyed.

"Someone said she is a teacher from another village." Neela stopped her prattle to squint over at Divena. "I am as tall as you are, and you are skinnier than me. But you are very much older than I am. Is your grandmother ever going to find a husband for you?"

A deep blush burned over Divena's face. What a thing to say! Neela may be young, but even she should know better than to hurt others with her tongue.

"I have no time to talk today," Divena snapped. Without waiting for a response, she rushed on ahead.

By the time Divena got back to the last cluster of huts at the end of the road where her grandmother lived—downwind from the upper castes who didn't want to smell the stench of polluted people—the full water pots weighed heavily on her shoulders. The sun glowed above the horizon. The day had begun.

The first thing Divena noticed was a thin line of smoke rising from the cook pit beside her grandmother's hut. She grabbed a firm hold on the water pots and jogged the rest of the way, sloshing water all over herself.

"*Ammama!*" she cried when she saw the hunched form of her grandmother bent over the smoking fire. "You are well, then?"

"Take care with that water or you will have to go back and get more," the old lady scolded. "Of course I am well. I have no time to lie around and moan."

"I feared—"

"Feared?" Shridula straightened her back and looked up into the girl's face. "Did we not decide to do away with our fear?"

Even so, Shridula, who usually stood so strong and sure, trembled over the rice pot. Divena willed herself to not be afraid. She knelt down, took her grandmother's shaking hands in hers, and caressed them. How she longed to throw her arms around her *Ammama's* neck and beg her to stay well. But Shridula pulled away. The rice had begun to boil.

"You have work to do, Divena," Shridula said.

Divena did. She had peppers to pick from their large vegetable patch. Spinach leaves to break off. Cucumbers to pull from the vines.

"Do not pick them yet," Shridula said of the cucumbers. "Let them grow bigger. You will get more money for them if you wait a few days."

Yes, but waiting was not always wise, either. Later others would also have cucumbers to sell at the market. Farmers and men with gardens. Shoppers preferred to buy from them. Divena only had an advantage if her produce appeared in the marketplace first, or if it was better, or much cheaper. Mostly her customers looked for cheaper.

When Shridula turned back to stir the rice, Divena tugged the two largest cucumbers from the vine and slipped them under her mound of peppers. Her grandmother need not know everything.

At the far end of the village market—past the farmers' carts loaded high with produce washed and stacked into neat piles, past the merchants' stands with sacks of spices and bags of nuts and stacks of fabrics, past stalls selling delicious things to eat, past the pleasant shelter of banyan trees—Divena unfolded her thin blanket and laid out her meager display of fresh vegetables. Not so many shoppers came all the way out to the market's fringes. Especially not the men with the most coins in their pockets. But the better spots were not for the likes of Divena.

"Look, I have ripe mangos today!" Selvi announced as she hurried to set up her own wares.

Divena looked longingly at her friend's golden fruit. She closed her eyes and breathed in the enticing fragrance. Selvi also had two fine stalks of red bananas, but it was the ripe mangos that called to Divena.

"My father says I am not to give anything away to you," Selvi said. "He says you must buy like anyone else." But then her eyes twinkled, and a grin spread across her face. "Do not worry yourself, though. I conveniently dropped one of the mangos on the road and it split open, so of course I cannot sell it. Later, when the sun gets hotter, we will share it." Selvi threw her head back and laughed out loud.

Divena kept her gaze away from the other sellers: women with baskets of gleaned custard apples, the milkman's wife with her cans of watered-down milk and hunks of cheese, the wrinkled old woman with purple-black skin who sold peppercorns—green, red, and black. All of them scowled at Selvi, even when she didn't talk noisily and laugh out loud. They whispered that she didn't keep her head lowered like a proper Indian woman of her low status. They murmured that her hair, bobbed to her shoulders and hanging loose, disgraced her. They looked through narrowed eyes at the stylish blue and white two-piece *salwar kameez* she wore instead of a traditional *sari*, and they clicked their tongues. "She watches television," they whispered to one another with knowing nods.

Divena liked Selvi and enjoyed being with her—most of the time. But she didn't want to bring shame on her grandmother, so she busied herself rearranging the vegetables on her blanket.

Selvi continued with her laughing chatter. People stopped to look over her fruit. If they turned to walk away, she pointed them to Divena's vegetables. Some of these shoppers actually bought a few peppers or a handful of spinach leaves.

One shopper selected fruit from Selvi's display and laid the pieces together in a pile. "Two ripe mangos," Selvi counted out loud. "Fifty *paise* two times. Don't they smell good? And two green mangos. Forty *paise* for each of them. Oh, and bananas, too. One, two, three, four, five, six, seven, eight. Eight bananas. Eighty-eight *paise* for them."

As Divena watched her friend, she also counted the total, but silently in her mind.

Selvi started to count on her fingers: "Fifty paise two times is one hundred *paise*. One *rupee*. Forty *paise* two times is, um, eighty *paise*. And eighty-eight more is, uh . . ." She shook her head in complete confusion, the same as she did every other day. Selvi never could keep accounts.

"Two *rupees*, sixty-eight *paise*," Divena whispered to Selvi. The same as she did every other day.

On the best market days, Selvi could earn as much as five rupees. Divena never did that well. "It is not your fault," Selvi assured her. "It is only that my fruit is so much better than your vegetables."

At the end of the day, Divena counted her coins: three *rupees*, eighty-one *paise*. A good day's earnings for her. "Will you watch my vegetables?" she asked Selvi. Then she slipped over to the tobacconist's stall.

A chew of tobacco, her grandmother's one vice. Shridula had stopped buying it when Divena came to live with her. More important to have rice, she said. She could chew *betel nut* for much less cost. But now and then she surely did enjoy a pinch of real tobacco. This would be a good day for Divena to surprise her with some.

"I hate the village," Selvi said as the girls started the trek back to their homes.

"Why?"

"It is so boring," Selvi said. "Nothing ever changes here. And it is filled with fools."

The sky glowed bright orange, as though the heavens were ablaze. "Oh, just look at the setting sun," Divena gasped. "The village does have—"

But Selvi interrupted, wrinkling her face to show her disgust. "Do not tell me you actually *like* that cluster of huts where you live!"

"It is not like or dislike. I understand life there with my grandmother. I feel comfortable with it. I know what is expected of me."

"Everything is different in the city," Selvi said. "If we lived there, we could ride the bus home from the market. Or get a ride on the back of someone's motorbike. Maybe even in someone's car. We would relax in a room with electric fans and read books to each other about strange places and new things. We might even *go* to some of those strange places!"

Divena didn't answer. But the expression on her face said, *Selvi does not know everything.*

"If we got sick in the city, we would go to a real doctor, not to Mahima with all her herbs and *mantras*. We would have real medicine, and we would get well quickly."

"Maybe."

With a giggle, Selvi whispered, "We would even talk to men."

Divena's eyes popped. "Why? What would we say to a man?"

"Anything we wanted! Maybe we would say, 'The sun is hot today.' Or 'These ripe mangos taste delicious.' Or maybe we would say, 'Can I ride on your motorbike with you?'"

Divena almost dropped the basket of vegetables off her head. "Really, Selvi, how do you think of such things?"

"Television. My father's friend has one, and sometimes I watch it. Many shows are about the city. In the city, girls do exciting things all the time. I wish we lived in a city."

Selvi and her father lived in a wood house with a courtyard, still at the *Dalit* end of the village, but in a better section than did Divena and her grandmother. Closer to the *Sudra*s, who might be poor, but were people of caste. Divena had never seen a television, but she did remember life in the city. People, people, everywhere. Filthy streets lined with lean-tos thrown together from sticks and palm leaves and discarded plastic bags. Her family had once lived in one of those lean-tos. Pigs and goats rooted about in the garbage piles, eating whatever they could find. Beggars clogged the streets. Beggars like her own blind sister.

"I like the village," Divena said.

"Divena! Divena!"

Selvi had already gone on to her father's house and Divena had just turned off onto the path to her grandmother's hut, when a figure ran toward her, head bare and *sari* flapping.

"Divena! You must come quickly!"

"Mahima?" Divena called out. "Is that you?"

"Quickly! Quickly!" Mahima cried. "Your grandmother is terribly ill. Hurry!"

4

March

"Humaya!" Ajay Varghese called out the passenger-side window of his pick-up truck. "How goes the rice planting?"

The mud-splattered overseer pulled his *chaddar* off his head and wiped it across his face. "The lower paddies are tilled and planted, Master Landlord. The upper ones . . ." Humaya spread his arms wide. "They are soaking with river water right now. As soon as it recedes, we will bring in buffalo and turn the earth. Then we can begin the planting up there, too."

"Good, good!" Ajay said. "With God's blessing all will be planted before the summer rains."

"Yes, Master Landlord," Humaya replied with a bow. "If the gods smile on us, it will be so."

Ajay motioned to his son Sundar to drive on toward the road. "Humaya had better be telling me the truth," he muttered.

Even at the age of forty-three, and despite his nearly bald head, Ajay Varghese boasted an impish, boy-like expression. His face was round and dimpled, almost sweet. He prided himself on looking the part of a modern-day businessman—

moustache and beard neatly trimmed, crisp Western-style shirt, trousers with a pressed-in crease.

"What is this?" Ajay grabbed the end of the white *chaddar* his son had draped around his neck. "Sundar! Do not wrap that around your head in a turban. It makes you look like an *Untouchable* laborer."

"It keeps the sun off my head." Sundar glanced at his father and struggled to keep from smiling. "Which is probably why the *Harijans* do it."

"*Harijans! Dalits! Outcastes*! Call them what you will, they are still nothing but *Untouchables*," Ajay grumbled.

That his eldest son would condescend to carelessly mix in with the laborers exasperated the powerful landowner. That his son cared not the least what others thought frustrated him beyond endurance.

Ajay took a deep breath. "You are my first son," he said to Sundar. "And in many ways, you are my best. Jeevak does a good job of working in the fields and pushing for more progress. Ramesh is intelligent in a bookish way. But you are the one who shows the greatest potential. Even so, you must earn the right to be the next landlord."

"Yes, Father," Sundar said.

Ajay shook his head and sighed. "That is all you have to say? At such a compliment, Jeevak would be kissing my hand."

"I am sure he would."

"You work hard and you reason well. But it is Jeevak who shows passion. Foolish, impulsive passion at times, but passion nevertheless."

Sundar said nothing.

"What I am saying is that you must think over all the ramifications of a situation before you act. Consider it from all sides, then take a wise approach. But—" He searched his son's face. Impassive, as usual. "I appreciate all you do, and do so well, my son. But how I wish you would . . . could . . . *care*!"

In the midlands of India's southern state of Kerala, under the distant shadows of the great mountain peaks of the Western Ghats, Varghese land spread out rich and fertile. While the landlord took his first son around his vast lands to inspect the property, his second son, Jeevak, sloshed through the rice paddies and directed the actual work. Charming Sundar drove the truck, his father by his side, offering advice; filthy Jeevak slogged through the stinking paddy mud and carried out his brother's ideas. Handsome Sundar rejected every young woman his father proposed as a wife; muddy Jeevak could not marry until after his older brother had wed.

"You!" Jeevak called to a gap-toothed man guiding a plow behind a water buffalo. "Keep that line straight!"

Up ahead, a group of women, each carrying a basket of sprouted rice seedlings, prepared to start the planting. "No, no!" Jeevak called out to them. "Do not plant until the field has been properly flattened!" But he didn't look at them. His eyes lingered on a comely girl of thirteen or fourteen.

Jeevak pulled his eyes away from the young girl. "Humaya!" he yelled. "What kind of overseer are you? This area is not ready for planting. Move those workers on until you have this paddy properly prepared. And get it done immediately!"

Humaya bowed and poured forth his profound apologies and gratitude for Jeevak's wisdom. The overseer shouted new orders to the workers. But as soon as Jeevak moved away toward the road, Humaya motioned for the laborers to resume work as before.

At mid-morning, Jeevak passed by a handful of women who were finishing up planting an especially fine paddy. Twenty-three women, muddy and perspiring, worked standing, their legs straight, bent over at the waist to reach the ground. The twenty-fourth, a fair wisp of a girl, crouched over her work in a most delicate way. Her straw hat had tumbled back, and wisps of fine hair curled around her lovely face. Her hair seemed to be streaked with gold, and her shaded face the color of ripe wheat blowing in the field. Pale skin . . . cultured ways . . . Jeevak felt certain that from somewhere deep in her past she must hold vestiges of high-caste breeding.

"You!" Jeevak called to her. "What is your name?"

The young woman looked up in confusion. "Baka, Master," she said.

"You need not work for the remainder of the morning, Baka."

Baka hunkered in the mud and poked another seedling into the ground.

"I am telling you to quit work for the rest of the morning!" Jeevak said again.

"But, sir, I still have planting to do."

"Go to your hut, clean yourself up, and take a rest." The other women turned to stare, which made Jeevak most uncomfortable. He cleared his throat and removed the gruffness from his voice. "The sun is too much for your fair skin. My father does not want his workers ill from the heat."

The laborers exchanged meaningful glances. Baka didn't move.

"Now!" Jeevak ordered. "Back to your hut with you!"

As soon as he could get away, Jeevak followed Baka to her stark wooden hut. He found her sitting on the bare floor, her face streaked with tears. She wore the same muddy *sari* she had on in the field, though she had scrubbed her hands and arms and combed the worst of the mud from her hair. Sighing, Jeevak decided, *Well, she is a laborer, after all.*

"You are quite beautiful, for one of your kind," Jeevak whispered. He knelt next to the lovely young woman and reached out to caress her creamy skin.

Baka pulled away.

"I would suggest you watch yourself!" Sharpness edged Jeevak's voice . . . cutting sharpness tinged with threat. "It is in my power to make your life here pleasant and easy. Or, if I choose, I can guarantee that you will be most miserable."

Baka winced in spite of herself. "I have a husband," she murmured.

"Do you now? Well, it really does not matter, does it? I own both of you." Jeevak pulled her roughly into his arms.

"Please, Master Landlord," Baka begged. "Please, no!"

But Jeevak had already pulled the dirty cloth of her *sari* off her head and slipped it down from her shoulders. He reached out to caress her.

"You insult me with your tears," Jeevak scolded. "Someone like you is lucky to attract a fine, wealthy, high caste man. Especially one as good-looking as I am." He grabbed hold of Baka's hair and forced her head back. "Look at me! Look at me and tell me how handsome I am! Tell me what a lucky woman—"

At that moment a chunk of firewood cracked against the back of Jeevak's head. For a moment he sat still and stared uncomprehendingly at Baka. His mouth worked, but he couldn't form any words. Then he slumped forward, his bleeding head in Baka's lap.

Baka leapt up, shaking uncontrollably. "What have you done?" she cried. "What have you *done?*"

"Saved your honor," said Kilas. "Saved my wife."

Baka covered her face with the edge of her *sari* and wailed.

Baka herself had run back to the paddy, screaming for help. The landlord, talking with Humaya, completely ignored the girl as he rushed to Jeevak. Together he and Sundar lifted Jeevak into the truck bed. All the way home, Ajay Varghese cradled his son's bleeding head in his lap.

That evening, as the doctor prepared to leave the landlord's house—Jeevak's head swathed in bandages, his stomach filled with strong drugs—Ajay Varghese said, "My son is a fool. But the workers belong to me. I have the right to do with them as I will."

"By what law, Father?" Sundar asked him.

"By the law of this village! By the law of our people! I am the landlord, so I need no other law!"

The landlord's punishment fell brutally. At Ajay Varghese's command, his servants dragged both Baka and her husband before him, their hands tied fast behind their backs. The landlord himself raised the stiff wooden switch his son used on the tough hides of stubborn bullocks and slashed it down across Baka's back. She crumpled to the ground.

"Stop!" Kilas cried. "It is against the law for you to do this to us!"

"The law! The law! Forget the law and ask us what is right!" To his servant, Ajay ordered, "Pull the shirt off his back!"

Ajay clenched his teeth and again raised the switch high. "I have the right to punish you, and I most certainly will!" He lashed a blow across Kilas's bare back. Kilas clenched his teeth and shuddered but did not cry out. Ajay struck another blow.

"We are your laborers, but you do not own us!" Kilas cried.

Another blow. Then another. Kilas fell to his knees. Another and another, until Kilas fell flat and lay silent on the ground.

Ajay turned his attention to Baka. "You! Get back up on your feet!"

He strode toward an old woman who sobbed as she stirred up an already prepared fire. Shoving her aside, Ajay grabbed the cool end of a red hot iron, ready and waiting in the pit. He jerked it from the fire.

"Get her up and keep her still," Ajay ordered his servant. "Hold her by her hair so she cannot move."

The servant hesitated.

"Do it!" Ajay commanded. "Now!"

The servant pulled Baka to her feet. She could barely stand, so he grabbed a handful of her hair and yanked it tight. As the old woman continued to wail, as the laborers stared in shocked silence, Ajay carried the sizzling iron to Baka. "Bow to Jeevak!" he ordered. "Jeevak is my son, and that means he is your master. Bow to him!"

Baka lowered her head, but as she did so, she spat out something unintelligible.

"Never again will you lure a high caste man to you!" Ajay roared. He pressed the glowing iron across the girl's tender cheek and down over her mouth. She let out a horrible shriek through blistered lips.

Then she fell to the ground unconscious.

After a most unsettling week, Ajay, enveloped in the heady spring scent of new jasmine blossoms, sat on a low-slung sofa pushed back into a corner of the veranda. His feet rested on his great-great-grandfather's exquisite Persian carpet. Ajay picked up his teacup and took a long sip. Tea, thick and sweet, exactly the way he liked it. Pale with rich water buffalo milk. He smacked his lips and said to his sons, "The planting goes especially well."

So rich and lush lay the Varghese expanse of land that it willingly produced two crops every year. Unless the rains or stifling heat came at the wrong times. Ajay had endured his share of grain shriveled in the fields or mildewed on the stalks. But that would not happen this year. This year he would fill his storehouse with rice and his coffers with *rupees*.

Weather. Crops. The state of the world. Ajay discussed all these topics with his sons. At the end of each day, they ate their evening meal together out on the veranda, or inside in the sitting room, depending on the weather. (Ajay refused his sons' pleas to invest in an air-cooling unit.) They lingered for hours afterward, drinking tea and watching the sun set. They talked of many things, but never of Jeevak's indiscretion, nor of the beatings that had followed it.

Kilas had spoken the truth; such behavior toward workers *was* against the law. But, Ajay reasoned, what else could a father expect from so rash a son as Jeevak? "I will get a girl for him," Ajay told his wife, Hanita. "An *Untouchable* woman, who has no husband and who knows nothing about the law. She will be his plaything, and he can do with her as he wishes."

"What do you intend to do? Kidnap a young woman?"

"No, no," Ajay said. "I am an honorable man. When I find the right girl, I will make her a loan that she cannot repay."

Ajay knew he must be careful. He must take his time and form a good plan. That was the only way to prove to everyone that he was still in charge. That nothing was done without his knowledge and approval.

As for this current embarrassment, clearly Jeevak had been at fault, and he must be made to pay. But what Ajay would do—and when—no one knew. The reckoning loomed heavy, but not one of his sons dared speak of it.

Bandages still swathed Jeevak's wounded head. As for Baka and Kilas, they no longer lived in the settlement. To add to the Varghese embarrassment, the day after the beatings, when everyone assumed they still couldn't walk, the two disappeared. One day Kilas stumbled painfully around his shack, and the next day both were gone.

One by one, the Varghese sons lifted their teacups and drank. To not speak of that disagreeable affair suited them fine. Except that they knew it to be only a matter of time. The discussion would come up, and when it did, their father's rage was sure to strike. Waiting was excruciating.

"Nothing in the village escapes my attention," Ajay stated to his sons.

Three teacups, clutched in the hands of his three boys, froze in dread.

"Nothing on my land or in my settlement passes without my notice. What kind of landlord would I be if I did not make certain of that? I am aware of everything that happens here."

Jeevak attempted to set his cup down, but his hands shook so violently he couldn't manage it. Sundar and Ramesh did their best to ignore their brother's distress.

"When I made that worker woman bow to you, Jeevak . . . You do remember that, my son, do you not?"

Remember? The horror of that moment would be seared into his memory forever.

"She said something to you. What did she say, Jeevak?"

Jeevak's trembling hands knocked his cup over. He grabbed at it, but the tea spilled into his lap. His father gazed at the puddle of milky tea as it spread out over his son's jeans. In the mildest of voices he asked, "Is something bothering you, my son?"

"I cannot recall her saying anything," Jeevak replied in a strained mumble.

Everyone knew that to be a lie. Everyone knew she had called Jeevak "the despicable son of the devil."

"Her husband," Ajay said thoughtfully. "His name slips my mind. What did they call him, again?"

Jeevak didn't even try to answer. He cradled his aching head in his hands and squeezed his eyes shut.

"Sundar, please tell your brother the man's name. He seems to be a bit forgetful this evening."

"Kilas," Sundar said. "His name is Kilas." Sundar kept his eyes fixed on his own teacup.

"Yes. Well. As it turns out, this Kilas is not just another *Harijan* raised to do as he is told. But I guess he already showed you that, Jeevak, did he not?"

Perspiration broke out on Jeevak's face. He folded his hands to keep them from trembling.

"This Kilas is of high birth. A *Vaisaya*, from the merchant caste. A student at the university who dropped out of school to pay off his parents' debt."

"That makes no sense," Ramesh protested. The youngest Varghese son also happened to be a university student. "Only a crazy person would willingly quit his studies to become a slave."

Slowly Jeevak shook his head. In a pained voice he said, "Such a beautiful girl. Like a goddess. I should have known she could not be a *Harijan*."

Ajay slammed his fist down on the table. "Does not one of you see the significance of this? That man quoted the law. He *knows*!"

"But that woman and her husband are gone, Father," Ramesh said. "Surely the matter is behind us."

"If only it were," Ajay said. "But outrage does not die easily. Outrage seethes. Outrage lies in wait."

5

March

Divena, trembling, kept her gaze away from Mahima. "Selvi says my *Ammama* needs a real doctor."

"Oh? And which *real* doctor would that be?" Mahima asked. "The one who treats only people from the high castes?"

"No, no. I only meant—"

"How would you get your grandmother to that real doctor? Carry her on your back?"

Tears filled Divena's eyes. "Selvi's father has a horse cart. Maybe he would—"

"Would Selvi's father also pay the real doctor the money the man would demand? Or perhaps you plan to go begging for a loan at the door of the landlord."

Shridula moaned as she tossed restlessly on her mat. Through parched lips, she begged for a cup of water.

"See how you have upset her!" Mahima scolded. "If you were a true blessing, you would not talk the way you do. After I make your grandmother well, surely she will change your name to something ugly."

Divena said no more.

"Hurry to the well," Mahima ordered. "I need more water. This time your grandmother's malaria is much worse than ever before, and her body is too old and too hungry to fight it."

Divena took up the water pots and, with hesitating steps, headed for the road. Darkness gathered fast. No one else would be on their way to the well at this late hour—at least, no one Divena cared to meet in the dark of night.

"Hurry!" Mahima called after her. "Your grandmother suffers!"

Every rustling bush Divena passed seemed to quiver with peril. Every shadow looked as though it sheltered menace. Even the trees that offered such welcoming shade from the glaring daytime sun, in the dark seemed to smell of danger. Divena quickened her pace faster and faster until her feet raced along the road.

Worst of all, Divena was convinced that everything Mahima said was true. Divena *had* no money for a doctor. The health clinic *was* far away. She did *not* have any way to get her grandmother there. Of course Selvi's father would not take her. Divena knew that. Anyway, surely Mahima must know the art of healing. The village respected her. Not only for her abilities, but also for her kindness. Divena determined that she would work out some way to pay Mahima. Whatever she asked, Divena would give her. Mahima would make her grandmother well.

Selvi did not know everything.

Divena passed the stand of *neem* trees and approached a stretch of flat rice paddies. She looked up and smiled appreciatively at the rising moon. Only a quarter moon, not even bright enough to cast shadows across her path, yet it gave off enough light to make it easier for her to walk along the road. Half-walking, half-running, Divena arrived at the well in record time. With no crowd around, with no one wanting to stand and gossip, she quickly drew the water and hurried toward home.

Going back home from the well, with the moon behind her, proved to be more difficult. The ruts in the road hid in shadows, tree roots that jutted out to trip her lay camouflaged in shade. It forced Divena to walk much more slowly and carefully. She also had to balance a full water pot on her head and another on her hip.

"So large a load for so scrawny a girl." Divena started at the sound of a man's voice close behind her. "I could carry one pot for you."

Selvi's father, perhaps? Or someone who recognized her from the market? With one hand, Divena grabbed hold of the water pot on her head; and with the other, she gripped more tightly the one on her hip. She stepped deftly to the side and looked behind to see who the stranger might be.

Knobby-kneed and a bit hunched, the man had his *chaddar* wrapped high around his shoulders and neck, instead of around his head like a turban, so that it obscured his face.

With a gasp of dismay at so mysterious a person, Divena attempted to bolt away.

But the man acted quickly. He leapt after her and seized her by the arm. The pot tumbled from her head, though she managed to grab it before it fell to the ground.

"Now look what you have done!" Divena cried. "My grandmother needs this water!"

"Let the medicine woman fetch it for her," the man said. "Why should you be her servant?"

Divena gasped in amazement. How did he know about Mahima?

That voice. The glare of defiance in those black eyes. Divena stared hard at the man who still gripped her arm.

"*Appa?*" she said. "Is that you, Father?"

Bark from the healing *neem* tree. Yes, that would be Mahima's first ingredient. Sick animals chewed on *neem* trees and then got well. Mahima had seen it with her own eyes. She would add an equal amount of the fleshy stems of *guduchi*. Mahima knew where to find the plants. She'd need cinnamon and cardamom, too, both of which she already had in abundance. Once she got the water, she would boil all the ingredients together and stir, boil and stir, until the mixture reached a syrupy texture. In another pot she would boil sugary palm tree sap down into *jiggery* and mix that with her medicinal concoction.

But Mahima couldn't get the medicine started until Divena got back with the water. What could be taking the girl so long?

Mahima glanced over to see the old lady staring at her with glazed eyes.

"Shridula?" Mahima said. "You are awake?"

"*Un . . . touchable*," Shridula mumbled. She struggled to sit up. "Do not call me *Harijan* . . . I am not a child of those gods. Do not call me . . . *Dalit*. I am not something broken. I will not be fixed."

"Come, come," Mahima soothed. "Lie back and close your eyes. It is the fever talking."

"No, it is me talking," Shridula insisted, "and I say I am *Untouchable*!"

"Lie back and close your eyes."

Shridula fell back onto her sweat-drenched mat, and her eyes drifted closed.

When Mahima went to collect the *neem* bark, she resolved that she would also get leaves from the sacred *neem* tree to lay before the goddess. In case her concoction wasn't strong enough. Shridula may refuse to worship the goddess, but

Mahima would do it in her place. Just as soon as Divena returned.

Puran did his best to straighten the hunch in his back and stand up taller. He pulled the *chaddar* down from his face and tried to remember how to smile. "Daughter," he cooed. "You have grown up so lovely. How I have missed you since that fateful day I agreed to allow your grandmother to have you for a while."

Divena glared at him. "You deserted me! You pushed Tanaya screaming into an orphanage, then you left me in *Ammama's* doorway."

"Only for a while, my dear," Puran insisted. The smile left his lips, and his eyes hardened. "Your sister is better off where she is. Forget her. But I have come back for you."

Shaking, Divena set the water pots on the ground beside her and struggled to think. Should she scream? No one would hear her. She must escape. But how? How? She couldn't think! Her feet felt like heavy boulders.

"Are you thinking of running from me?" her father taunted. "What a foolish girl you are. You have been along this road many more times than I. How is it that I am the one who knows there is nothing along here but rice paddies?"

Divena blinked away tears of desperation. "How did you know I would be out fetching water in the middle of the night?"

"I did not know, of course. Pure *karma* that I should see you." Puran laughed. "It would seem that the gods look more kindly on me than they do on you . . . Anjan."

Anjan? He knew so much about her, yet he would still call her Fear? Divena willed herself to stop trembling. She steadied her hands and picked up the water pots.

"Do not turn your back on me, girl!" Puran shouted.

Run! Run! Divena ordered herself. *Drop the water pots and run!* But her feet wouldn't move.

Puran laughed, his voice cruel and scornful. "Call yourself whatever you want, girl, but you are still Anjan." He reached up and adjusted his *chaddar* back into a turban. "You are still the fearful one. I always knew you would be."

Gripping the water pots, Divena leapt forward and flew down the dark road.

"Leave me, and you will never see Tanaya again!" Puran yelled after her. "Your sister will be gone from you forever!"

As the stars began to fade, Divena lay down beside her grandmother on the soggy sleeping mat. "Mahima is boiling medicine for you, *Ammama*," Divena said. "Soon you will be well again."

Shridula reached over and laid her hand, hot and trembling, on Divena's arm. "I am old and tired," Shridula murmured. "I have lived a long time. Please, send Mahima away."

"No!" Divena exclaimed. "She will make you well and you will live much longer."

Shridula clutched the girl's hand. "I do not want to waste what little money we have on medicines and healers."

"*Ammama*—"

"I have nothing to pay for a dowry for you, my blessing." A sob caught in the old woman's voice. "How can you hope to marry with no dowry?"

"Not now," Divena pleaded. "We will talk about it later, when you are well."

"By then, I will have *less* than no money."

Tears filled Divena's eyes. But her thoughts were not on the lack of a dowry. Not about a life with no husband or children. Her thoughts were on her father out on the road waiting for her, watching everything she did. He knew where they lived. Of course he knew. He had left her there. But she mustn't talk of it to her grandmother. Not now, while she lay so sick.

"It is no good to marry a man who costs nothing, for he will be worth less than nothing as a husband," Shridula said in an urgent gasp. "He will spend his money on gambling and drink. He will leave you alone to watch your little ones starve."

"Please, *Ammama*, not now," Divena begged. She pulled her hand away. "I will get you a drink of water, then you can sleep some more."

With quiet desperation, Shridula grabbed at Divena. Her words tumbled out so fast that Divena could hardly follow them. "Any boy worthy of you, my sweet girl . . . his family will demand a bicycle and a wristwatch and a radio. His family will insist on a fine wedding with a feast for everyone he knows and everyone he does not know. I can never give such things. Never!"

"It is not important to me now," Divena said. "We can talk about it later."

"There will be no later," Shridula moaned. Tears streaked down her wrinkled cheeks. "You must give up all hope of marrying. You must forget ever having a son to care for you when you are old like me. A hut in the *Untouchable* section is all you will know. I am sorry, my blessing. I am so sorry!"

As the stars faded from the sky, as another dawn broke, Divena watched and waited. Her ears picked up every crackle of broken twig and flutter of bird's wing. If her father came, she decided, she would scream for help and hope her neighbors would come running. Her grandmother wouldn't like it, of course. Women should speak softly, she said. Always. They should be polite and affectionate to everyone . . . Except behind a person's back. Then women could gossip and pass along all kinds of stories. But they should never shout like men, or laugh loudly the way Selvi did.

Surely, though, it would be different if her father came after her.

But Puran didn't come.

Though it took hours of boiling, Mahima finally finished preparing the medicine. A sweet and spicy aroma filled the air, like mangos boiled in curry. Strong enough to soothe, and warm enough to comfort.

"Drink it, *Ammama*," Divena urged. She raised the cup to her grandmother's lips. "Sweet with palm sugar and spicy with cinnamon. Mmmm. Drink it."

Shridula swallowed the portion Mahima set out for her, smacked her lips, and asked for more.

"Soon," Divena said. "And soon after that, you will be well."

"Soon I will die," Shridula said. "Because I am too poor to stay alive."

❧

Divena knew every rut in the road between her grandmother's hut and the well, every curve and every turn. She had once bragged to Selvi that she could walk it with her eyes closed. But this morning everything seemed different. Beyond the clutch of *Dalit* huts where she and her grandmother lived, on both sides of the road, dusty brush lined the packed dirt. A knobby-kneed, hunch-backed little man could easily climb into the brush and hide. With most of the trees long since cut down for wood, the land lay in barren shades of brown and sandy tan. Barren, yet rich with hiding places. The stand of sacred *neem* trees, for instance. Or the old goat shelter, now abandoned. Even the stinking gully villagers used as a lavatory.

It was Divena's world. The only thing she knew. Except the part before, of course, when she lived in the city with her mother and father. But that she chose to forget. And her blind sister. Divena could not bear to think about her.

Selvi might think she knew Divena, but Divena knew better. "I already know how to read," Divena whispered to the empty road. "*Ammama* taught me." Puran also thought he knew her, but he most definitely did not. "I will not be afraid anymore, Father," she said. "I will not!"

Divena fixed her gaze on the horizon. She hoped her father *was* lurking about somewhere. She hoped he could see her walking tall and without fear. She hoped he could hear her voice.

"I will not marry a worthless man!" she shouted. "And I will not be *Untouchable*!"

6

April

Divena shaded her eyes and stared up at the morning birds as they flitted across the newly risen sun. How could it be that she never realized how startlingly fine they were, silhouetted black as they cut through the shimmering sky? She never realized, of course, because she never walked to the well so late in the morning. Not in normal times.

In normal times, by this hour she had already returned to the hut with her water pots full, and had finished picking vegetables from the garden. By the time the sun rose above the horizon, she had set her feet in the opposite direction—toward the market.

But these were not normal times.

Not that the days of her grandmother's illness were any less busy. No, just different. At first dawn—or whenever her grandmother roused herself—Divena poured her a good dose of Mahima's medicine. Shridula did feel better. And the better she felt, the more she needed to talk.

"Wait until I get back from the well," Divena promised, "after our rice is cooked, after the vegetables are made ready for Selvi to take to the market. Then I can sit with you and we will talk."

Every day Divena made the same plea to her grandmother. Yet every day the old lady had a story she felt she simply had to tell, or a bit of wisdom she must impart, or a pressing question that couldn't wait. "About the kindling twigs," she might say. "I do not believe I ever told you my secret place for finding the best ones." Or, "The beggars along the road, Divena. You must be careful of them!" Or—quite often—"I think I would feel so much better if I had a bit of tobacco. Not much, mind you, only a small pinch. Ahhhh, how pleasant even to imagine it."

Only one more swallow of Mahima's medicine remained. Two swallows at the most. After she gave her grandmother that last bit, Divena decided, she would not get more. She couldn't even afford to pay Mahima what she already owed. Instead, following the healer's example, Divena planned to brew her own healing tea from *neem* tree blossoms and herbs. She would also boil *guduchi* stems and fruits, and mix them into their rice. That's what old Arpana advised. Surely a woman who had lived as long as Arpana must know the healing secrets of a healthy life.

"Who did you see at the well?" Shridula called out—the same question she asked every time Divena returned with the water pots full. "Did you hear any new gossip to tell me?"

"No gossip," Divena said. "Only that silly Neela again." Divena sat down on her grandmother's mat. "She is hardly more than a child, *Ammama*. How can she be as tall as I am?"

"Because you are short and scrawny," Shridula said.

Divena inspected the protruding bones on her elbows and wrists, and sighed in exasperation.

"It is not your fault, my dear," Shridula quickly added. "It is because of that wicked father of yours. When you should have been eating and growing, he let you starve."

"We all went hungry then," Divena pointed out.

Shridula reached out and took hold of Divena's hand. "Did I tell you about the years I lived as a slave to the landowner?"

Oh, yes. Her grandmother had told her many times. Divena cast an anxious glance at the unpicked vegetables.

"He took me away from my mother and father." Shridula grasped Divena's young hand in her gnarled ones and held it tight. "He made me his daughter's personal servant. It was better than working in the fields, but I still belonged to him."

Divena looked at her grandmother's weathered face, her stiff gray hair and watery eyes, and tried to see that young girl she had been forty years earlier.

As though she could read her granddaughter's thoughts, Shridula hastened to say, "It is all different now." She sighed and closed her eyes. "Some things are different. Not everything."

"Rest, *Ammama*," Divena said. "Selvi will be here soon. I must get the vegetables ready for her to take to market. After she is gone, after I finish cooking our morning rice, I will sit beside you and you can tell me more about those days." Divena patted her grandmother's hand and gently pulled away.

Pepper plants that reached out into the open field behind Shridula's hut hung heavy with spicy goodness, with peppers hot enough to burn the toughest of tongues. Juicy cucumbers hid among the leaves that snaked around behind the hut. Divena cut the best of the vegetables, though not too many peppers. Selvi couldn't carry an entire load because she had her own fruits to take to the market. When Divena pulled up some of the thick onions that grew among the other vegetables, she laid a plump one aside for her own rice pot. Divena searched through the last of the spinach leaves, but she could find none worth cutting. The sun had grown so hot it scorched every one of them.

A few ripened tomatoes showed red on the vines. It used to be that no one ate tomatoes, but now more and more people stopped to get a few for their dinner pots. Only a year ago, Divena had brought home a pile of spoiled tomatoes that some vendor had left beside the road, and she threw them into the field. Now the plants filled an entire section. She wouldn't be sending tomatoes to the market this day, though. They would make the basket too heavy for Selvi.

Divena came back to the sleeping mat, her full basket as colorful and beautiful as though it were filled with flowers. She kissed her grandmother's head and gently said, "Rest a bit longer. I will start the cooking fire and put rice in the pot to boil."

Shridula sat up, her eyes glowing like a civit cat in the dark. "Freedom is your most valuable possession, my blessing," she said. "Freedom from landowners. Freedom from husbands. And freedom from silly old women."

Divena laughed out loud. "No, no. Not from you, *Ammama*. I never want to be free from you."

As usual, Divena heard Selvi before she saw her.

"Look what I brought today!" Selvi called out as she hurried down the path toward Shridula's hut. "A ripe mango!"

Even Shridula, who did not particularly like Selvi, couldn't keep from smiling.

"And I brought these, too. Mango leaves for your doorway. They will beckon the goddess and persuade her to quickly bring good health back to your house."

Divena looked at her grandmother and shrugged. "It cannot hurt."

As she and Divena hung the leaves, Selvi called back to Shridula, "You really should go to the goddess shrine and make a sacrifice. How can you expect the goddess to look with favor on you when you do nothing for her?"

Shridula's face hardened. "Whatever food we have, we eat. As for coins, we have few. And not a single one to waste on prayers offered to a piece of carved wood!"

Selvi shrugged. "But then, you are the one who is sick, no? It would not hurt you to burn a stick of incense at the goddess shrine, or to break a coconut at her feet. It might ward off the evil eye that seems to be focused on you."

"Stupid girl!" Shridula lay down and turned her back.

"I gathered some green cardamom for her," Selvi whispered to Divena. "It is good for the teeth, and it takes away the poison of a snake bite."

Perplexed, Divena said, "Her teeth are fine. And she has never been bitten by a snake in her life."

"I know. I only thought that anything that could help one part of a body must surely be good for the rest. I could also bring you some—"

Whatever else Selvi might have brought dissolved in the sudden raucous whistle and call of kites as they soared overhead. "Those birds are an omen—" Divena gasped. She stopped herself before saying *of death*. She grabbed up her basket of vegetables and thrust it toward Selvi. "Go!" she implored. "Quickly!"

As Selvi hurried toward the market, Shridula pulled herself up from her sleeping mat. "Perhaps this morning I will make the rice. It is my job."

"No, *Ammama*, I am here," Divena said. "When you are better, we can go back to our old way of doing things."

Shridula looked down at her worn hands—at her knobby fingers, bent and stiff. She folded them in her lap, but quickly unfolded them again. "Your silly friend might be right," she said. "After we eat our rice, perhaps we should take our mango to the shrine and offer it to the goddess. It cannot hurt."

Divena tiptoed to the sleeping mat. Even though she carried bowls of hot rice for their breakfast, it pleased her to see that her grandmother had fallen back asleep. But before Divena could tiptoe away, Shridula opened her eyes.

"Pleasant morning, *Ammama*," Divena said with a smile. She handed Shridula one of the bowls, then sat beside her on the mat, her own bowl in her lap.

The old lady held the rice close to her fading eyes and examined it. "It is fancy this morning," she said.

Divena smiled. Onions . . . Peppers. . . Green stems from the *guduchi* plants . . . Three ripe tomatoes . . . A pinch of curry. "It is special rice," Divena told her. "I made it to help you get well. It is healing rice."

Shridula pinched a small bite of the special rice between her shaking fingers and hesitantly lifted it to her mouth. She wrinkled her nose, but instead of complaining, she took a second bite.

"I wish I had sent you to school," Shridula said in a soft, quavering voice. She started to put another bite of rice in her mouth but put it back in the bowl instead. "I always thought that to send a girl to school must be a waste of money." She sighed. "Keep her at home so she can learn to be a good wife and mother . . . that is what I thought. What man cares if his wife can read?" Shridula carefully licked her fingers. "I was wrong, my blessing. Things are not the way they were when I was a girl."

"Oh, *Ammama*, no other girl I know is as fortunate as me. You taught me to read! You gave me the Holy Bible your father gave you, and you taught me to read it in English."

For several minutes they sat in silence, Divena eating and urging her grandmother to eat, Shridula managing to take two more bites.

"Whatever comes, I am not afraid," Shridula said. "I am glad you came to live with me. You really are my blessing."

Tears filled Divena's eyes. She tried to keep her face down so her grandmother wouldn't see.

"I wish I could have been better to you." Shridula shook her head sadly. "I wish you did not have to work, work, always work."

Divena swiped at her eyes. "You have made my life happy, *Ammama*."

With a shudder, Shridula laid her head back and closed her eyes. "I wish that father of yours had brought your sister to me, too."

Divena did not trust herself to speak.

"I know nothing of my other granddaughter," Shridula said with regret. "What did her parents call her?"

"Tanaya. You would have loved her. Tanaya is the pretty one—rounder than me, and lighter colored. She laughed all the time, and she sang as sweetly as a bird. That is why she is blind."

Shridula's eyes opened wide. "What do you mean?"

"Tanaya had a beautiful face, and she sang so sweetly," Divena repeated. She spoke slowly, as though she were selecting each word with careful precision. "But my sister did not make a good beggar. Not until they took away her eyesight. Then everyone loved her."

Shridula began to tremble. She wiped her mouth on the skirt of her *sari*. "Do you mean to tell me that my daughter—

my Ritu—blinded her own child to make her into a good beggar?"

"No, no," Divena protested. "*Amma* did not do it. She cried and begged *Appa* not to take Tanaya to the uncle who made good beggars. But *Appa* said she could bring in enough money to feed all of us. And I think she did." Divena began to weep. "But if she could do that, why would he give her away to strangers?"

Shridula stared at her granddaughter in shocked silence.

Eighteen *rupees*. Mahima looked at the scratchings she had made on a piece of paper, then at Divena's signature across the bottom. Yes, the girl owed her eleven rupees. Divena had paid three *rupees*, and promised to pay the rest. But not now. She had told Mahima as much. Mahima laid the signed agreement aside.

Mahima was a healer, just as her father had been and her grandfather before that. But in their day, people respected healers. If they didn't have the money to pay, they sold a bracelet or a special pot or even an animal. Whatever it took, they paid the amount the healer asked. Not in this day, though. Now people said, "Would you take vegetables as payment?" or, "I will pay later when I have the money," or simply, "I will go and see a real doctor. I will save my money and get modern medicine."

The system had worked better for her father and grandfather than it did for Mahima. Before the landlord had grown so greedy. Before Ajay Varghese raised the price of rice so high that the poor could barely afford to eat, let alone pay for a healer's medicines.

Yet when Landlord Varghese approached Mahima with a business offer, she saw it as a playing out of her *dharma*, her own path to righteousness. The gods and goddesses knew she had to eat.

So with every full moon, Mahima assembled her signed agreements that remained unpaid and took them to the landlord to see if any of the debtors interested him. Those he chose, she in turn pushed to secure loans from the landlord so they would have the money to pay her bill. Some suddenly found they did have a way to pay, after all. Others, faced with the specter of having to deal with landlord, maneuvered other methods of raising the money. But for every person who agreed to get a loan from the landlord, Ajay Varghese paid Mahima twenty-five *rupees*. Twenty-five! Plus the debtors paid her what they owed her.

The landlord wasn't likely to choose Divena, of course. He wasn't likely to want a scrawny girl and an old woman. But, since Mahima had three other names to take to him, she figured she may as well take Divena's name, too.

"Please!" Divena begged her grandmother. "If you insist on making a sacrifice to the goddess, I will make it for you. You should not walk that far."

But she may as well have been talking to a rock in the road. Shridula smoothed out her badly rumpled *sari* and rebraided and secured her long hair. She splashed water on her face and arms. Then, taking up the mango Selvi brought, she announced, "I am ready to leave. Will you come with me or shall I go alone?"

Divena heaved an exasperated sigh.

Actually, the shrine was not that far away. It had been set up along the narrow path between the cluster of huts where Shridula lived and the main road. Even so, by the time they got there, Shridula could barely walk. But instead of heeding her granddaughter's plea to sit and rest, she went directly to a woman selling offerings for the goddess. She selected two handfuls of marigolds and three pieces of juicy pineapple. It cost her four *rupees*, twenty-four *paise*.

Carefully, Shridula struggled to arrange a circle of marigolds on the ground before the shrine. Inside the circle she placed the pieces of pineapple, and at the very center, the precious mango.

Divena clenched her teeth and refused to help. Never had she had the good fortune to taste pineapple. Such a treat cost too much to eat.

"Come," Shridula offered. "You may lick the nectar from my fingers."

Her grandmother meant to be kind. Divena knew that. But all the same the girl turned away in disgust.

As they struggled home, Shridula leaning heavily against her granddaughter, Divena asked, "Are we Christians or Hindus?"

"We are Christian Hindus."

"That makes no sense. You and I read the Holy Bible together. We love the teachings of Jesus, and we hate the teachings of caste. So why are we not Christians?"

"Because we are Indians."

"The holy scriptures of the *Vedas*, which we are not even allowed to read, say we are foul and loathsome people who must keep to our place. Our punishment is for sins we cannot remember, we are told, so we do our best to avoid new sins that will bring us back in another life as a rat or a cockroach, or, even worse, as a *Dalit* woman again. I do not want to be Hindu."

"Neither do I," said Shridula with a weary sigh. "But we are Indian. We have no choice."

Shridula sagged, almost too exhausted to speak. Divena tried not to let her grandmother see her frustration.

"You are more Hindu than Christian," Divena said. She couldn't help herself. "With all the money you paid, you will surely be much better tomorrow."

Shridula struggled to straighten up and walk by herself.

"I did not pray for me," she said. "I prayed for Tanaya."

7

April

As the sun began to set, Selvi came by with Divena's vegetable basket. It looked to be still nearly full. "A gift for you from old Arpana," Selvi said as she handed a pot to her friend. "Pickles made from green mangoes and tamarind. She said you should eat them with your rice."

"I boiled tea with herbs," Divena said with a smile. "I will bring you a cup."

Selvi, her eyes bright with anticipation, moved closer to Divena. "Do you remember the fisherman, Bechan?"

Divena shook her head, but Shridula said, "Yes, yes. Thin with long, wavy hair and red eyes. I remember him."

"Yes. Well, he went fishing in a pond on the other side of the village, and when he got back to his hut he found it burned to the ground."

Shridula clapped her hands together in dismay and clucked her tongue.

"So much money he had saved for his daughter's wedding, too! Now it is nothing but ashes," Selvi said. "And all because the pond he fished in supposedly belonged to the landowner

Varghese. The landowner insisted that old Bechan trespassed on it."

"They do have that right," Shridula said. "That is how it has always been. Bechan should have known."

"And a woman laborer who works for the landlord. Everyone is talking about her, too. The landlord burned an ugly scar across her face, all because she rejected his son's advances."

Divena shifted uncomfortably and said nothing. She looked up at the last streaks of color in the sky.

"I must go," Selvi said. "Oh, your earnings for today!" She pressed coins into Divena's hand before she turned for home.

Divena opened her hand and looked at the coins. "Two *rupees*, twelve *paise*," she said. "Half the amount it cost to buy the gifts for the goddess."

Shridula slumped with the weariness of the day. "Freedom is your most valuable possession," she repeated. "Freedom from landowners. Freedom from husbands. Freedom from silly old women. And freedom from the endless demands of gods and goddesses."

Sundar scraped up the last of his breakfast *sambar* with a *chapati* and reached for the water pot to wash his hands.

"Very soon a new family will come to the settlement," Ajay Varghese said. He pushed his plate back and waited for Sundar to finish washing. "When you go to the paddies, tell Humaya to ready an empty hut for them. The one next to the path that leads out to the fields."

Sundar wiped his face with the damp towel. "Not that hut, Father." Sundar didn't look at Ajay. "We must have that hut torn down."

"Do not start with that again!" Ajay pounded his fist on the table. "You are not the landlord yet. My word is still law here, and I say we will not destroy a perfectly good hut!"

"It is not perfectly good," Sundar said. He made a careful effort to keep his voice even and controlled. "Every time the workers pass by it—which is every day on their way to the paddies—they whisper the names of Baka and Kilas. And each time they whisper those names, their tone grows more reverent than the time before. Lately, with those names come vows of revenge."

Ajay growled out a laugh. "You know nothing of what is said in the settlement!"

"I do know, Father, because I listen. That hut is a point of loathing to the workers. For us, it is becoming an ever-greater humiliation."

"You have no right to talk to me this way!"

"Destroy the hut, Father," Sundar implored. "Allow that wound to heal."

Sundar had not only showed himself to be the brightest of the Varghese sons but also the most perceptive. His father did not hesitate to tell him as much. Sundar consistently found better ways to bring productivity to the land. In the eight years he had worked with his father—ever since he was a boy of sixteen—the harvest yield had grown with every season's crop. Because of his business sense, his father had been able to add four more rich fields to the family's holdings. Their workers presented them with fewer problems, and throughout the village, the Varghese family had gained prestige and respect.

"The new laborer. Is he a carpenter?" Sundar asked.

"No," Ajay answered brusquely.

"No? I thought we agreed we would get a carpenter. What is he, then?"

Ajay hesitated. "It is not a 'he.' It is a young woman."

"What?!" Sundar exclaimed. "She will be worthless to us!"

"Not worthless," Ajay said. "She will keep trouble away."

Sundar's eyes narrowed, and he glared at his father. "Is the young woman for Jeevak?"

Ajay said nothing.

Back when Ajay first told Sundar he would have the honor of following as the next Varghese landlord, Sundar stammered out his doubts. "Nonsense, my boy!" Ajay had said. "You will be the best landlord in the memory of the village. That is, if you can relax your grip on those tight principles of yours."

"Do not do this thing," Sundar warned his father.

Ajay breathed deeply and let out an exasperated sigh. "My son, I appreciate your desire to be a fair man. I have that same desire. But you must understand: our workers are not like us. They are poor and dependent and grateful for the debt relief we give them. Yes, we need them for our purposes. But they need us even more. Remember, they came to us for loans. We did not go to them."

"This is not my point, Father. I—"

"Surely it is no cruelty to expect debtors to pay according to the agreements they willingly signed. And in the process of paying their debts, we have every right to expect them to work for us faithfully and dependably, and in an obedient manner. We have the right to expect them to meet our needs, whatever those needs might be."

Sundar's face hardened. He pushed his chair back and fixed his father in a steady gaze. "Is it not a cruelty to force ourselves upon their women? And to beat and mutilate them when they resist our advances? To force them to subject themselves to Jeevak's passions?"

"Unfortunate things happen, my son. Unpleasant circumstances do present themselves. The important thing is that we hold our heads high and maintain control of what is ours. And we must do it any way we can."

"No, Father. To me the important thing is that I avoid the compromises that stain our family. The important thing is that I be able to hold my head high before both the great and the small."

Ajay shook his head and gulped in one deep breath after another. Sundar understood. It was what his father always did when he struggled to control his anger.

Even so, Sundar did not back down. He held his father's gaze steadily.

"Destroy that hut, then, if that will make you happy!" Ajay exclaimed as he bounded to his feet. His chair crashed to the floor behind him. "Crawl on your knees before the *Harijans*, if that is all the pride you have! Whimper and beg like a stray dog if you must!"

Sundar neither moved nor changed his expression.

"Do whatever you want! Earn the respect of every low caste and *outcaste* in the village. But do not wait for respect from your own kind." Ajay frowned. "And do not make the mistake of trusting the workers when your back is turned."

The Varghese family identified themselves as Christian. Everyone in the area knew that. The family could trace their roots all the way back to Saint Thomas, disciple of Jesus the Christ, who brought Christianity to South India in the first century. Every Varghese child heard the story—sometimes told with great pride, but more often in recent generations with a few snickers. Always, however, told with a we-are-better-than-the-Hindus air.

Even so, except for baptisms at birth and rites at death, for the most part Christianity meant little more to the Varghese family than freedom from dreary Hindu rules. Varghese men did take great pleasure in their platters of meat.

Sundar's grandmother Sheeba Esther had been an exception. She used to call her first grandson Sundar Samuel. "Listen for God to speak to you, Sundar Samuel," she would say to him. But Sundar had been quite young at the time. And though he longed for it, he never had heard God tell him anything. It seemed to him that God had no voice at all. At least not that could be heard in the disharmony of the Varghese household.

"Yes, Sundar, destroy the hut." Jeevak sneered at his brother. "Hundreds of other huts will still stand in the settlement. I can easily find the ones that suit my purposes."

Sundar didn't look at his brother. Instead, he stepped off the veranda and headed for the garden.

"You are not the only son of the landlord!" Jeevak called after him. "You may ride around in the truck with Father and whisper in his ear, but I am the one who slogs through the mud and does the real work!"

Sundar didn't slow his pace.

"This entire problem is really your fault!" Jeevak ran after his brother. "I think you refuse to marry the girls Father chooses for you just so you can frustrate me and laugh! You know I cannot marry until after you."

Sundar stopped and turned to face his brother. "It cannot be a battle of us against our laborers, Jeevak. Maybe that is how it used to be when Father was a child, but not now. Everything has changed. If we want to—"

"I get blamed for this, but it is all your fault!" Jeevak bellowed. "You are nothing but a stubborn, selfish pig!"

Had Brahmin Rama sent word that he intended to visit, every Varghese man would have found a pressing need to be off the veranda and away from the house by the time he arrived. But Rama had been spiritual head of the village for many years. He knew better than to announce his comings and goings to the landowner. By the time Ajay saw him approaching, leaning heavily on his walking stick and supported by his first son, Brahmin Vrispati, the landlord had no time to escape.

"Ahh, the good Brahmins," Ajay Varghese sighed in a voice that would fool no one.

Brahmin Rama chose to ignore the insult, and also the slight of not being invited to join the landowner on his veranda. Rather than argue, Rama simply made his way up the steps and sat down uninvited. He lifted his face to the sky, surveyed its stark blue expanse, and said, "The afternoon will be extremely warm. Even so, we should be able to have a comfortable hour together here in the fragrant shade of your jasmine vines."

To look at Brahmin Rama, slight and bone-thin, one would think him too frail to walk the road and climb steps to anyone's veranda, even assisted by his son's strong arm. But then, the Brahmin had always been slight and bone-thin and frail-looking. Back when he was a young man, everyone throughout the area knew him, not for his looks but for the beauty of his Vedic chants. And old and bent as he had become, his voice still had a wonderfully melodious ring to it.

"You have come to regale us with more tales of your pilgrimage along the great Panch-kos to the Holy Ganges, I presume?" Ajay asked. A mocking comment, since Brahmin

Rama had taken that pilgrimage close to half a century earlier and had told and retold every detail of the trip.

"Perhaps another time," Brahmin Rama said with a smile. He chose a seat for himself on a mat in the corner, facing the landowner's chair. Vrispati sat beside his father. "No, today I have come to offer you counsel on the matter of brutality at your settlement."

Ajay stiffened. "In that case, you might as well not waste time making yourself comfortable. My settlement is not a matter of concern to you."

"But of course it is," said the Brahmin. "As the spiritual guide—"

"I am not Hindu!" Ajay snapped. "I do not consider you my spiritual guide."

"As a Christian, then," Brahmin Rama said. "Do you see your actions as ones that follow the teachings of Jesus?"

"I will not listen to this! Leave my house!"

Neither Brahmin moved. "You are correct to suggest that the Vedic culture is slipping from its rightful place of importance," Rama said. "This son beside me, my eldest, studies *Sanskrit*, but my youngest son does not. By his own choice, yes, but a choice heavily influenced by a lack of funds. The idea of oneness that currently afflicts India is most unfortunate. It produces endless struggles to erase the differences that have guided our society for thousands of years by means of religious and moral laws."

Ajay leaned back in his chair and assumed a look of boredom.

"What used to be right is no longer right," Brahmin Rama said. "What used to be fair is fair no more."

"We are still caste and they are still *outcaste*," Ajay said. "Nothing can change that."

"Eat, eat, eat!" Ajay ordered his sons. He motioned to the platter of savory stewed lamb set out before them, steaming with the fragrance of onions proudly pulled from the ground. "Eat, and rejoice in being Christian!"

Ajay sat at the table, Sundar and Ramesh on either side of him. Jeevak, sullen and brooding, hunkered alone at the far end of the veranda.

"Old Brahmin Rama came by today with his son," Ajay said. "He had it in his mind to scold me about the troublemakers in the settlement. Of course, I would hear none of it."

"Why do you even listen to that old fossil?" Ramesh asked.

"Because the village reveres him. We do not need to stir up any more animosity from the villagers."

"The hut is gone," Sundar offered.

"The village!" Ramesh sneered. He whipped his fingers around his plate and lifted a bite of lamb and rice to his mouth. "The village will never change. Endless gods and goddesses, and dried-up old Brahmins who have never done a day's work, and cowering *Harijan* beggars who line the road with their hands stuck out for pennies . . . Forget the village!"

Ajay cast his youngest son a scathing glance. "Perhaps you also forget that our land surrounds the village. Were we to forget the village, your brothers and I, who would pay for you to attend the university? Who would pay for you to pretend you are not Indian?"

"Do as you will," Ramesh said with an insolent shrug. "Slosh in the paddies and destroy offending huts and argue with the Brahmins and fight over who gets to be the next landlord if you want to. Not me! I will become an engineer and—"

"If you pass the exam," Jeevak said.

"If I pass the exam. If I do not, I will go to the city and work with one of the new computer companies. Either way, I will get myself far away from this prehistoric village where nothing ever changes."

Ajay helped himself to more lamb. "You say the hut is gone, Sundar? Good. Maybe the village will be satisfied and Brahmin Rama will leave us alone."

On the night of the full moon, Mahima walked to Ajay Varghese's house. She stood beside his veranda and waited for the landlord to come out. At long last, Ajay stepped through the door and called to her, "Come! Sit. Show me what you have for me."

Mahima laid out four signed agreements, all overdue. Pointing to the first one, she said, "This is a potter. He has a wife and three daughters. His debt is eighteen *rupees*."

"What is the debt for?"

"His wife. She was injured in a fall."

"She has recovered?"

Mahima hesitated. "No. She can no longer walk."

Ajay pushed the agreement back. "I do not need a worker with an injured wife and three daughters."

Mahima showed him two others. Ajay accepted a young man with a forty-two *rupee* debt whose wife had died, but he rejected a woman with two young sons, a recovering husband, and a debt of fifty-one *rupees*.

"Is that all you have?" Ajay asked.

Mahima hesitated. "I do have one more," she said, "but I do not think it would interest you." Ajay waited. "An old woman and her granddaughter. Maybe the old woman could watch over babies and her granddaughter could work in your paddies? The debt is only fifteen *rupees*."

Ajay squinted thoughtfully. "What is the girl like? Sturdy? Dark, I suppose?"

A *Sudra* servant girl, her hair hanging down her back in one long braid that reached almost to her waist, paused on the other side of the door to listen.

"No, no," Mahima assured Ajay. "Divena is small and slender and of medium color. But she is strong."

"Pretty?"

"Well, yes." After a moment's hesitation Mahima quickly added, "And she is strong. Responsible, too. And she is used to hard work. She grows vegetables and sells them at the marketplace."

Ajay leaned back in his chair, a smile spreading across his face. "Divena, you say? I want this girl. Promise her whatever you must to get her signature on an agreement."

"I cannot be certain she will accept," Mahima said. "She is a determined girl."

"Get her for me and it will mean fifty *rupees* in your pocket. Double what I usually pay you. I want that Divena here immediately!"

The eavesdropping *Sudra* servant stifled a gasp and slipped away from the door.

8

April

Walking along the road in the cool of the evening, before she reached the unpleasantness of the lowest huts in the *Dalit* section, Divena closed her eyes and breathed in the fragrance of the final days of spring. Already the road had begun to bake into dust, but she didn't look down at her feet. She looked up at the ripening mangos nestled among the tree leaves, the syrupy-sweet scent of their nectar hanging in the gentle breeze. Divena paused and considered how she might climb up and pull one off, maybe two or three.

"You can smell, but you cannot taste!" A hefty woman, dark and round, stood beside the closest of the houses, her hands on her hips.

"I have peppers," Divena offered. "And onions. Fresh and ready for your rice pot. Would you like to make a trade?"

The woman's eyes narrowed suspiciously. "Let me see what you have."

Divena lifted the basket from her head and showed off the vegetables left over from the market.

"Four good peppers and two onions for one mango," the woman said.

"Seven good peppers and three onions for two mangos," Divena countered.

The woman squinted up into the tree. "One good mango and one overripe mango."

Divena smiled. She chose seven beautiful peppers and three round onions, and handed them to the woman.

The rest of the way home, Divena's basket seemed much lighter. She didn't even notice the stink of the lavatory gully when she passed by. She could smell just one thing: the sweet perfume of ripe mangos.

She found her grandmother hunched over the cook fire, stirring their evening rice pot, just as she had always done before her sickness. In the glow of the setting sun, the sight of *Ammama*'s shape by the fire struck Divena as almost heavenly.

"I brought us a treat!" Divena called.

Shridula turned and smiled. It occurred to Divena that she had seen her grandmother smile more since her illness than in all the years she had known her before.

"A ripe mango," Shridula said with a laugh. "Its sweet syrup reached me before your sweet words."

Divena set the basket in the shade of the hut. Shridula, still staggering slightly, came over to choose a vegetable or two to drop into her bubbling pot.

Shridula no longer burned with fever, nor did she shake with the shivering chills that had so rattled her. Crushing headaches, which had once made her cry out in pain, had faded away. Even so, she did not seem the same as before. She seemed weary, unsteady on her feet. Divena had suggested asking Mahima for one more pot of her medicine, but Shridula insisted, "No, no. Your teas and fancy rice do me just as well. Mahima can get her money from someone richer than us."

As Shridula looked over the produce, she smiled and said, "You did well at the market today. Not one tomato left in the basket. And still we have plenty of vegetables for our own rice pot." She bent over the basket and gently ran her knotted fingers over the vibrant kaleidoscope of vegetables.

"More than four *rupees* today, *Ammama*," Shridula said proudly.

They were so busy talking together that neither saw the knobby-kneed man with a crooked back approach. Not even when he crept in close. He knew how to stay in the shadows. He watched as Shridula selected two small peppers and a stunted onion. Only when Divena drew the coins from inside her clothes and held them out to her grandmother did he step forward.

"Do you have a plate of rice for your father?" he asked Divena. But his eyes were on the coins in her hand.

"I missed you too much to stay away from you," Puran said as he pressed another handful of Shridula and Divena's dinner into his mouth. "When you were young, I thought it would be better for you to be with your grandmother. But you are no longer a child. I can make a home for you now."

Shridula leaned forward and stared into the face she no longer recognized. "Where?" she demanded.

Puran paused mid-bite and defiantly returned her stare. "Where, what?"

"Where is the home you have to offer her?"

Puran hunched over his plate and scooped up another bite. "I did not say I have a home. I said I can make a home."

"How will you do that?"

His eyes flashing, Puran's stare turned hard. "Do not question me, old woman. I am Anjan's father."

"Her name is Divena," Shridula informed Puran. "I have cared for her for five years, since the day you deserted her at my door. I most certainly *will* question you. Old man."

"I have a skill," Puran said. "I sharpen knives. Repair tools."

"Where is your whetting wheel?"

"I am not so foolish as to drag a whetting wheel along behind me. I have it safely stored in the next village. No one else there is doing the type of work I do, so I make plenty of money."

Shridula looked the shabby man up and down. She made a face and said, "Oh, yes, you do look like a rich man!"

Puran popped another bite into his mouth, then turned to Divena and grinned. Rice grains hung from his unkempt beard. "I will save a dowry for you, Daughter."

Divena didn't answer him.

"No longer will you have to work at the market every day. You can cook for us and clean the new house I will build. But first, we will go together and get your sister. She will keep us happy with her beautiful songs."

Shridula tried to lunge at Puran. "You have eaten our rice. Now get away from my house!"

But Divena rushed to her father. "*Appa?* You really can find Tanaya?"

"I know exactly where she is. At the orphanage where I left her for safekeeping." Puran looked down at Divena's hand that still clutched the coins. "But I am afraid it will cost us to get her back. Those at the orphanage who have been caring for her will expect me to pay them. Everything costs money."

Instinctively, Divena pulled her hand away.

"I emptied my coin purse along the road," Puran said. A look of sad contrition fell over his face. "So many beggars. I understand how such poverty feels, and I could not pass them by. The gods will reward me, I know that to be true."

"Get out! Get out!" Shridula yelled. She pushed forward and swatted Puran across the head.

"Stop!" Divena cried. "What if he is telling the truth, *Ammama?* I may never get another chance to find my sister!"

Shridula scraped the last spoonfuls of rice from the pot and divided it into two small bowls. One she handed to Divena.

"I decided I did not want a second wife, after all," Puran said. "I only want my two lovely daughters beside me."

Shridula moved around behind Divena and slipped the mangos into the folds of her skirt. She stepped into the hut and pushed the golden fruit back behind the rice bag.

"You are not yet at the best age to marry, Daughter," Puran said to Divena. "I will have time to save a nice dowry for you. Many fine young men live in my village, and I intend to look each one over carefully."

Shridula sat back down beside Divena and picked up her own bowl of rice. Frowning, she mumbled, "Hardly enough rice left to be worth the chewing."

"We really must leave immediately," Puran insisted. "The moon is still bright, a fine time to walk. Best to do in the cool of the evening—but not too late."

Shridula set her empty bowl down on the ground and glowered through the firelight at the hunched man.

"Do you have a better *sari* than that one you are wearing?" Puran asked his daughter. "A colorful one, perhaps? Clean, with no tears?"

Divena pulled self-consciously at the tatters in her dingy *sari*. She opened her mouth to apologize that she owned no other garment, but Shridula interrupted her.

"Which village did you say holds your whetting stone?"

Puran shot the old lady an irritated look. "The next one over. On the other side of the landlord's fields."

"If you leave now, will you not get there long before dawn? After the moon has set and it is too dark to see?"

"A good time to arrive," Puran said. "Besides, I cannot walk fast. My back, you see. And my poor, bent legs."

"Perhaps, if you wait a day or two, we could get Divena a new *sari*. Red or orange, maybe. She would also have time to wash in the river and make herself more beautiful."

Divena stared at her grandmother.

But Puran's eyes flamed with excitement. A sly smile crossed his face. "Yes, yes," he said. "What is one more day? What are two more days?"

"I could put oil in her hair to make it glisten," Shridula said. "Perhaps a bit of kohl on her eyes and red stain on her cheeks. She will be beautiful."

"Yes!" Puran breathed. "Beautiful!"

"That large village beyond the temple. I have never been there, but I hear tell it is a wonderful village. I know it is far from here, but would that not be a better place to settle? I should think you would earn more money there."

"That is exactly why we must leave as early as possible! As soon as you get the new *sari* and prepare the girl. To get to that village before the heat—" Puran stopped short. He knew he had said too much.

Slowly, painfully, Shridula lifted herself up. Her voice came in a menacing growl. "You would dare to sell my blessing to a brothel?"

"She is mine!" Puran bellowed. "She belongs to me! I will do with her as I wish. Get out of my way, old woman!"

"What is the problem?" The potter from across the road, a dark man with bulging muscles, ambled over. With each step, his heavy stick thudded on the ground. Two strong sons followed close behind their father.

At the same time, two other men started down the path toward them, both calling out Shridula's name.

Puran jumped up and ran. "I know your village, old woman!" he called back. "Not always will someone be so close at hand!"

"He does not know where Tanaya is, does he?" Divena asked through her tears.

"No, I am certain he does not," Shridula said.

"I will never see my sister again."

"We will pray that God will protect her."

"Her voice is so beautiful. I wanted you to hear her sing."

Shridula reached out and laid her hand on the girl's arm. "I already know its sound. I hear it every day in your own beautiful voice."

Divena buried her face in her hands and wept.

Shridula got up and disappeared into the hut. When she returned, she announced, "Our stomachs are empty and our hearts are sad. Now is the perfect time for us to eat our ripe mangos."

9

May

When Divena arrived at her regular place at the market, she cast a melancholy glance up at the sky. All around her vendors sweated under shimmering rays of heat, even though the sun hung just above the horizon.

"Maybe today I will take my vegetables to the other side of the market," Divena announced. "Maybe I will go and lay out my display in the shade of the banyan trees, under the branches that reach out and grab hold of each other to make a canopy of shade."

"Ha!" laughed old Arpana. "The sellers over there would throw you out before you set your basket down."

"Why should I cook in the sun while the weavers and bakers and milkmen lie back in cool breezes?"

"Because they are *Sudras* and you are a *Dalit*," Arpana said. "That is why."

Divena wrinkled her nose and made a face. "They look like us. Some are even darker than you."

"But they are not like us," said Arpana. "Try to sit down in the shade of their trees and you will find that out quickly enough."

Selvi spread her blanket out next to Divena's. "Do not waste your time talking to that old woman," she whispered. "What does she know? One time she tried to drown herself in the river."

Divena turned away from both of them and spread out her cloth. Of course, Arpana spoke the truth. But Divena had no interest in listening to her, nor to Selvi, either. Not this day.

The milkman's old mother laid out packages of curd cheese wrapped in banana leaves. On each side she placed a plate of *ras-gola*. One time Divena had bought two of those round boiled cheese balls as a special treat for her and her grandmother. Divena closed her eyes and licked her lips. She tried with all her might to recapture the sweetness of the syrup, the spongy softness of the cheese ball as it melted on her tongue. Maybe . . . if she could sell many vegetables today . . .

But of course she would not. The sun would grow hot, the shoppers would rush for home, and she would gather up her wilting produce early with little to show for her day at the far end of the market.

"How much would a new *sari* cost?" Divena asked.

"More *rupees* than you have," Arpana told her.

"But how much?"

"Go and see," Selvi suggested. "Go look at the weavers' booths."

"No!" Divena exclaimed. "What would people say if they saw me there?"

"Then you sell my fruit for me, and I will go. I do not care what people say."

In Selvi's long absence, Divena sold enough of her friend's fruit to earn Selvi close to three *rupees*. For herself, she sold nothing but a handful of peppers for thirty-two *paise*.

Divena carefully put the coins away. When she looked up, she noticed a woman standing off to the side, watching her.

A *Sudra*, with her hair in a long braid hanging down her back almost to her waist. Divena, uneasy after the recent events, purposely pulled her attention back to the vegetables she had for sale. But the woman with the braid slipped closer until she stood at the edge of Divena's cloth.

"Hot peppers?" Divena asked her.

The woman leaned down and whispered, "Watch out for Landlord Varghese. You are not safe!"

Divena stared at her in confusion. "What? You must be mistaken. I do not know the landlord."

"But the landlord knows you . . . Divena. Be very, very careful."

Selvi hurried back, bursting with new gossip. "The weavers do not weave cloth anymore!"

Divena glanced over at her. Only for a moment, it seemed, yet when she looked back for the woman with the braid, she was gone.

"How can that be?" Arpana asked Selvi. "I saw them hanging up *saris* and *kurta* shirts and *mundus* when I came in."

"Yes, but not from the weavers. All that comes from the mill. I heard shoppers sneering that the work and fabric were not nearly so good, but they bought anyway because of the good price."

Divena tried to push the *Sudra* woman's warning out of her mind. Nothing but silly babble. "How much for a *sari*?" she asked Selvi.

"Nine *rupees*. But the weavers charged almost twice that much."

"Red *saris*, too?" Divena asked. "And orange?"

"Any color you want." Selvi gave Divena a curious look. "Why are you so interested? Have you been saving your money to get a new *sari*?"

"Of course not," Divena mumbled. "Where would I get nine *rupees* to spend on such an extravagance? Next you will accuse me of putting oil in my hair and kohl on my eyes and trotting to another village to sell myself!"

Maybe someone said something after that. Maybe someone asked a question. Divena didn't know. Her mind was spinning over the warning of the woman with the long braid. That woman had called her by name. She had said, "Divena." How could she have known her name?

A woman stopped by Divena's display looking for unscorched spinach leaves. A man asked about lentil beans. Another looked to make a trade for his collection of wild herbs. "What a worthless day," Divena grumbled.

At mid-morning, four tribal women came along. Black-skinned and wild-haired, each one lugged an enormous basket of dried fish. They sat down cross-legged, all in a row. The shoppers breathed a sigh of relief. Finally, something to stir up a bit of interest. Everyone always expected to get a better bargain from women sellers than from men. And with four women together, surely each one would compete with the next to offer the best price.

As one, the tribal women began to shout—first among themselves, then at the shoppers. But it soon became apparent that these women knew well how to strike a hard bargain. They all shouted out the same price. Not one of them would come down so much as two *paise*.

"I have news to tell you," Selvi whispered to Divena.

But with the fish sellers yelling and the shoppers shouting back at them, Divena shrugged and shook her head. She couldn't understand a word Selvi said.

As the sun burned hot and shoppers drifted away to sit under the shade trees, Divena looked sadly at her still-full basket of shriveling peppers.

"Come, let us go," Selvi whispered to her. "I have something important to tell you."

"Please, no more gossip," Divena begged.

"Not gossip," Selvi said. "Real news."

In the next village over—the village where Divena's father claimed to have his whetting wheel—a university professor and his wife would be starting a class, Selvi said. "They will teach the laborers that belong to that landlord how to read and write."

"It is not true," Divena said. "My grandmother told me about landowners. None of them would allow such a thing."

"He does not like it, of course, but there is nothing he can do about it. The professor has as much political power as the landlord does. And he is high caste, the same as the landlord."

"I do not believe it," Divena said. "It is nothing but more foolish gossip."

"How do you know? I think we should go. Maybe we will learn to read."

"I already know how to read," Divena stated.

Selvi laughed out loud. "Of course you do not! And you are cruel to make fun of me, Divena! Go or stay, I do not care. I will be there, anyway."

When Divena didn't answer, Selvi said, "The first class is tomorrow evening. Go with me. We can see for ourselves if the gossip is true."

"I do not want to walk that way in the dark," Divena said. She shivered at the thought of meeting her father on the road.

"We will be together," Selvi assured her. "Imagine! Soon we can be free like the women on television!"

Divena whipped her fingers through her boiled rice. She could not stop thinking about her father. As she lifted a bite to her mouth, a lovely tune her sister used to sing tumbled through her mind. She sucked the curry from her fingers and looked at her grandmother.

Shridula lifted herself up and poured water into a clay cup.

"*Ammama*, what does it mean to be free?"

"It means you do not belong to anyone."

"I do not belong to anyone now, but I cannot do whatever I wish. Today, I could not go to the better end of the market and spread my cloth out under the banyan trees."

"And you fear your father," Shridula said.

"Yes."

Shridula sat down beside Divena. "When I was your age, I thought I knew what it meant to be free. Get away from the landlord and I would belong to no one but me, that is what I thought. But then I lived with Miss Abigail for a long time. Her mind had left her, poor lady. I needed to watch over her and do her bidding, even when her bidding made no sense. And my father. He loved me very much, but he also told me what I could and could not do because he felt certain he knew best. When he told me to marry, I married. Then I did the bidding of my husband, who loved me not at all. When he left and my sons died and your scheming father took my daughter away as his wife, I found myself captive to the endless struggle to keep from starving."

"And then I came," Divena said.

"Yes. But perhaps it is not good to be completely free. Perhaps completely free means completely alone and completely empty."

Divena slipped her fingers around her bowl and scooped up every last bite of curry. When nothing remained inside the bowl, she ran her finger around the edges in search of hidden grains of rice.

"You do not like Selvi, do you?" Divena asked as she sucked her fingers clean.

"A good Indian woman should be content and not complain," Shridula said. "To be content with your lot in life is to be happy."

"You were not content to live as a slave to the landowner."

Shridula contemplated this for several minutes. "You are right," she finally said. "But I know what is expected of a woman—to keep a good house, not to quarrel with others, not to talk with a big mouth. Selvi does not know these things. She holds her head high and shouts and runs about like a horse. Most likely, she will be reborn as an Untouchable woman once again."

"I thought you did not believe all that about rebirth and *karma*."

"I do not," Shridula said. "But it does not hurt to be careful."

"Selvi wants to be free."

"Hmph!" Shridula grunted. "Really free or free like the women she sees on television?"

"Now that the sun grows so much hotter, market days are not as long," Divena said. "Shoppers do not want to stay out in the afternoon heat. Tomorrow I want to go to Selvi's house after the market and visit with her. I can sleep in her courtyard and take my leftover vegetables back to the market the next morning."

Shridula set her rice bowl down beside her. "Will you see what plays on that television she watches?"

Divena shrugged. "I do not know. Maybe."

"Be careful, my blessing," Shridula said. "Be very careful. Freedom can be a dangerous thing."

10

May

Because we cannot ever hope to leave the village if we cannot read, and do not tell me again that you already know how to read, because I know that is only you bragging. If you really could read, I would have known it before now. I do not only mean reading in the Malayalam talk, either. I mean reading in English—at least I think in English. Because one time I saw on television . . ."

For the entire two hours it took the girls to walk to the neighboring village, Selvi hardly paused her talking long enough to grab a breath. Divena reminded herself to say, "Hmmm," now and then, or occasionally, "I agree," but mostly it made no difference whether she said anything or not. Selvi seemed happy enough to listen to herself talk.

Which suited Divena perfectly. She had so much going on in her mind that she found it a comfort to be spared the frustration of being interrupted by conversation.

". . . because, even though we are nothing but *Dalits*, a real teacher will know how to help us understand things like counting without making mistakes and adding the cost of bananas and mangos, which you can already do at the market, but I never learned to do it, and that is why I will . . ."

Divena felt terrible about deceiving her grandmother. She determined to immediately tell her the truth—unless this evening turned out terribly and she decided to never go back to the class again. In that case, she could see no reason to tell her grandmother anything about it at all.

". . . not really in the settlement where the workers live, because I am certain they would not dare to meet there, but it has to be somewhere close by, not too far from the road. I do not suppose it is the sort of thing we should ask about, but I do not want to wander around too long, so maybe if we . . ."

Divena had no idea where they were going. Although she had only been in the village five years, she could not really remember being anywhere else. Except for her terrible memories of the city, but that did not help her here. She was not at all certain that she and Selvi would simply happen upon the class.

". . . when the wife of the teacher walked through our town, which is how I heard about all this, and so I do have an idea what she looks like and who she is. Not that I actually met her, or even saw her. If I had had that chance, I would have told her straight away that you and I wanted to come, but by the time I understood who she was and what it all meant . . ."

In the end, they had no trouble finding the class. Not far off the road, a short distance before they came to the village landlord's fields, Divena spotted the group sitting together under a large *neem* tree. When she pointed it out, Selvi nodded enthusiastically. She recognized the teacher's wife.

In fact, the fine lady turned and looked their way. "Come!" she called to the girls. "Do join us!"

That's when Selvi fell silent. Throughout the entire class, she could not manage to speak one single word.

"I am Professor Chander Menon," the teacher said. He stood tall and distinguished in his carefully pressed trousers and starched *kurta* shirt. His hair, gray at the temples, was neatly trimmed, and his moustache was well groomed.

Divena whispered to Selvi, "He does look like a professor."

"My wife is Rani Menon," the professor said. "We both count it a privilege to be here with you."

Eighteen people, all sitting cross-legged on the ground, narrowed their eyes and stared at him suspiciously.

"You will learn to read," Professor Menon said. "I cannot express the opportunities that will open before you when you master reading. We will also learn basic English."

"Why?" demanded a scruffy man who hunkered up close. "We are not English."

"Nor am I," said Professor Menon. "But English is the language of education in India, and also our language of business and law. If you wish to live free in this country, you must know English."

Divena, her eyes open wide, leaned forward to better hear.

Professor Menon held up a card. "Can anyone tell me what this says?"

"Tea!" several people called out.

"Yes! You know that word because of the advertisements you see along the streets."

By the end of the evening they could also read: soda water, coffee, soap, telephone. "Watch for English words and copy them down," the professor said. "When my wife and I come back in three days, we will read your words, too."

Chander Menon asked who in the group had access to a television. Two men raised their hands. Selvi did not. He asked who had access to radios. More than half raised their hands. Divena did not.

"If the master knew we were here, he would not even allow us to have food," one woman remarked.

"You have a right to learn," Professor Menon said. "That is the law of India."

"Not on the landlord's land," rumbled a man with a deep voice. "Here the landlord is the law."

"Nowhere in India is a landlord the law," the professor insisted. "Landlords do not like that, but they know it is true. It is important that you know it, too."

The men and women glanced doubtfully at each other. No one seemed quite convinced.

"But we are Untouchables, sir," said a man with two hugely protruding front teeth.

"No, sir, you are not," said the professor. "Not by Indian law. You are rightfully listed as being in the "Scheduled Castes." You are rightfully called *Dalits*, a word that comes from the *Sanskrit* for 'crushed' or 'downtrodden.' It is a name your people chose for themselves to describe the situation of their lives. They wanted to replace the terms *Harijans* and *Untouchables*, words they hated."

"Whatever they call us, to them we are still untouchable," the man with the big front teeth insisted.

"They are wrong," said Professor Menon. "You have been told that God does not love you. You have been told you were born to serve the upper castes. You have been told you have no rights. I am here to tell you none of that is true. God loves every one of you. You were born to serve only God and to live free. Indian law gives you rights; you only need to understand what they are and how to use them."

A young man called out from the back, "Who do you work for?"

"My wife and I work for no one," the professor said. "We come to you on our own."

"Why?" demanded the young man. "Why do you come here?"

Professor Menon took a handkerchief from his pocket and wiped his eyes and his mouth. "May I tell you a story? A young man, also a *Dalit*, wanted very much to be free. He owned a piece of land, but he had no money to plant crops on it. So he went to the landlord and asked for a loan. The landlord loaned him ten thousand *rupees*. 'I can pay you everything when I harvest the crops in six months,' the young man told the landlord. He worked hard and his harvest proved to be a fine one. But as soon as the rice stalks were cut, the landlord came and took every last grain for himself. 'I just increased your interest to 50 percent,' the landlord informed the young man."

"Yes!" the man with protruding teeth called out. "That is exactly what our landlord does to us!"

"The young man planted a second crop on his land," the professor continued. "He worked twice as hard and so his harvest boomed twice as good. But once again the landlord came and took it all. 'How can I afford to plant another crop if you continue to take everything?' the young man pleaded. But the landlord ignored him. He took the young man's entire second harvest."

"That young man was foolish," rumbled the deep-voiced man. "He never should have trusted the landlord!"

"Four times the same thing happened," Professor Menon said. "Four times the young man worked from daybreak to dark. Four times he brought in a wonderful crop. And four times the landlord took it all away. By then the young man had paid back three times as much as he had borrowed. Yet the landlord said, 'You still owe me money. Pay me or I will take your land, too.'"

"It is not fair!" Divena exclaimed.

"No, it is not fair. Nor is it lawful," said Professor Menon. "That is why I am here."

In the gathering shadows, a young man pulled himself up on a walking stick. "I will tell you why I am here. I studied at the university, but I could not be happy because my father and mother worked so hard for the landlord to pay the money they borrowed so I could attend the university. They did not owe much money, but every time they nearly finished paying off the debt, the landlord added more charges."

"Yes!" the scruffy man called out. "He does that to me, too. He does it to all of us!"

The young man continued talking, as though he hadn't heard the interruption. "I quit school to work in my parents' place, so I could pay off their debt. My beautiful wife, with her pale skin and soft hands, went with me, to work by my side. But the landlord's son looked upon her with wicked eyes. Despite her pleas and entreaties, he forced himself into her hut and laid his hands on her. He could do no more than that, though, because I came in and hit him in the head with a block of wood."

The class, which had fallen silent, roused up and cheered. But the professor held up his hands. "Let the man talk," he insisted.

"For defending my wife, the landlord beat me so badly that I now have trouble walking. But my poor wife . . ."

He turned to his reluctant wife and urged her to her feet. A horrendous fiery-red scar ripped across her face—under one eye, over her cheek, and across her lips.

"My name is Kilas," the young man said through his clenched jaw. "My wife is Baka. That is why we are here."

11

May

With the walk back from the neighboring village so long and dark, the girls didn't reach Selvi's house until deep into the night. Even so, despite her exhaustion, Divena slept uneasily in Selvi's room. The sound of the electric fan whirring overhead disconcerted her. Long before dawn she lay fully awake, wishing she could see the stars overhead. Was her grandmother also lying awake? Thinking about her grandmother set Divena to worrying all over again. Suppose *Ammama* were thirsty. Who would carry her water pots to the well and fill them for her? Or if she were hungry, who would boil a pot of rice for her? Would they know to drop in the peppers and onions she liked so much?

All day, the sun had burned hot. Even so, Divena took no comfort in the fan's cooling breeze that ruffled her *sari*. She could not stop thinking about her grandmother. In the heat of the day, *Ammama* must have looked anxiously over the garden plot and seen the vegetables wilting. How concerned she must have been!

Divena eased herself up from the sleeping mat, taking care not to awaken Selvi. Carefully she pushed aside the curtain that separated her friend's room from the front of the house. She stepped softly to the door and eased it open, then hurried across the courtyard. Once her feet sank into the thick dirt of the road, she broke into a run and didn't stop until she reached the path that led to her grandmother's settlement of huts. When she could see her grandmother's dirt yard, she paused to compose herself. Then, taking one silent step at a time, she crept over to the sheltered area where her grandmother slept.

Shridula lay perfectly still on her sleeping mat, her eyes closed and her breathing slow and regular. Divena paused to think: If she could creep into the hut and get the water pots, she could go on to the well and be back by the time her grandmother awoke. Maybe she could even have the cooking fire started and—

"You are here," Shridula said.

Divena gave a start. "Yes, *Ammama*. I will hurry on to the well."

"Good. When you get back, I will have our morning rice ready. Then we can talk."

Divena knew her grandmother. The old lady spoke with the voice of one who had lain awake all night. She spoke with the voice of one filled with suspicion and worry. It would not be an easy day.

"The dawn is especially brilliant this morning," Divena said lightly when she returned from the well. She had taken both water pots and filled them to the brim.

Her grandmother did not sit hunched over the cook fire as usual, which meant she had been waiting for Divena to return.

"You and your marketplace friend," Shridula began. "You and that one called Selvi. Did you look at her television together?"

"Yes," Divena said. "Well . . . no. Not exactly. I am not as interested in it as she is."

Shridula lowered her head, raised her eyebrows, and peered up at her granddaughter. Divena knew perfectly well what that look meant. Her grandmother didn't believe a word she said.

"The television tells about life in the city, and it shows Bombay movies, and talks about the Bollywood cinema stars," Divena said. "Unimportant things. That is to say, not anything about us. It does not tell about anything in our lives." She could hear herself talking too fast. *Slow down! Slow down!* "What I mean is, the television shows nothing about our kind."

"Our kind? What do you mean by 'our kind'?"

"*Dalits*," Divena said. "From our end of the village."

Shridula said nothing. She simply fixed her eyes on her granddaughter and waited.

"Selvi likes that sort of thing. What the television shows . . . well, it is all stories about people who live in the city. And popular singers, of course, and Bollywood stars and all. Selvi likes all that." *Slow down! You are talking too fast!*

"If you did not look at the television, then what did you do all last night?"

"Well, we talked. Selvi and I. About the market and people we see there. And also . . . uh . . ."

Shridula, eyebrows still raised, kept her gaze fastened hard on Divena.

"Did I tell you that four tribal women—the wives of fishermen, I suppose—came to the market yesterday?" Divena asked in desperation. "I thought I might try to trade with them—some of my vegetables for some of their fish, you see—but I . . . I . . ."

Shridula watched her in silence.

"Oh, this is no good!" Divena cried in exasperation. She dropped down beside her grandmother. "Selvi and I went to the village next to this one. I did not want you to know because I feared it would upset you. A professor and his wife are teaching classes over there. Not on that village landlord's land, but most of the people who come belong to the landlord."

Tears filled Shridula's eyes, and she began to tremble. "You do not know what you are doing, my granddaughter. The landlord will crush them. And if you are there, he will crush you, too. You must never go again!"

"No, no, *Ammama!* It is not the same landlord you knew. It is not even the family of that landlord."

"Every landlord is the same, my child. You do not know. They can look like regular high caste men. They can talk kindly and do generous things. But they are moneylenders. To talk kindly and appear generous is their job. They will do anything to hold onto their money and their power."

"I know, *Ammama*. I know. It is only that . . ."

"No, you do not know! You have not seen the cold cruelty of a landlord's face staring at you. You never watched a landlord whip a boy until he struggled to cling to life. No, Divena, you do not know!"

"We are doing nothing to the landlord, *Ammama*. The professor is only teaching us to read."

"You do not need to go there. Stay here and read with me!"

"You told me yourself that you are forgetting your English."

"Now I remember it. It has all come back to my mind this very minute."

"*Ammama!*" Divena said with a laugh. She got up and carried one of the water pots over to the cook fire. She filled the cooking pot and set it on the hot flames. "It is not only to read," she said. "It is to read and to understand."

"Understand what?"

"Understand what we can be," Divena said.

Shridula tried to get up and move over to the fire, but her hands shook uncontrollably and her legs would not support her. "We are what we are, Divena." It sounded more like a plea than a statement. "Wise women accept their lot in life."

"You did not," Divena said.

"Please," Shridula begged. "Please, my blessing. Do not make trouble. Especially not on the land of a powerful landlord."

From its special place under the lowest wooden shelf on the back wall of her hut, Shridula pulled out the Holy Book that the English missionary Abigail had given her father when he was just a child. Her father had taught her to read it, and when his eyesight dimmed so that he could no longer make out the words, he had given it to her. "Keep it safe," he told her. "These are the words of life. These are the words of hope."

Shridula blew off the thick coat of dust that covered it. "You and I have not read this for a very long time," she said.

"We used to read it together every evening," Divena recalled. "Well, mostly you read and I listened."

"But not for long. Very soon you started to recognize common words, and when we came to words you knew, you read them. Remember?"

Divena smiled. "That is the same way the professor teaches us. We read the words we already know."

"Then he must be a very good teacher," Shridula said.

"Look! Here is the mango leaf we used to mark our place," Divena exclaimed. "The book of John, chapter eight."

"You read," Shridula said. "My eyes are too dim to see the words anymore."

Divena leaned forward and traced the lines with her finger: *Jesus went unto the mount of Olives. And early in the morning he came again into the temple, and all the people came unto him; and he sat down, and taught them.*

Stumbling over only a few words, Divena read about Jesus and the woman taken in adultery.

He that is without sin among you, let him first cast a stone at her.

"He did not say anything about *karma*," Divena said.

"Certainly not. Jesus did not believe in *karma*."

And they which heard it, being convicted by their own conscience, went out one by one, beginning with the eldest, even unto the last: and Jesus was left alone, and the woman standing in the midst.

"I do not think those men were high caste," Divena said.

"No. If they had been high caste, they would not have listened to Jesus at all. They would have told him to leave them alone because they were the ones who made the laws. They would have scolded him for questioning them, and they would say they were right because their way is always the right way."

When Jesus had lifted up himself and saw none but the woman, he said unto her, "Woman, where are those that are thine accusers? Hath no man condemned thee?" She said, "No man, Lord." And Jesus said unto her, "Neither do I condemn thee: go, and sin no more."

Divena stopped and stared at the words on the page before her.

"Was that the woman's *dharma*, then?" Divena asked. "Her own law of righteousness? Why else did Jesus not tell her to do good things and sacrifice to the gods and goddesses to accumulate *punya*?"

"I do not know," Shridula said.

"But would she not be punished for the terrible things she already did? In her rebirth, would she not come back as a cockroach or something?"

"No, because Jesus forgave her," Shridula said. "He took her sin away, just as though she had never done any wrong."

Divena pondered a moment. "Why did we stop reading this Holy Book?"

"Because my eyes could no longer see the words clearly," Shridula said. "Read some more."

Divena continued to read about Jesus and his teaching. *Then said Jesus to those Jews which believed on him, If ye continue in my word, then are ye my disciples indeed; and ye shall know the truth, and the truth shall make you free.*

Again, Divena stopped reading.

"I want to be free, *Ammama*," she said. "But with everyone telling me different things, how can I know the truth that will make me free?"

Shridula shook her head. "I do not know," she said.

"I want to go back to the class again," Divena insisted.

"You already know how to read."

"It is not only reading."

"This is India," Shridula said. "Throughout all time we have depended on the landlords for our lives. At long last, everything is changing, but we must be patient. We must allow it to change in its own time."

"But can you not see? It is not enough to simply wait," Divena pleaded. "If we sit patiently and wait for something to happen, nothing will ever change."

"It is better now."

"I know it is. Maybe I can have a job growing a mango tree, like Selvi does. Or raising two goats, like the widow woman with six children. But just having a job is not enough. I want to live without being frightened and humiliated. I want to move about my days without having to hide from the landlord's son, or fear that a red-hot iron will sear a scar across my face."

Shridula stared at her granddaughter. No longer did she see a scrawny, lost child. No more a desperate waif. The girl seemed to grow larger and older right before the old woman's eyes. Shridula wiped her face with the edge of her *sari* and squinted her filmy eyes into focus. How had she failed to notice that her Divena had grown into so strong a young woman?

"I was not always an old woman," Shridula said. "I remember being young like you. Back then, other laborers feared freedom. Even my own father. He did not know where to go or what to do."

Smiling at the memory, she wiped her face again.

"My father said we would starve if we left the landlord. I said I would collect custard apples from the trees and take them to the market. And I did, too. The first time someone tossed me a coin for a handful of those shriveled-up old things, I wept. Never before, in all my life, had I seen a woman paid for her work."

"I want to go back to the professor's class," Divena said again.

Shridula sighed. "You will do as you wish. Whether I want you to or not."

12

May

The hot season blasted into the village with a vengeance. Already sizzling when Divena left for the market, the temperature continued to climb.

Although Divena warned her grandmother to stay in the shade, Shridula struggled out to the garden field and poured the last of the water from the water pots over the drooping vegetable plants. She started with the peppers and moved on to the cucumbers, then over to the tomatoes. But by the time she reached the tomatoes, the peppers were already dry again and showing signs of shriveling. Shridula looked helplessly at her empty water pots.

Pick the peppers and cucumbers before they are ruined, Shridula told herself. After that she would fill the pots at a nearby muddy pond and water the rest of the garden. When Divena came home, she could go to the well for drinking water. Shridula knew she must keep the vegetables as damp as possible, or Divena would have nothing to take to the market.

Shridula was well acquainted with hot weather. She had endured it every summer of her life. Some years were hotter than others, of course. Like this day. The sun so scorched the air that the old woman found it difficult to take a proper breath. Gasping, she shuffled along the rows, picking pepper after pepper after pepper. The plants flourished in full sunlight, which had been wonderful at the beginning of the season, and would be wonderful again in the fall. Now, however, they panted for relief. Her hands started to shake and her face felt as though she had bent too close over the cooking fire. *I will finish these peppers and stop*, she promised herself. *Just work to the end of the row and no farther.*

Halfway down the row, Shridula fell to her knees. She did manage to drag herself back to the shade of her hut, but there she collapsed onto her sleeping mat. She shook her head and mourned, "All those peppers picked, and I left the basket in the sun."

Then she covered her face and cried.

As the heat soared, shoppers at the marketplace picked up their pace. They hurried to grab necessities, then to head for the shade of their courtyards and trees. Only a few considered peppers to be a necessity. By noon, almost all the shoppers were gone.

"I will not stay here in the hot sun when no one is around to buy from me," Divena informed Selvi.

"My father will not want me home early," Selvi lamented. "I have no choice but to stay."

By the time Divena started home, almost no one remained out on the road. The soft dirt had all been kicked away by the rush of so many feet and the ground below lay hard baked and dry.

"Is that you, Divena?" Jincy, a neighbor woman, shaded her eyes and called out from her doorway. "Come and sit in the shade with me. Talk for a bit." Jincy grabbed for her toddling son and balanced him on her hip.

Women had often called for Divena to sit a bit and tell them all the latest marketplace gossip, but Divena always thought up some reason to hurry on her way. But this day burned too hot for excuses. Eager to get out from under the sun, even for a few minutes, Divena joined Jincy in the shade. She took the baby onto her lap and asked, "Would you care to buy some fresh vegetables?"

"I hear that Christian missionaries are teaching classes on land that belongs to the landlord," the woman whispered in a conspiratorial tone. "Did you hear anything about that at the market?"

"They are not Christian missionaries," Divena told her. "They are teachers from the university. And they are not holding their classes on land that belongs to the landlord. But it is true that they are teaching classes."

Divena played with the baby as the woman sorted through her vegetables. "Oh, oh," the woman said, clicking her tongue. "The landlord will not like the teacher being there. He will not like that one bit."

When Divena left, she had another eighty *paise* in her hand, as well as an invitation from Jincy to come by with her vegetables and gossip any day, at any hour.

Divena had not walked far when Etash, an old woman busybody with faded eyes and frizzed gray hair, called her name. "It is too hot to be out under the sun!" Etash insisted. "I saw you talking to Jincy. Come and sit with us. Tell us what you know, too."

Divena fingered the eighty *paise* she had gotten from Jincy. "Only for a short time," she said.

When Divena got closer, she saw that three other old women also sat in the shade of Etash's *neem* tree.

"So, the landlord drove the teacher away, did he?" Etash asked. "That is how we hear it."

"No, no," Divena said. "The teacher is still there."

"Well, the landlord *will* drive him away," a withered wisp of an old woman stated.

"And so he should," insisted the one beside her. "We have our ways. Who does he think he is to come here and stir up trouble with new ways?"

"His way is the way of hope," Divena said.

"Hmph!" Etash grunted.

"We should not fear every change," Divena said as she pushed her basket over toward the women.

When Divena left the old women, her basket felt considerably lighter, and she had another five *rupees* and fifteen *paise* tied up in the corner of her *sari*.

Yet another neighbor lady—Chitra, a short, round mother of a whole brood of little ones—busily swept at her dirt yard, all the time watching Divena. Two small children worked alongside her while two tiny ones played in the dirt. When she saw Divena leave Etash's hut, Chitra quickly beckoned to her. She, too, talked and bought.

Another woman, Beena, stopped spreading her wash over the side of the veranda to listen, then she also bought Divena's vegetables.

Beena's young son called out to her. He had plastered the mud walls of his mother's hut with free advertising posters of athletes and pop stars. How old must a boy be to attend the teacher's classes, he wanted to know.

By the time Divena finally reached home, Shridula had recovered enough to act as though nothing had happened and she had only been napping. But Divena had other matters on her mind. She untied the knot on the edge of her *pallu*, the loose end of her *sari*, and poured out her earnings. Seven *rupees* and eight *paise*. She grinned at her grandmother's astonishment.

"All in one day?" Shridula exclaimed.

"Maybe I will not go back to the marketplace," Divena said. "Why should I?"

"For days, everyone in the settlement has been whispering about that new teacher," Jeevak reported to his father, the landlord. "Now they speak openly of him. They say if the laborers in the next village can learn to read, why can they not do the same?"

"How do you know this?" Ajay demanded.

"The overseer's assistant told me. Crispin. He says the younger workers are especially agitated. And the women, too. The women! He says they are saying if they finish their work, it is their right to do as they wish with the time left over."

"They are my laborers!" Ajay exclaimed. "They have no rights!"

"Actually, they do," Sundar said.

Both his father and his brother turned on Sundar. "What are you now? One of them?" Ajay demanded.

"I am not saying it is a good thing, only that it is their right. The Constitution of India says so."

"Listen to him, Father!" Jeevak exclaimed. "He would go against his own family and side with a bunch of *Harijans*. I say he has no right to—"

"No, no. What Sundar says is true," Ajay said with a sigh.

"Probably nothing but idle gossip, anyway," Jeevak said. "Those laborers of ours should be too busy to talk. I will say as much to Crispin."

Ajay rubbed the well-trimmed whiskers on his chin and shook his head sadly. "I know of this teacher. He comes from the temple village. That is where that gang of filthy *Untouchable* boys got on a full bus and caused so much trouble."

"I did not hear about that," Jeevak said.

"The *Harijans* had to stand, of course, and let their betters sit. But when the bus hit a deep rut, they fell directly onto the high caste young men."

"Fell? Ha!" Jeevak sneered. "Fell on purpose, no doubt."

"The *Harijans* quickly got off the bus. But of course the high caste boys were angry. And rightfully so. They set out after those *Untouchables* and gave them a sound beating."

"Understandable," said Jeevak.

"Certainly understandable. But this professor, this Chander Menon, encouraged the *Harijan* villagers to march off to the police and demand justice. Justice! The police kept the lot of them jailed overnight to give them time to come to their senses, but they continued their demands. Finally the high caste men of the village offered the troublemakers twenty thousand *rupees* to drop their complaint."

"Twenty thousand *rupees*!" Jeevak exclaimed.

"That is not the worst of it. Those *Untouchables* had the nerve to refuse the offer! They said the high caste young men must apologize before they would accept."

"Apologize!"

"Here is the most shocking of all: those young men *did* apologize. They crawled and groveled before the *outcastes*, then they handed them the money."

"We would never give in to such humiliation!" Jeevak exclaimed. "I say we hire *thags* to chase that teacher down and beat him so badly he will never again dare to set his foot anywhere in this district."

"No, no," said Ajay. "We will go to Landlord Dinish Desai and demand he take responsibility for his laborers. He allowed this problem to start on his land, so he must stop it."

"And we will tell him exactly what will happen if he does not," Jeevak insisted. "We will—"

Ajay turned his back on Jeevak. "Come!" he ordered Sundar. "We will go there at once. You and I."

Although Dinish Desai owned most of the land in the next village, through the years Ajay Varghese had found little reason to make contact with him. Ajay considered the man a fool. Not a thoughtful, progressive man like himself. Every time Ajay's wife Hanita had been with child, he made use of the new ultrasound equipment available for those who could pay for it. When it showed a baby girl on the way, he insisted Hanita have an abortion. In this way, Ajay had made certain his wife only bore him sons. But Dinish Desai's wife had borne him three girls before his one son, which meant he must constantly be on the search for qualified, but reasonably priced, grooms.

When Ajay Varghese and Sundar arrived at the landlord's home, Ajay's first words to Desai's servant were, "My visit has nothing to do with marriage."

Dinish Desai, ever hopeful, still rushed out to the road to meet them.

Ajay glared at the ridiculous little man who walked as though he were made of wood. Still, he could not help but look with envy at Desai's curly black hair. So full a head irritated him no end. "I must have a word with you," Ajay said brusquely.

Dinish Desai's young son ran out of the house and stood by his father's side. "Who are those men, *Appa*?" the child asked.

It dawned on Ajay that the landlord himself had absolutely no clue to his identity. Ajay stretched to his full height, raised his head high, and announced, "I am Ajay Varghese. Landlord Ajay Varghese. And this is my first son, Sundar." Ajay looked down at the little boy beside Desai. The child couldn't have been more than eight or nine years old. Ajay smiled and added, "This is the first of my three strong and extremely intelligent sons."

"Of course!" Dinish Desai answered. "Come! Please come and sit. Let us talk." Dinish Desai, bowing and bobbing, invited the two to a table situated in a nicely shaded corner of the veranda. He called to his servant, "Bring us tea!"

Dinish Desai looked at Sundar and grinned.

"This is indeed a fine son you have there, Varghese!" He winked and added: "Might it be that you came to talk with me about my eldest daughter?"

"No!" Ajay said a bit too quickly. "No, I have come to talk about that teacher you allow to work among your laborers."

"Oh, no, no," Desai said. "You have been misinformed. I have nothing to do with the professor. He is not allowed to so much as set his feet on my property."

Ajay's impatience grew with his irritation. "You have everything to do with him!" he exclaimed. Ajay had more to say, but Dinish Desai's servant appeared with a tray laden with tea and sweetmeats.

"Thank you," Sundar said most politely.

Ajay gave a curt nod and continued. "You have everything to do with that teacher, Desai, because it is your laborers he teaches."

"That is his right," Dinish Desai said. "And it is the right of my workers to sit before him and learn, so long as they do it only after their workday is completed."

Ajay, struggling to keep his composure, gulped in one deep breath after another.

Sundar glanced at his father. "It is what the professor is teaching them that is the cause of our concern—"

"I can speak for myself!" Ajay snapped to his son. "Dinish Desai, you know as well as I that *Untouchables* have certain customs and rules by which they must abide. When they stay in their place, all runs smoothly. But when someone such as your professor comes in, they—"

"He is not my professor." Dinish Desai's voice had lost its friendly tone.

"He *is* your professor because you are the one who abides his presence!" Ajay yelled. "If you did not, he would leave and go elsewhere."

"The law says he has the right to—"

"The law, the law! When it comes to the backward castes, *we* are their law!"

"Now see here," Landlord Desai said. "I have received you into my home and offered you generous hospitality. I do not intend to allow you to return that generosity with a pompous browbeating."

Ajay pounded his fist on the table. The teacups jumped and sweets fell off the plate. "You are the one who must listen, Mr. Landlord! Pay close attention to me. You depend on a good harvest in the spring and a good second harvest in the fall, the same as I do. The same as every landowner in the state of Kerala does. Unless you control your laborers, all of us will suffer. And I am warning you: None of us will allow that to happen!"

Dinish Desai leaned back and smiled. "Ajay Varghese, you are allowing yourself to get worked up over nothing. If you are not careful, your heart will explode from too much worry."

Ajay gulped a breath.

Sundar said, "Think about what we say, Desai. That is all we ask. Only that you consider—"

Ajay jumped to his feet. "We served you fair warning, Dinish Desai. Stop harboring and encouraging that teacher. And rein in your workers, or we will do it for you. And if you force that, you might well be reined in along with them!"

"Now, see here," Landlord Desai sputtered. "That teacher has done nothing illegal. Nor have my workers. Nor have I. Do not come to my house and threaten me!"

"This is not a question of legal or illegal! India is caste, and caste is India. Writing a law does not change thousands of years of culture."

Dinish Desai chuckled. "You really are quite the spectacle, Ajay Varghese. In the end, we—you and I—"

Ajay shook with fury and his face burned crimson. "Whatever you do, I will know. I . . . will . . . know . . . *everything*!"

The more Ajay's face contorted in rage, the more he sputtered out equally contorted words. And the more Dinish Desai laughed at him.

Sundar took his father's arm and pulled him toward their vehicle. "Get in the truck, Father," he said. "You did all you could."

"I will gather up *Sudras* and be back!" Ajay shouted as he struggled against Sundar. "They will be only too happy to help me."

Sundar pushed his father into the truck, then ran around and climbed in the driver's side. He started the engine.

"I will know *everything*, Dinish Desai!" Ajay called. "I make it my business to know!"

As Sundar started down the road, Landlord Desai's guffaws rang out behind him.

For a long time, neither Ajay nor Sundar said a word. Ajay struggled to regain control of himself, and Sundar had no desire to risk irritating him further. It wasn't until they were back in their own village and almost to their house that Ajay finally spoke.

"An *Untouchable* politician—"

"*Harijan*, Father."

"A *Harijan* politician came back home to his little village to open a hospital. He received warm welcomes from everyone who once looked down on him. People like us. They served him a fancy lunch and listened to what he had to say. When he got ready to leave, another *Untouch . . . Harijan* . . . walked into the room through the back door, his head bent low. The politician said to him, 'You do not have to come in the back way with your head down anymore. I was once like you, but look at what I have made of myself.' The *Harijan* said to him, 'I do not mean to be a bother. I only came to get my plates and cup. They borrowed them to serve your lunch to you.'"

Ajay laughed out loud. He laughed until tears rolled down his cheeks. He continued to laugh as Sundar stopped the truck beside the veranda. Ajay chortled all the way into his house.

13

May

Old busybody Etash, with hands like gnarled tree roots, pushed back a shock of frizzled gray hair. "That other landlord in the next village must be a kindly man," she said to Divena. "The landlord here would never allow anyone to come in and teach his laborers to read."

"That landlord there does not allow the teacher and his wife to step a foot onto his land, either," Divena said. "But neither does he force them out."

"Laborers who can read." Etash shook her head in wonderment. Slowly she counted out four coins and handed them to Divena. "Imagine that. Laborers who can read."

Divena smiled at the old woman. "Enjoy the cucumbers and peppers, Auntie," she said. "And I thank you for sharing your shade with me."

Old Etash raised the edge of her *sari* and swiped at the perspiration that dripped down her face and off her nose. "Go home to your grandmother, Divena. You should not be out in this heat. And you should not leave your poor *ammama* alone."

Divena smiled. By spending her mornings visiting with the neighbor women, by holding their babies and gossiping while they sat in the swept dirt beside their huts and looked through her assortment of fresh vegetables, she earned more money than she ever got sitting at the market day after day. And she got home in time to cook rice for Shridula's supper, and to make certain her grandmother had plenty of water.

On class days, Divena hurried off to meet Selvi for their trek to the neighboring village. But the walk took so long the girls always arrived late.

"We read the word *computer* at the last class, yet several of you brought it again this evening," said Professor Chander Menon. He held high a card with the word printed on it so all could see. "You are right, it is an important word. And every year it will become more and more important."

The professor laid the card aside and picked up another one. "Malik. I believe that is your name?" He pointed to a tall young man in the center of the group. "Are you the one who brought us this word?"

Malik nodded.

"Would you do us the favor of reading it to us?"

The men and women scooted in close and squinted up at the writing on the card. Malik answered, and so did everyone else: "Coca-Cola!"

"Yes," said the teacher. "Good choice of a word, Malik."

Divena and Selvi self-consciously eased in behind the others.

"Welcome!" Professor Menon called out with a smile. "Did either of you bring a word for us to read?"

Selvi fixed her eyes on the ground and said nothing. But Divena held up a scrap of paper. Rani Menon smiled as she took the paper and carried it up to her husband. The professor nodded enthusiastically and copied her word onto a card.

"Who can read this?" he asked as he held it up.

"That is a wicked word," spat Kilas, the man who walked with a crutch. "It says *moneylender*."

"We may not all be able to read the word, but every one of us understands it," Malik said.

"It means 'cheat,'" called a man in front of Selvi.

"No," said the professor. "It only means one whose business is to lend money. Such people can play an important role in a village."

"Money lenders abuse us," insisted a young woman who looked old. "We know it, but we can do nothing to stop it."

The professor nodded. "Yes, yes. Many of you have signed your futures away by putting your thumbprint on an agreement you cannot read."

Class members nodded knowingly.

"Or your father signed your futures away. Or perhaps your grandfathers did."

Women and men called out their agreement, "Yes, yes! This is what happened!"

"It is not the wisest way," the professor said. "Nor is it the most fair."

"Fair? We hear that India is booming," Malik said. "If that is so, it is paid for with our blood and our labor."

"They call us *Harijans*," said the man in front of Selvi. "We say, no, we are *Dalits*. But what difference does it make what they call us? An *outcaste* is still an *outcaste*."

Professor Menon leaned forward. "Listen," he said. "Learning certainly means reading and writing and counting and figuring. But it also means finding out how to protect yourselves. And most of all, it means understanding the rights you already have under the laws of India."

Two dozen faces stared blankly. They had no idea what this professor might be talking about.

"The Constitution of India has special provisions that ban *Untouchability*, no matter what name others call it," the professor explained. "The Constitution also allows for special considerations for people from *Scheduled Castes* and *Scheduled Tribes*. That is what you are now officially called."

"What does that mean?" Selvi whispered to Divena.

But Professor Menon answered. "It means free education. But only for a fortunate few."

Selvi gave a start and glanced around. Her face blushed crimson.

"It means that a certain number of government jobs are reserved for *Dalits* like you. And it grants you special representation in the Indian parliament."

"Guaranteed by the Constitution, you say? And yet, look at us." Malik's voice again. "Say what you will, but look at us. We are *untouchable* laborers. Now and forever, that is what we are."

Chander Menon shook his head sadly. "The problem is that words alone, even when they are written down in a constitution, cannot change tradition. Illegal or not, many of you are bonded laborers who cannot leave the landlord's settlement."

Many in the group murmured and nodded their agreement.

"Others of you live outside the village, in a section reserved for *Dalits*."

Kilas positioned his crutch and struggled to his feet. "But if those words are in the Constitution, why can we not go to the police and bring charges against the ones who keep us from our rights?"

"You can," the professor said. "But that does not mean the police will register your complaint. Or that they will investigate your case."

"Then we can go before the Magistrate and file charges!" Kilas insisted.

"Yes, you most certainly can. Though, to be honest with you, few *Dalits* ever manage it get that far."

Malik jumped to his feet and forced his way past those sitting around him. "If what you say is true, then I waste my time here. And you waste your time, too, Professor Teacher."

"No, no!" Chander Menon insisted. "The more you can read, the more you will understand about your rights. The more you understand, the more you will be able to control what happens to you."

The murmuring grew louder, everyone talking at once.

"Some people say you are dangerous to us," the man with big teeth called out.

"We are not," the professor said. "We are only dangerous to those who would keep you enslaved. Only to those who want things to stay the way they have always been."

"If you are dangerous to the landlords, they will fight back," said a tall, thin young woman named Maya. "Are you afraid?"

"There is always danger in change," the professor said. "But that must not stop us. India has lived in fear far too long."

The professor looked over at Divena and Selvi. "But let us talk about now. Are you two also from the landlord's labor settlement?"

"No, we are not laborers. Our names are Divena and Selvi, and we come from the next village down the road." Everyone turned to stare at the girls. "We try to walk fast so we will not miss any of the class, but the journey takes us too long to get here on time."

"Ah, but perhaps you need not walk all the way. It may be possible for you to ride the bus. Please, sit with my wife under the tamarind tree. She will give you a bus schedule and show you how to use it."

"Why do you help us, Mister Professor?" Kilas demanded. "Who pays you to come here?"

Chander Menon smiled. "No one pays me. I come because I want to. I help you, because it is the best way to help India."

The bus schedule did indeed seem a wondrous thing. But the bus stopped in only one place in the village. Although it seldom arrived on time, anyone not ready and waiting when it did come did not get a ride. Also, it cost money to ride the bus. And a rider must know the rules, such as that *Dalits* must stand up in the back and leave the seats free for upper caste people. Oh, and the bus did not stop for passengers at night.

"I think we will walk home," Divena said with a sigh.

The moon had not yet risen when the girls left, which meant a dark night sky.

"We are more extraordinary, we are more powerful, when we act as one," Selvi proclaimed, echoing the professor. "That is true. I am glad you are with me, Divena. I would not want to walk this way alone."

Divena shivered at the very thought of walking by herself on that dark road. "We should be quieter," she said. "And walk off the road where we would be hidden by the brush. In case my father is around."

"You worry too much," Selvi said, but in a whisper. She readily followed Divena off the road and quieted her chatter.

For a long while the two girls walked in silence, each lost in her own thoughts. They crossed over a rise in the road and headed down into a heavily overgrown gulley that ran across the road. If the rains came heavy this year, that gulley would turn into a rushing river and would carry away much of the tangled brush. If that happened, the road would have to be closed, always a major inconvenience for anyone going in or out of the village. The only other way through was a paved district road, but it too was often closed. Anyway, it would take the girls far out of their way and make their trek much longer.

"I think I did very well this evening," Selvi whispered. "I knew every one of the words on the professor's cards. And, really, reading that bus schedule is quite easy if we—"

"What is that?" Divena whispered.

"What is what?"

Divena stopped and pulled Selvi down into the brush between the rise and the gulley where they could not be seen so easily. "Over there." She pointed off to the side. "Farther down the gulley, to the left."

Selvi gasped.

"Shhhh!" Divena slapped her hand over her friend's mouth.

Selvi pushed her hand away. "I see them, all hunched down."

"They have their lanterns turned low," Divena breathed. "I think they are hiding there."

"And, look," Selvi whispered. "Is that a pile of rocks? And sticks?"

"They must be waiting for someone." *That Sudra woman with the braid down her back. What was it she said? "Be careful. The landlord knows you. Be very careful."*

"We have to get away from here!" Divena eased up and pulled Selvi to her feet. But then Divena suddenly grabbed her friend and pushed her back down. "Maybe what they are waiting for is the professor and his wife." Divena, shaking, fought back tears. "You heard what he said tonight. We must go back and warn them!"

"No!" Selvi begged. "The men might not even be waiting for them."

Divena tugged on her arm and pulled her up again.

"Maybe they just—"

"Shhh!" Divena warned. "Stay in the bushes and be quiet! We must not let them know we saw them."

The girls crept back up to the top of the rise. Once on the road, on the other side, they broke into a run. When they could run no more, they slowed to a walk, gasping for breath.

"I do not think those *thags* are even waiting for the professor!" Selvi insisted.

"Whether they are or not," said Divena, "the professor will know the right thing to do."

The moon, newly risen on the far side of a stand of trees up ahead, cast eerie, swaying shadows that looked like bony fingers reaching out to them.

"I want to get *home*!" Selvi cried. Her quaking voice sounded strained, even to her. Giving up all pretense of bravery, she begged, "Please, Divena! We should turn back."

"Look!" Divena cried. "Headlights!"

❧

When Professor Menon saw the girls in the road waving wildly, he stomped on the breaks. Rani Menon threw the jeep's door open and exclaimed, "Oh, you poor girls! Walking all this way in the dark! Get in and the professor will drive you to your village."

"No, no! You do not understand," Divena pleaded. "You must get off the road! A crowd of men lie in wait on the other side of the rise. We think they are waiting for you!"

"We cannot go back," Professor Menon said. "This road is the only way through tonight. Protestors of some sort have blocked the district road." Divena tried to object, but the professor said, "We will trust God to take us safely across."

"Get in," Rani Menon said to the girls. "You will be safer inside the jeep than out in the open."

Selvi eagerly climbed in. "I never rode in a jeep before," she said. "Come on, Divena."

"But the *thags*. They are waiting in the gulley!"

"Then we must not delay another moment," the professor insisted.

Swallowing the fear that rose up inside her, Divena climbed in beside Selvi and slammed the door shut.

The professor stepped on the gas and the jeep slowly moved forward. Selvi grabbed Divena's hand and squeezed hard.

Just when Divena thought the jeep ride might not be so bad after all, Professor Menon stomped the gas pedal to the floor. With a sudden roar, the jeep lunged forward. Selvi screamed and clawed at Divena's arm.

The jeep roared to the top of the rise. Instead of slowing down, it flew right over the gulley and bounced down on the other side.

From their hiding place, the armed *thags* gasped. Once they regained their senses, they jumped up and gave chase. But the jeep had already roared out of sight.

14

June

"I heard about all the excitement," old Etash called up the road to Divena. "Come, come! You must tell me everything that happened." Divena's story so enthralled Etash that she wanted to hear it all over again: the men hiding in the ditch and the jeep flying over them. So enthralled was she that she almost forgot to buy vegetables. Divena reminded her.

At Jincy's house, Divena began her visit by setting her basket down in front of the woman. Divena picked up Jincy's little son, who loved playing in the dirt, and tickled his stomach.

"*Thags*, you say?" Jincy exclaimed. "Oh, Divena, you are so brave! I would have run away as fast as I could." Jincy bought eight peppers, three cucumbers, and a squash.

As usual, Chitra busily swept the dirt from her hut and back to the road where it belonged. But as soon as she saw Divena coming, she laid down her broom and called out, "Is it true? Are you really a great hero? Come and tell me everything. Everything!" So, with one of Chitra's babies playing at her feet and the other climbing up her legs, and with the older children gawking at her—one with his finger in his mouth—Divena repeated the entire story.

Woman by woman, house by house, Divena worked her way along the road. At each stop, before she told her story, she laid out her basket to show what she had for sale. To the women's delight, the story got more exciting with each telling. By the time Divena got to Beena's house, both Beena and her son stood by the road waiting with eager anticipation. "I wish we had a picture of you," said Beena. "A big picture we could paste up on our wall with all the other pictures of important people." Beena bought the last of the peppers Divena had collected that morning.

But Divena wasn't the only one telling the story. Selvi sat at the market, repeating the adventure again and again, to anyone who would listen. But in her version, she played the part of the fearless one who courageously prodded her frightened and reluctant friend Divena to help her save the teacher.

"Why do you go to those classes, anyway?" a small man with a leathery face asked Selvi. "If you were my woman, I would keep you at home where you belong."

"Then I thank the gods I am not your woman," Selvi answered. "If your woman ever did go to the class one time, even you could not keep her from going back!"

Shoppers turned to gape. The leathery man frowned and spat on the ground.

"Times have changed, Uncle," Selvi hurried to add in a softened voice. "This is a new India."

At the lowermost of the Varghese rice paddies, a sturdy young worker called Sakaraj paused in his labors to straighten his back for a moment. How it ached! As long as he had already made the effort to stand upright, he pulled off his *chaddar* and mopped his burning face. Turning toward the distant mountains, he shaded his eyes and searched for any sign of an early cloud.

"Not a rain cloud in the sky," Crispin, the assistant to overseer Humaya, called to him. "It is too early for the rainy season. Look again next month."

Sakaraj shook his head. He refolded the *chaddar* and wrapped it back around his head as a turban. "I may not be alive next month."

"Of course you will be," Crispin assured him. "Only the rich can afford to die young."

"Then I am doomed to live forever." Sakaraj picked up his hoe. The assistant to the overseer laughed and moved on down the row. But Sakaraj called after him, "Or maybe I will stop work in time to visit the reading class in the next village."

"Ha!" laughed a gray-haired man with no front teeth. "Better chance that you will grow rich enough to die young! Still, it might be worth a try."

Crispin winced. "Watch your words, both of you! If Master Landlord hears of you saying such things, you will both wish you were dead." He glanced around at the other workers. All of them had paused to watch, everyone with rapt attention. All of them listened to every word.

"Forget the teacher in the next village!" Crispin warned. "All of you, forget him. That is an order!"

In the shady mango grove in front of the first house in the village's *Brahmin* section, old Brahmin Rama sat straight and stiff on his mat, with all three of his sons gathered around him.

"Not one more word about that new teacher," said middle son, Brahmin Satpathi. "We all agree he should be driven out of the area."

"Whether we talk of him or not, no one drives him away. He continues to do his damage," said Brahmin Arjund, the youngest of Rama's sons. Arjund shook his head sadly. "I proudly wear the *sacred thread* of the *Brahmins*. I read the *Vedas* in the holy language of *Sanskrit* and I pray to the gods. I ritually bathe every morning and I remain pure in all ways. Yet I can barely afford to feed my family."

"We live in puzzling times," Brahmin Rama said.

"We used to understand what was expected of us, and what we could expect in return," said Satpathi. "But right is no longer right, and wrong is no longer wrong."

"I hear the gossip," said Brahmin Rama. "I know the damage the teacher does."

"Then why do you not stop him, Father?" Satpathi demanded. "You are the only one strong enough to challenge him."

Brahmin Vrispati, the eldest son, laid a faded red ribbon inside his book to mark the place where he had been reading. He shut the book with a sigh. "That teacher has broken no Indian law."

"He teaches the *Harijans* to read, does he not?" Brahmin Satpathi exclaimed. "To read! They are nothing but laborers. What need have they to read?"

"First, they learn to read, then they will leave the fields and take the jobs intended for people of caste." Brahmin Arjund didn't attempt to hide his bitterness.

Brahmin Rama looked up at his first son, a tall and most serious fellow. A confident man. Compassionate and fair-minded. "You wear the *sacred thread* proudly, Vrispati," he said. "Your brothers also wear the *sacred thread*, of course, and they, too, know the *Vedas*. But you are the one who will succeed me as spiritual leader of this village. Already you serve beside me. Tell your brothers: what are they to do?"

Brahmin Vrispati did not immediately answer. But Arjund, the youngest son, said, "I have two sons of my own. Two sons I cannot afford to train in the ways of the *Brahmins*. It is not right."

"Today it is the fault of a professor teaching Landowner Desai's laborers to read," Satpathi said. "Tomorrow it will be *Harijans* taking over the village. The Wheel of Fate moves against us, Father. Soon the qualities that define us as the most important caste will fade away until all of India forgets we ever existed."

Brahmin Rama nodded his agreement. "Already the landlords have more influence than we do, even though they are still our inferiors in every way."

Ajay Varghese walked to the edge of the veranda just as an overripe mango dropped from a tree and splattered on the baked earth. He made a face. Fruit dropped faster than the servants could collect it. What had started as a refreshing fragrance of spring blossoms and had ripened into a luscious aroma in early summer was now but a stinking pile of rotting fruit.

"The sun has no right to scorch us this way!" Ajay grumbled.

He was not the only irritable Varghese. "You can sit in the shade and fan yourself, or go inside and sit under the electric fan," Sundar said with a frown. "What of the poor laborers who struggle in this heat to chop weeds from the rice paddies?"

Ajay cast a scathing glance toward his son. "What of them? They are laborers. It is their job to labor. If it upsets you, go send one of them to the shade and you take his place in the paddy. But as for me, I will stay on the veranda and fan myself."

Ajay Varghese complained about the heat because it made him too angry to bring up his real grievance. The professor's reading classes now seemed to be the rich gossip of two entire villages. Even worse, Ajay Varghese knew this same whispered gossip had infected his own laborer settlement and even now spread through it as quickly as a wind-blown fire.

"That man is too incompetent to rightfully call himself a landlord!" Ajay exploded. "Weak and useless, that is what! He will be the downfall of us all."

Sundar sat back and sighed. "What do you suggest we do, Father?"

"Call the authorities!"

"And tell them what?"

"That the fool Dinish Desai is upsetting the order of his own village and ours as well!"

Sundar wiped his perspiring face. "As I understand it, the teacher has not set his foot on Desai's property. And the workers only attend classes after dark, on their own time, after their work is done. Nothing illegal about that."

"Those workers belong to Desai! It is his right to refuse to allow them to leave his property."

Sundar didn't immediately respond. What could he say? His father had grown too agitated to think rationally.

"I can tell you this: Things will be different among my laborers!" Ajay insisted. "I will not tolerate another word from them about teachers or reading or the rights of *Harijans*. If my laborers think they have time for such foolishness, I will instruct Humaya and Crispin to send them to the paddies at dusk. They can spend their nights guarding the harvest against thieves, then go back to the paddies in the morning."

Sundar sucked in a deep breath. "Father, Indian law is on the side of the teacher. Legally, bonded labor no longer exists in this country."

"The laborers do not know that."

"But the teacher does," Sundar said. "Most assuredly, the teacher knows. And so does the Magistrate. If a complaint were brought before him, what might he do?"

Yes, most definitely the Magistrate and the teacher knew. And now, so did every person who attended that professor's class—including that *Harijan* girl, Divena.

Finally, Ajay had managed to repair the damage his foolhardy son Jeevak had caused. He had designed a well-thought out plan. He had even given instructions that a hut be made ready for a girl whose job it would be to satisfy his son. Ajay had even selected the perfect girl and had offered Mahima fifty *rupees* to secure her. And now, after all that, he found himself blocked from claiming what rightfully belonged to him. Divena knew too much. And with Professor Chander Menon involved, Ajay did not dare to move against her.

At least, not yet.

"I wish you could go to the class with me, *Ammama*," Divena said as she lay on her sleeping mat beside her grandmother.

"It is too late for me. Old people cannot learn."

"But you already know how to read. And you know enough English words to read the Holy Bible, and even to understand some of it."

"If I already know, why should I go to the class?"

Divena propped herself up on her elbow. "Professor tells us much more than how to read words, *Ammama*. Did you know that the Indian Constitution gives us rights? Even though we are *Dalits*? We can claim those rights, but it is not easy. *Brahmins* and landlords and others in the upper castes do not want us to know—"

"Enough!" Shridula ordered. "You talk too much, Divena."

"I am only saying it to you."

"No, not only to me. You speak your mind to every woman in the village, and every woman in the village loves to gossip and pass along what you tell her. Do you not know that troublemakers also have ears?"

"I only talk to my friends. And the women who buy our vegetables, of course. And—"

"And, and, and! In time, everything you say will reach the ears of the landowners. And the ears of the *Brahmins*, too."

"But—"

"Someone already tried to beat up the teacher. Those *thags* might even have killed him. What do you think will stop them from trying again?"

"But Selvi and I only—"

Shridula clasped her granddaughter's hands in her own. "You do not know what they will do, Divena. Please, please . . . You cannot know."

15

June

Divena, her empty water pots balanced on her head and hip, turned around at the sound of her name. "Mahima! Are you also going to the well? But you have no pot with you!"

"No, no. I wanted to talk to you about your debt to me."

"I now sell my vegetables to neighbors and not at the market, so I earn more money," Divena said quickly. "I can give you four more *rupees* on my debt. Let me see . . . Fifteen, take four away, is eleven. Only eleven *rupees* I still owe you."

"Fifteen," Mahima said.

"Fifteen? No, no. See, if you take four away from fifteen, which is what the debt is now, you have eleven left."

"Fifteen," Mahima said. "Four more *rupees* for interest."

Divena stopped and stared in confusion. "Interest? You never charged interest before."

"I do now," Mahima said. "Because people do not pay me what they owe me."

"We did not agree to that," Divena objected.

"We agreed you would pay, which you have not done. So I am charging you interest."

Hot blasts of summer heat had already parched the lush countryside to a barren brown. His irritation rising, Landlord Ajay Varghese clenched his teeth and glared up at a scrawny vulture that dared circle overhead, squawking out in harsh, thirsty shrieks.

"What do you mean, a worker disappeared? Workers do not simply disappear!" Ajay struggled to contain his growing anger. "They do not walk away from their work in the middle of the day and vanish."

"Maybe someone helped him run away," Ramesh suggested. "Who could it have been?"

Ajay's hands shook, and he gulped for breath. "Of course someone helped him! But I do not care about that. The important thing is to find that laborer! Find him and drag him back to me for punishment."

"Humaya will to be hesitant to do that," Sundar told his father.

"Why?" Ajay demanded. "Because he fears that any person he sends out to bring the runaway back might also vanish?"

Sundar looked at the ground and said nothing.

Ajay uttered a strangled cry of fury. "*You* go and find him, Sundar! Surely we can trust you to return. Drag that *Untouchable* back to me. When he gets here, I guarantee you I will see that he is soundly punished—and in the presence of the entire settlement, too. If I must punish him, we might as well also make an example of him."

For several minutes, Sundar continued to sit in silence. Finally, he fixed his eyes on his father and said, "Crispin. Crispin is the one who left."

"What?!" Ajay roared. "Crispin is second only to Humaya! Why would he risk running away?"

"Because he is an ambitious man who hears the talk of freedom. Because . . ." Here Sundar's voice hardened. "Because of what Jeevak did to the bonded woman. Because he still seethes over the punishment that left her husband lame and her with a scar burned across her face."

"Ridiculous!" Ajay waved dismissively. "I say it is the fault of that teacher, and of that foolish coward Dinish Desai who tolerates him. Yes, it is the fault of that stupid fellow who refuses to control the laborers he owns!"

On the other side of the village, Kilas dared to pause in his work long enough to lean against his hoe and mop the sweat from his burning face. He looked about him at the rice paddy that belonged to an especially haughty *Sudra*, and smoldered with resentment. That *Sudra*, who had at first been so reluctant to hire a man with a lame leg, now kept him limping along the rows chopping weeds, hour after hour after hour. Kilas pleaded for water. He begged for a short rest in the shade.

"Drink less and work faster," the *Sudra* ordered. "If you do not like the work conditions here, go find someone else to hire you."

"It is not right. It is not fair," Kilas fumed—but carefully and only under his breath.

Long after dark, when Kilas finally limped back to the shack where he and Baka lived in hiding, his anger exploded. "Why should we live like this? Why should we suffer for someone else's sins?" he demanded of his wife. "What the landlord's son did to you was against the law. What the landlord did to both of us was also against the law. I will go to them, and I will demand—"

"You heard the teacher." Baka ran her hand along the ragged scar across her face. "The police will do nothing."

"Even landlords must mind the law."

"Did you not hear what the teacher said, Husband? The police will do nothing for us!" Baka reached out and touched her husband's arm. "What is done is done. At least we are free from the landlord."

"And what of my lame leg and your scarred face?" Kilas replied bitterly. He tossed his crutch into the corner and sank down on the floor. "We will never be free from them."

"I care nothing about the actions of a couple of angry laborers," Ajay Varghese insisted to his sons. "I care even less about a neighboring landlord too stupid and too weak to act on his own behalf. But I do care about what affects me and my family. I will not be forced into a compromise!"

Sundar wanted to point out to his father that in this current situation Ajay could not claim to be totally innocent. He longed to argue that to act was one thing, but to act wisely was quite another. Yet Sundar knew better than to offer his father an opposing opinion, so he kept his mouth closed.

Jeevak, however, jumped in immediately. "You are exactly right, Father. You have no choice but to act."

Sundar's eyes hardened. "It would seem to me that you have already done enough acting for all of us, Jeevak. You are the one who stirred up all this resentment by your outrageous behavior. Were you also responsible for those *thags* that lay in wait for the teacher? Could it be that you actually planned to have him killed?"

"Who are you to accuse me?" Jeevak demanded. "You know nothing! Even if you were correct—which you are not—

everything you say I did would be within my right. According to Hindu teaching and our own tradition, *Untouchables* were put on this earth to do the jobs no person of caste would ever do. You and I are here to make sure they do their jobs."

"You are fearless, Jeevak," Ajay said, "but you are not wise. Sundar, you are wise, but you lack the determination to act. And you, Ramesh." Ajay gazed disdainfully at his youngest son's denim jeans and American-style shirt with the top buttons undone and the sleeves rolled up to his elbows. "Do you even desire to be Indian?"

"That is not fair!" Ramesh protested.

"At least I do something." Jeevak glared back at Sundar. "At least I get my hands dirty. At least I try."

Outrage does not die easily. It may lay buried for a very long time, giving others the idea it has gone. It may be so still it allows the perpetrators to hope everything is back to the way it was before and that all will be forgotten. But those who harbor such hopes are wrong. Outrage does not die easily. Even when it is buried deep, it seethes and grows.

"No!" Baka cried as she grabbed Kilas by the arm. "Please stop plotting against the landlord. If you do not stop, something worse will happen to us!"

Kilas jerked free of his wife's grip. "Do you expect me to cower in this sweltering shack and do nothing?"

"The landlord has such great power," Baka pleaded. "If you think the police will turn their backs on you now when the law says you are right, what do you imagine they will do if you act against the law? If you seek revenge on one so rich, who wields such influence, consider what he might do to the likes of you!"

But Kilas had already made up his mind. "When Landlord Varghese's orphaned niece married, Crispin sent me to prepare the field for the wedding feast." Kilas closed his eyes and spoke slowly, as though he were seeing it happen all over again. "Every day, the landlord's wife dressed up in fine silk and flaunted her wealth of gold jewelry. So much gold! Necklaces, rings, earrings, nose rings—"

"Yes, yes. We know the landlord is rich," Baka said with irritation.

"He can well afford to pay us the fine the law says he owes us," Kilas said. "But of course he will not. And his police and magistrate friends . . . They will not make him pay. So he leaves us no choice. I myself will levy a fine against him for his deeds. And I will collect it. Myself."

Baka gasped. "You mean *steal* from the landlord?"

"Not steal," said Kilas. "Take what is rightfully ours. In gold jewelry."

Tears spilled from Baka's eyes and traced down along her scarred cheek. "These are not the words of my husband," she said. "Kilas, this is not you speaking."

Sundar, choosing his words carefully, said to his father, "The *Harijans* do not know what the Constitution of India says about them. If they cannot read, it is almost impossible for them to—"

"Exactly. And that is how it should remain," Ajay insisted. "Really, Sundar! Next you will argue that we should read all of our private papers to them to ensure there is nothing they do not know."

"Everyone gains sometimes and everyone loses sometimes. It must be so for the sake of a united country."

"Pshaw! If all of us blessed by God and born into the upper castes must give up what is rightfully ours for the sake of unity, I say we do not want it!"

Jeevak laughed out loud. "Well, do listen to that son of yours, Father. The one you intend to follow you as landlord. The gallant son. He would give away his own birthright in the name of unity!"

"I only mean to say—" Sundar began. But his father interrupted him.

"Enough! Our privileges are not up for barter. What we can do is put an end to our own laborers' idle chatter and wasted time. And we can stop outside agitators from coming here—by which I mean, that professor."

Ajay paused to compose himself.

"We are more commanding if we stand together and act as one," he continued. "But even without the help of others, we can prevent this from going any further."

"And you suggest we do that by going against the law?" Sundar persisted.

"That will not be necessary. The law has so many loopholes we can obey it and still accomplish anything we want."

"They have their *dharma*, but we have ours," Jeevak said.

"The Hindu teachings say any actions we take are divinely mandated," Ajay said. "On that point I am inclined to agree. God is with us!"

"Well, then," said Jeevak, "let us take action!"

"Not you," Ajay told his second son. "Not any of you. Not the *Brahmins* and certainly not that worthless landlord Dinish Desai. No, I will take care of this problem myself."

16

June

Divena started out early in the morning, the same way she did every other day—with her vegetable basket filled and balanced on her head. Carefully she picked her footing through the deep ruts baked into the road. Still, she dared not slow down or she would not be able to finish her rounds before the hot morning burned away into the searing heat of the afternoon.

Each of her customers watched the road, waiting for Divena to come. But it wasn't her vegetables that called to them. The women eagerly awaited her in the hope of hearing new gossip they could pass along through the settlement. It was worth the cost of a few extra peppers or tomatoes.

"Has anyone in your class lived as long as me?" old Etash asked Divena. Then she leaned close and whispered, "Tell me, did the *thags* really threaten to beat the life out of you? Who do you suppose sent them to lie in wait?"

Chitra asked, "Do women ever bring their children to your class with them?" She handed one of her little ones to her daughter and lifted the fussy one onto her hip. The youngest she carried tied to her back. "What if those *thags* come back again, Divena? What will you do? Are you afraid?"

"How old must young ones be to go to that class of yours?" Beena asked. Divena said she didn't know. Beena leaned forward and whispered, "You know my Aneesh. He is a very smart boy. Perhaps one of these days you will take him along with you. You could teach him English on the way."

"What a brave girl you are!" Jincy told Divena. "What exciting stories you have to tell!" She leaned in close. "Can you tell me one that no other person has ever heard?"

Before Divena finished half her rounds, her vegetables lay wilted in the basket. By the time she got back to her grandmother's hut, the peppers were all but roasted.

"You talk too much, Divena," Shridula warned. "The wrong person might hear you."

"I only talk to the women who buy vegetables from me. How could the wrong person hear that?"

"I do not know how," Shridula answered. "But I do know this: the wrong people always hear."

Under a blinding hot sky, the rice paddy Ajay Varghese inspected seemed to float in and out of focus. He squeezed his eyes shut and tried to shake the vision from his head. But when he opened his eyes, he could see nothing but an endless expanse of dry rice stalks stretched out before him. Carefully, Ajay pulled his hand along the closest stalk, then he looked with dismay at the rice grains he held. Roasted. Every one of them roasted. The sun burned so hot it had baked the rice right on the stalk. Ajay tossed the ruined rice to the ground and called out a curse on it.

The heat melted everything into one shimmering blur. Sundar had convinced his father to wrap a *chaddar* around his head before he ventured out to the paddy in the middle of the day. It did keep him more comfortable, Ajay had to admit that. Still, he hated wearing a turban that made him look like one of the laborers stooped over on the other side of the fence. Ajay wiped his hand across his sweaty face and down over his dirty working clothes. He looked toward the road, hoping to see Sundar and the truck.

". . . yes, Baka and her husband! That woman who now wears the landlord's scar burned across her face."

Laborers in the next row, evidently talking to whomever would listen. Ajay hunkered down so they couldn't see him.

"How do you know it was her?" another laborer asked.

"Those two *Harijan* women that go to the reading class in the next village. They saw Baka and Kilas with their own eyes. And that is not all those women had to say. I heard—"

Ajay shook with fury. He would punish every one of those blathering fools. They were supposed to be putting their energy into the work, not gossip. Humaya, too. And Gheet too, who had replaced Crispin. Yes, the overseers would certainly pay! He would—

". . . the father to the one called Divena came back to the village." A different voice said this.

"The family of Divena's mother used to belong to this landlord."

Divena! Could that be what the worker said? Ajay dropped to his knees and crawled closer.

"A sneaky sort, her father. Calls himself Puran." That third voice again. How Ajay wished he could look over the fence and see who was doing all that talking! ". . . would happily sell his own mother for the right price. That is the talk."

For the first time since he stepped out to survey the damage to his rice paddies, the hint of a smile touched Ajay Varghese's lips.

As quickly as he could, without attracting attention to himself, Ajay made his way out of the paddy. Sundar had parked the truck a short way up the path.

"Sundar!" Ajay called. "Get me home!"

"But what about Jeevak? He is still somewhere in the paddy."

"Go now! You can come back and get Jeevak. When you find him, bring him to me. Immediately!"

In spite of the withering heat, Ajay refused to go inside his fan-cooled house to wait for his son. Instead he paced back and forth across the veranda. Back and forth, back and forth. Each time he turned around, his impatience burned hotter.

Ajay was still pacing when Jeevak hurried up the steps. "What is it, Father?" he asked. "Sundar said you wanted to see me immediately."

Ajay took his son by the shoulder and pushed him toward the sofa in the corner.

"What?" Jeevak demanded.

"All this trouble over that teacher, Chander Menon? It is of your making," Ajay insisted in a gruff whisper.

"What? I have nothing to do with him, or with anything else—"

"Can you not understand? Your reckless behavior has compromised me among the laborers!" Ajay paused to make certain that the severity of the problem got through to his son. Then he added, "You owe me a great debt."

Jeevak opened his mouth to protest further, but his father continued without a pause. "Help me—help all of us—and I will erase every trace of your debt."

"What do you want me to do?"

"Find the location of the stranger who calls himself Puran, father to Divena," Ajay said. "If you can do that, I will never again speak of your foolish actions."

"Go toward the *Harijan* settlement, on the far side of the village," Ajay Varghese ordered Sundar from the passenger seat of the truck.

Sundar didn't want to go. He had seen his father with Jeevak, whispering and murmuring plans. He saw his father clap him on the shoulder as if no problem had ever existed between them. After that, Jeevak walked around with a most unsettlingly satisfied look on his face. Something would happen soon. Something that had been carefully kept from Sundar. Then, in the midst of all that suspicion and secrecy, Sundar had been told to drive his father in the truck to . . . somewhere.

"You have business to attend to?" Sundar asked as lightly as he could manage.

"Yes," Ajay said.

"Has it to do with the classes that teacher conducts on Dinish Desai's land?"

Ajay grunted and focused his attention out the window as Sundar started the truck's engine.

For quite some time, they traveled in silence. When they crossed the river, Sundar ventured, "The water is low. The stubborn heat will not give up its hold on us."

This time Ajay didn't even bother to grunt.

"Stubbornness is a destructive trait," Sundar said. "It is so in the weather, and it is even more so in those who must endure the weather."

Ajay stared out the side window.

"If you intend to search out the home of the scarred woman and her lame husband, I must tell you—"

"Of course I do not!" Ajay snapped. "What could I possibly get from them?"

Sundar knew he should hold his peace. Already he had said too much. He knew that. Yet he could not stop himself. "We may be able to control our own workers," he said. "But if you strike out beyond them, Father. If you try to control—"

Ajay's face flushed crimson. "I am the landlord," he said in a low growl. "You may be my son, but you still work for me. You will go where I tell you to go, and you will do what I tell you to do. Without argument and without wearying me with your thoughts and opinions."

For a long while, Sundar said no more. As they passed the last of the *Sudra* land, he asked curtly, "Do you command me to take the bypass road, or to go through the *Harijan* settlement?"

"Through the settlement," Ajay said. "All the way through. When you get to the other side, keep on going until I tell you to stop."

"I suppose I will know where we are heading when we get there." An edge of sarcasm sharpened Sundar's words.

"I suppose you will," Ajay said.

Sundar drove on through the *Harijan* settlement at the far end of the village, and on past an assortment of scattered shacks. They passed a string of children in gray and blue uniforms on their way to school. They passed a boy struggling to prod a herd of lazy water buffalo in the direction of the river. They zipped past a group of giggling girls with water pots on their heads and left them covered with dust. They passed a thirsty dog with his tongue hanging out. Finally, after they passed the last house that could possibly be considered part of the village, Ajay pointed to a clump of trees set off the road and said, "There."

Sundar cast a puzzled look at his father.

"Quickly now! Turn off the road and drive over to those trees."

❧

"Puran!" Ajay Varghese called as he pushed his way through tangles of dry brush. "Show yourself, Puran! I have a business proposition for you."

Sundar looked on with growing apprehension. His father seemed to be heading for a crudely constructed shelter of sticks and branches. Set back from the road, all alone in a grove of trees, it looked to be purposely hidden away.

"Puran! Show yourself!"

"Father, what are we doing?" Sundar asked yet again. And yet again, Ajay ignored him.

"I have money!" Ajay called out.

A rustling sound came from behind the shelter. Something moved in the pile of brush. Puran stepped out and brushed off his *mundu*. He tried to stand straight despite his hunched back. "What do you want with me?" Puran demanded. "Do not ask me anything until you show me the money!"

"My money is safely hidden until we make a deal," Ajay said with a note of disdain. Sundar didn't miss it. Neither did the hunchbacked man.

"Speak fast or leave me be," Puran demanded.

"I am a landowner, a man with honor, prestige, and power." Ajay smiled and spoke easily, "Your daughter is the one called Blessing, is she not? Divena?"

Puran's dark eyes flashed with suspicion. He didn't answer.

"Yes. Well. I know her to be your daughter. And a fine worker she is, I am told. Tireless and successful."

Puran said nothing.

"May I come right to the point? Puran, I would like to buy your daughter from you."

"Father!" Sundar gasped.

Squinting his eyes and searching Ajay's over-friendly smile, Puran asked, "How much would you pay me?"

"Two hundred *rupees*."

Puran's eye lit up. The shadow of a smile touched his lips—though it looked more like a smirk.

"Father," Sundar whispered through clenched teeth. "May we please step aside? I would like to have a word with you."

"She is my darling," Puran intoned. "My hope for the future. I could not possibly let her go."

Ajay pushed Sundar aside. "I do understand your concern." He gazed at the rude shelter. He lifted his eyebrows and glanced around at the brambles. "Perhaps two hundred fifty *rupees* would make the separation less painful for you."

Eagerness glowed in Puran's eyes. "She is flesh of my flesh, and in any normal situation I would refuse to let her go for any amount of money. Yet you take advantage of my weakened state. The ground is dry and the trees bare, but a man must eat."

"Most certainly," Ajay agreed. "A man must eat."

"Father!" Sundar hissed. "I will not be a party to this."

Ajay closed his eyes and rubbed his chin as if deep in thought. "Of course I understand. For I, too, must eat. But I must also feed my entire family. Even so, I am a generous man. I might be willing to put aside what is fair and offer you as much as three hundred *rupees*. Three hundred, but not one *paise* more."

Sundar's eyes flashed in undisguised revulsion.

Puran shook his head and pondered. "She is my only child," he said. "The light of my life, and—"

"Not one *paise* more than three hundred *rupees*. If the answer is yes, we will sign an agreement between us. If the answer is no, I shall be on my way."

"If I had anyone else—" Puran began.

"Not one more *paise!*"

"I see you to be a kind and honest man, sir," Puran said. "I know I can trust you to do what is right by my dear daughter."

Ajay smiled. "I already have an agreement written up. You are free to read it before you sign your name, of course. If you cannot sign your name, you can mark it with your thumbprint. I brought an ink pad with me."

"I may not be able to read," Puran huffed, "but I can write my name."

"Fine, fine!" Ajay said. "There is one more thing, though. I know how elderly people are, and as I understand it, your daughter currently lives with her grandmother. Surely the old woman will feel uncomfortable confronted by a man of caste. I must include a requirement that you fetch Divena and bring her to me."

"I will not be a part of this," Sundar stated. He turned his back on his father and walked away in disgust.

"The law is unfairly stacked against us," Ajay Varghese said to his son.

Sundar, his lips tightly pursed, swerved sharply to avoid a stray dog that wandered into the road. He didn't answer his father.

"That Divena talks too much," Ajay said. "It is my right to defend myself and my position in whatever way I can."

"'Everyone practices untouchability,'" Sundar said. "The workers say that is what the teacher tells his class."

"See? Do you see? That is exactly the kind of troublesome remark I am forced to struggle against!"

"Everyone does," Sundar said. "Without even thinking about it. We give them the job of cleaning the toilets. We keep them enslaved in our settlements and force them to work even through this debilitating heat. We would never consider touching them. Well, Jeevak does, but I would not think that to be a point in our favor."

"Enough from you, Sundar! I live in the real world, where real people must deal with the very real society in which they live."

"Thanks be to God you were not born a *Harijan*." Sundar's sarcasm cut deep.

"Now, see here!"

"I do see, Father. I see very clearly. May God forgive us for our lack of humanity. May God forgive me for my lack of courage."

17

June

In the heat of summer, Divena had taken to grabbing up her water pots and leaving the hut well before dawn, then hurrying back with the full pots before the sun had a chance to rise and scorch the air. Shridula had their morning rice ready and waiting when she returned.

"Selvi arranged for a farmer from the market to drive us to the next village in his truck," Divena said between bites.

Her grandmother frowned. "Trucks go too fast. Could your friend not find a farmer with a bullock cart?"

Divena laughed. "We only need to walk one way, and that will be after the sun goes down and it is not so hot."

"You should not be walking the road after dark. Too many things can happen."

Divena shrugged and kissed her grandmother's cheek.

After Divena left, Shridula went out to the vegetable garden behind the house to see what could be salvaged for Divena's rounds the next day. Under the merciless sun, too many red peppers wilted before they had a chance to mature, and cucumbers withered on the vines. Still, Shridula managed to find two dozen nice-enough peppers, cucumbers, and onions, and a pile of overripe vegetables she thought Divena might be able to sell cheap. She was just on her way to the pond, which was now more mud than water, when she heard the door to her hut squeak open and shut with a soft thud.

Cautiously, Shridula eased around to the side and peered toward the door. It squeaked open again and Puran stepped out.

"How dare you come into my house!" Shridula demanded.

Puran, smiling, held out his hand. "I look forward to talking with you, mother-in-law." His voice dripped as with rich, melted *ghee*.

Shridula glared at Puran's dingy *mundu*. He wore it folded in half, like a short skirt—the way the *Sudras* wore theirs when they worked their fields. Most disrespectful in the presence of a woman. Most insulting, the way he displayed his crooked legs and knobby knees. With a small flick of his fingers he could have easily loosened that *mundu* and it would have fluttered down and covered his legs. But Puran did not.

"Get away from here!" Shridula ordered.

Puran dropped his ingratiating tone. "I have not come for you, old woman. I demand just one thing: that you return my daughter to me!"

"I will do no such thing," Shridula said. "Leave my house this minute!"

"It is my right to claim her. She belongs to me!"

"Divena belongs to no one. She is a woman now, and she thinks for herself."

"I demand to speak with her!" Puran lifted his head and shoulders in an attempt at a threatening stance.

Shridula turned her back and picked up her broom. "You cannot," she said as she began to sweep the dirt around the front of the hut. "Divena is not here."

"Where is she?"

"I do not know." Shridula swept at the packed dirt with a vengeance. "And if I did know, I certainly would not tell you."

"Then I will wait for her to come back," Puran said. "The landlord and I had struck a deal."

Shridula gasped.

"Anyway, I am hungry this morning." Puran said. "Cook rice and peppers for me."

Shridula straightened her back and turned to face the bent little man. "If you wait, you will do it far away from here," she said. "And I will see you starve beside my fire before I cook one more grain of rice for the likes of you!"

Ignoring her, Puran settled himself on a large rock next to the cooking fire. "This will do me fine," he said. "I will wait right here until my daughter gets home. She will be pleased when she hears the fine arrangements I made for her. I am not without a bit of influence, you understand. In fact, it is my full intention—"

But Puran had no chance to state his intention. Shridula dumped the freshly picked vegetables onto the ground, and, taking a mighty swing, she hit Puran across the face with the basket.

Puran jumped up in surprise. But he stumbled over the rocks and fell backward to the ground.

Shridula grabbed up a handful of stones.

"How dare you—" Puran sputtered in indignation.

Muttering insults, Shridula pelted him with the rocks.

"Ow!" Puran screamed. "Stop that! Ow . . . ow! Stop!"

"I did not like you when my husband arranged for you to marry my Ritu," Shridula yelled. She picked up a larger rock and threw it at Puran's head.

Shrieking, Puran struggled to get to his feet.

"I liked you even less when you took my daughter away from the village." Another rock hit Puran in the side and knocked him back down.

"I despised you when you abandoned your little girl in my doorway."

Shridula picked up a rock so heavy she struggled to lift it.

"And now . . . now that you have come on a wicked errand . . ." Shridula stepped up beside Puran.

"No!" he cried, cringing. "I will leave. I will not bother you again!"

Shridula dropped the rock on Puran's leg.

"Owwww!" he shrieked.

Shridula, gasping for breath, stepped back against the side of the house and eased herself down to the ground. "I do not want to become like you," she whispered. Tears filled her eyes and trickled down her wrinkled cheeks.

"What is going on?"

Shridula looked up to see her neighbor, the potter, staring down at her. She motioned to Puran, who lay in the cook pit, wailing in anguish. The potter strode over and gazed down at the battered man. "You!" he exclaimed. "You dared to come back again?"

"Keep that crazy woman away from me," Puran pleaded. "She almost stoned me to death!"

The potter lifted his heavy stick from off his shoulder. "Almost? Perhaps she needs help to finish the job."

An old man hurried down the road with his grandson, the goat herder, right behind him. "What is all the commotion?" he asked. "Is someone hurt?"

The potter's wife, who had followed her husband, knelt down and wiped Shridula's face with a wet cloth. The milkman's old aunt hurried over and offered her a cup of fresh milk.

Puran, moaning, pulled himself upright. The potter glared at him and ordered, "Stop that noise! Your leg is not broken—yet. If you have any sense, you will get yourself up and away from here before someone does the job right."

Puran tried to pull himself to his feet, but he could not. The potter grabbed his arm and shoved him upright. Puran shrieked in pain, but stopped abruptly when he saw the crowd that had gathered. They did not look the least bit sympathetic. In fact, they looked angry—threatening, even. Many carried heavy sticks.

"Get away from here!" the potter ordered Puran. "And do not come back."

Puran started to limp away, but he stopped and turned to glare at Shridula. "This is between my daughter and me, old woman," he said. "Do not come between us."

When Divena got back from the class, she took care not to make any noise that might disturb her grandmother's sleep. She eased herself down to her sleeping mat and closed her eyes. Shridula reached over and took her hand.

"*Ammama!*" Divena said. "I thought you would be asleep."

"I have hardly seen you today," Shridula said. "I thought we could talk."

Divena turned over to face her. "Oh, *Ammama*, I learned so much tonight! In the cities, like the one where I once lived, sacred cows roam free and eat tons of grain while people starve on the streets. That is true! I remember seeing all those old, skinny cows everywhere. Some even got bites of coconut. Even pineapple!"

"Divena," Shridula said, "today—"

"And the rats, *Ammama*. They eat so much food that if it were all put in train boxcars, they would reach all the way across India!"

"Something happened here today," Shridula insisted.

"But even as the professor told us about the rats, people started to complain. They said every rat had to be protected because it might be someone they knew who was on the way to *Nirvana.* That is not in the Holy Bible, is it?"

"No. No it is not. That is what Hindus believe, not Christians. And that is why . . ." Shridula stopped abruptly and squeezed Divena's hands. "Your father came here today. He wanted you. I do not know what would have happened if he had found you here. Oh, Divena, he is a dangerous man!"

Divena stared at her grandmother. "But . . . he is gone now?"

"Yes. But he will be back. I know he will. And he wants you."

"Did you tell him where I had gone?"

"Of course not. But he will find out. Everyone in the village knows where you go. Everyone is talking about you and Selvi and your classes."

"Yes," Divena said.

"Please, do not go to the class anymore," Shridula pleaded. "Please, my blessing!"

"But if I do not go, when he comes back, he will find me here."

"If you do go, I will worry until you get back home to me. And what if he waits for you in the dark? I could not send the potter to help you, because I would not know anything was wrong."

Divena and her grandmother lay silently side by side in the dark, each lost in her own thoughts.

After several minutes, Shridula suddenly said, "A warning signal!"

"What?"

"A warning signal. If you see your father, you can give the signal and I can get the potter to hurry out and help you."

"Yes," Divena said. "I could scream, 'I see a rat!' "

18

June

"I am not my father!" Sundar Varghese told himself. All the way back from the meeting with Puran he repeated the affirmation in his mind, and he continued to repeat it throughout his sleepless night.

As on most nights, Sundar and Jeevak slept outside on the veranda, just as generations of Varghese men had done before them. Their father, who firmly refused to consider air conditioning, slept in a fan-cooled room, a luxury he believed should be reserved for married men. Married men and students, evidently, for Ramesh had his own fan-cooled room.

Come dawn, Sundar repeated—more frantically than ever—"*I am not my father!*"

On the other side of the veranda, Jeevak lay snoring on his sleeping mat. Sundar could hear the cook rattling pans in the kitchen as she began to prepare Sunday breakfast, but no one else seemed to be moving about. He got up from his mat and walked quietly to the bathroom, where he splashed water on his face and ran his fingers through his hair. He stared into the mirror and insisted again, "I am not my father!"

Sundar jogged to the shelter, where he had parked the truck. Again he repeated the *mantra*, but this time out loud: "I am not my father!"

Sundar did not intend to head for his father's rice paddies. Certainly he had no interest in seeing Puran, a man he considered absolutely despicable. Without making a conscious decision to do so, he headed down the road toward the next village. Toward Dinish Desai's land. Perhaps the professor would be there, and he could talk to him. Perhaps they could reason together. Maybe.

At the edge of Desai's land, Sundar parked the truck and got out.

"Did you come to shout curses at my father?"

Sundar gave a start. The young son of Dinish Desai, standing almost behind a tree, stared hard at him.

"No," Sundar said. "I, um . . . I only . . . um . . ."

Sundar looked down at the soccer ball beside the boy's feet. "Do you play soccer?"

"Not very well."

"It is hard to practice alone," Sundar said. "Kick the ball over here to me."

The boy kicked the ball, but it bounced low and rolled off to the side. Sundar jumped forward and scooped it up high with his foot, then leapt up and rammed it with his head. The ball flew back to the boy. The boy kicked it back—wide again, but higher. Sundar jumped up and hit the ball with his knee, sending the ball flying back to the boy. The boy ran for it, but he tripped on the ball and fell flat.

"You are good!" the boy exclaimed.

"You are not bad yourself. More practice . . . that is all you need."

"Are you here with that other landlord?" the boy asked.

"Not today. Today I am by myself."

"If you are looking for the class, they are not here."

"No. No, I am not looking for the class."

"Are you looking for the church, then?" the boy asked. "It is somewhere in the pepper grove. I do not think you can drive there, though."

Sundar stared at the boy.

"They think my father does not know about it, but of course he does. He found their church hidden away where the path goes in two directions. It is right there, but pushed back into the dark part of the forest. That is what my father says."

Sundar nodded.

"Anyway, my father does not care about that church. He says the more they sing their songs and chant their prayers, the less trouble they will cause him."

"Yes," Sundar agreed, laughing. "I think your father is quite right. And very smart, too."

"I can get him for you," the boy offered.

"No, no," Sundar said quickly. "I must be leaving." He climbed back into the truck. "Thank you!" he called to the boy.

Divena gazed around the empty clearing. "I told you no one would be at the class today! We walked all this way for nothing. I told you the teacher would not come on the weekend."

"But that tall woman, Maya," Selvi said. "I heard her tell Baka she would see her at the meeting on Sunday. I was afraid they were getting together without us."

"If they are, the meeting is somewhere else."

"Yes!" Selvi said. "That must be it. They are meeting somewhere else. Maybe in Landlord Desai's settlement?"

"Not there. He would never allow it."

Selvi dropped down and rubbed her forehead. "Oh, you are right," she said with a sigh. "We walked all this way for nothing."

"Maybe we will find some custard apples to pick," Divena suggested. "Or wild nuts. Something different to sell. I hardly have any good vegetables left in the garden. At least then our walk would not be wasted."

"They grow peppercorns here," Selvi said. "We could pick some green and sell that."

"What? If they catch us taking their peppercorns—"

"If they catch us, we will say Maya invited us."

"But . . . that is not true!"

Selvi laughed. "Not altogether true, but true enough."

Divena opened her mouth to protest, but Selvi pressed forward toward the pepper groves.

Sundar made his way down the narrow path. Dinish Desai's son had told him the church was a long way in. Even so, he worried as the path narrowed to a trail. The trees grew thicker there. That encouraged him, for the child had said the church was hidden in the dark part of the forest. Sundar watched for the place where the path went in two directions.

Far down the trail there did seem to be a bit of a side trail. Actually, little more than a narrow footpath that seemed to be seldom trod. Sundar stopped and searched through the vine covered trees for any sign of a building. None.

But as Sundar moved on down the trail, he heard what might be the soft mumble of voices. He retraced his steps, but still saw nothing but vines. This time he followed the narrow footpath. That's when he saw it, carefully tucked back among the thick trees. Only a simple thatched-roof building, really. Three walls with the back open for air, and a rolled-up mat attached just under the roof line that could be dropped down and serve as a back wall in case of rain. About a dozen men and women sat on cloths spread out on the dirt floor, a cluster of children in front of them. Sundar didn't walk right in. Instead, he eased into the shadow of thick trees where he could watch and hear, but where no one would be likely to notice him.

Several pairs of sandals lay in a neat row outside the open back wall. Of course the sandals would be there. Indians had too much respect for religious gatherings to wear shoes inside.

Men and women, their heads bowed in reverence and eyes squeezed shut, murmured prayers. Up in front, the children did the same, only with their hands folded. One little fellow kept an eye open and peered around at all the other worshippers. Sundar couldn't help but smile.

When the praying stopped, two young women stood up and began to sing. Sundar didn't look at them, though. He stared at the creamy-complexioned woman off to one side, all alone. An ugly scar marred her once-beautiful face. It had to be Baka! Sundar couldn't bear to look at her, so he swept his eyes over the other worshippers. In the back corner, he spotted Baka's husband, Kilas.

To Sundar's surprise, Chander Menon, the professor, stepped up to the front. He was a tall Indian man with a light complexion, dressed in Western trousers and a fine Indian *kurta*, yet Sundar had failed to notice him among the darker-skinned laborers. His wife, too. She sat in the corner in the front.

Professor Menon opened his Bible and read: *Verily, verily, I say unto you, He that entereth not by the door into the sheepfold, but climbeth up some other way, the same is a thief and a robber.*

But he that entereth in by the door is the shepherd of the sheep. To him the porter openeth; and the sheep hear his voice; and he calleth his own sheep by name, and leadeth them out. And when he putteth forth his own sheep, he goeth before them, and the sheep follow him: for they know his voice. And a stranger they will not follow, but will flee from him: for they know not the voice of strangers.

"I read from the book of John, chapter ten, verses one through five," Professor Menon said. "Jesus is the door. Jesus is the way to know God."

Sundar leaned forward to better hear. A large leather Bible lay on the second shelf of the bookcase in his family's sitting room, but no one had opened it for a very long time. Long ago, his grandmother used to read to him from that Bible. He remembered hearing about the Good Shepherd. But never had he heard anyone talk about what it meant. Or what any Bible verses meant, for that matter.

"My family is Hindu," a man said to the professor. "Are you telling me they are trying to enter God's sheepfold by the wrong door?"

The professor smiled. "A great Indian *sadhu* by the name of Sundar Singh, who lived almost a hundred years ago, said, 'Christianity is the fulfillment of Hinduism. Hinduism has been digging channels, but Christ is the water to flow through these channels.' Sadhu Sundar Singh pointed out that Hinduism has many beautiful things. Perhaps your family has found those things. Yet, as the great *sadhu* said, 'But the fullest light comes only from Jesus Christ.'"

A Christian holy man, Sundar thought. *Imagine that! And he shares my name!*

As the little congregation sang and clapped their hands, Sundar eased in closer. In one way, he found himself drawn to these people. But at the same time they repulsed him. They were so backward, the way they talked and acted. So dirty. So simple.

❧

"The shade of all these trees feels wonderful!" Divena sighed.

"I am glad to be off that blistering road," Selvi agreed. "How I hate the smell of hot dirt!"

At first it seemed as if the trees were so close together they might squeeze the narrow path completely away. Yet when Divena looked up, she could see large patches of blue sky. "This is not a forest," she said. "It only looks that way because the pepper vines grow so thick and tall around the trees."

Divena reached out and ran her hand along the rough bark of a nearby tree trunk. Perfect for winding, climbing pepper vines. "Look," Divena said. "Bunches of green pepper berries."

"Once the rains start, those little clumps will grow and grow until they hang from the vine in long strands," Selvi said. "If we could come back then—"

"Listen!" Divena said. "Someone is singing!"

> Vazhiyum sathyavumaayavane . . .
> Nin thirunaamam vaazhthunnu.

"Grab some of those bunches of green pepper and run!" Selvi cried.

But Divena stood perfectly still and listened:

> Father and God, your kingdom come.
> Your will be done forever, on earth as in heaven.

"I think they are Christians," she said.

"Then Christians believe the same as Hindus," Selvi insisted. "The gods ordain our lives, forever and ever, and so does the Christian god."

"I do not understand. Why, then, do the Christians pray for God's will to be done? I mean, if the will of their God is already set, why do they pray and ask him to do it?"

"Come, we must leave here!" Selvi demanded. "Hurry!" She grabbed Divena's hand and pulled her back up the pathway, toward the road that led home.

Jesus the Christ, Son of the only God, offers love and promise and dignity and freedom. That's what Professor Menon said. And everyone in the church clapped with joy. *Of course they would*, Sundar thought. The people were all *Harijans*. They needed such words of hope to carry them through their wretched lives. But he wasn't a polluted *Harijan*. He was *Kshatriya*, part of a great caste descended from kings and warriors.

Sundar had intended to hang back and watch for an opportunity to talk alone with the professor. He wanted to explain the problems the man's presence caused in the villages. Perhaps even to ask him a question or two. Only to get a different perspective, of course. But the young woman Baka stood up again and began to sing:

> Thiruninavum divya bhojyavumaay.
> Ee ulkathin jeevanaay.

Sundar could not bring himself to look at her scarred face. Yet despite the injustice she had experienced, she dared to sing those words. How could it be?

You are a loving God.
You give us eternal life.

Too shaken to stay, Sundar Varghese slipped out through pepper vines and ran up the path.

"I am not my father!" he proclaimed.

19

July

"We worked all day yesterday and half the night opening trenches to bring river water to the dry paddies," Sakaraj told Humaya. "The rice grows as well as is possible with everything so dry. So why do you force us to work endlessly in this cruel heat?"

"I do not give the orders," the overseer told him. "Master Landlord does."

"Then tell Master Landlord we refuse to work ourselves to death!"

An old man with no teeth stood up behind Sakaraj. He hesitated, running his hand through his bush of gray hair as he shifted from one foot to the other. "Paddies are already weeded good as ever," he said slowly. "I am too old to work under this burning sun. Especially when there is no good reason for it."

"I say we both rest ourselves in the shade," Sakaraj said to the old man.

Other voices called out their agreement.

"It is not your choice!" Humaya insisted to them. "It is not mine, and it is not yours, either."

"Tell the landlord to read India's Constitution," Sakaraj said. "Tell him that!"

Humaya, taken aback, stared at the defiant young man. He spoke to Sakaraj, but he intended his message for all of them. "I tell you to get yourselves out to the paddies and back to work!"

"Even if you make us go," Sakaraj said, "you cannot make us work."

Ajay Varghese sat on the veranda going over his accounts with Sundar when Jeevak came back from the fields. "I ordered the trenches open," Jeevak said.

Sundar looked at him in amazement. "But the river already runs dangerously low."

"We have no choice." Jeevak spoke to his father as if Sundar weren't there. "The paddies are dry, and still there is no sign of rain."

"You did the right thing," Ajay told his son. "We must ensure that the harvest is a good one."

Jeevak dropped down and sat across from his father. "The dry ground is not the only problem. More and more laborers refuse to work."

"Because there is nothing for them to do," Sundar said. "The paddies are weeded—for the most part. And now that river water is coming in, what work is there for them to do? Especially in this oppressive heat."

Jeevak turned on his brother. "I did not say they had no work. I said they *refuse* to work!"

Ajay slammed his accounting book closed. "This idea of rights had gotten way out of hand. It is not up to our laborers to decide when and where they work. Or even *if* they work. We tell them, they do not tell us."

"Perhaps we would do well to go out there and listen to what they have to say," Sundar suggested. "They can easily finish whatever work needs to be done in the fields during the cool morning hours and then rest out the hottest part of the day. In the late afternoon, they can do such things as repair the broken sections of fences, prepare the tools for harvest, maybe—"

"We do not listen to the workers," Ajay repeated. "They listen to us! Whether or not the paddies are in need of work makes no difference. If they dare to refuse to work, then we will make certain they *do* work!"

Jeevak smirked. "Is it your wish, Brother, that we look like that cowardly Dinish Desai?"

"We will stop the rumblings and complaints immediately," said Ajay. "Every rebellion has its leaders, and—"

"Rebellion?" Sundar said. "That seems awfully strong for what is happening in our paddies."

"Absolutely not! To refuse to work is to rebel. And every worker who participates will be punished as a rebel! See to it, Jeevak."

Despite Humaya's pleas: "Yes, the days are hot. The sun is torture to me as well. But this is still the hot season, so it is to be expected. Please, do not be persuaded to ignore the landowner."

Despite his warnings: "The master will be most furious. You do not have to work hard, but we must not let the landlord find the paddies empty of workers. Anything he does in his rage will be trouble of your own making."

Despite Humaya's threats: "To obey the landowner is our job. If the master comes and you are not out there, I will tell him I tried to persuade you but you refused. I can lose my position as overseer, but you can lose your lives."

Despite all this, the weary workers turned their backs on the overseer and listened to Sakaraj. "It makes no sense for you to work," he insisted in a fiery voice. "These days are too hot for meaningless labor. We will not cooperate!"

"We must do something!" Humaya told Gheet. "The blame for this will be laid at our feet!" But with growing dismay, they watched helplessly.

The laborers headed back to the settlement to sit in the shade, sip water, and gossip. They talked of the heat, of course. And of their ever-lighter food pots. They talked of difficult growing seasons from the past. And they talked of the teacher in the next village, and what it could mean to them to learn to read and write.

"I might get me some chickens to raise," said the old man with no teeth.

"Maybe I could cultivate some of those wild pepper vines," suggested a short man with skin almost black.

"We could go together and get us a few cows and start a dairy of our own," an energetic young man suggested.

"It does not matter what we do," the toothless man said. "The important thing is that we would be the bosses of us. Whatever money we earned, we could keep in our purses."

"But we cannot do any of those things," Sakaraj pointed out. "Because we cannot go to the classes and learn how."

Humaya lowered his head into his hands and wept for what he knew would come.

When Jeevak arrived at the laborer settlement, he came with servants bearing whips and lashes. He drove in and stopped the truck next to the well. Men, clustered together under shade trees, ceased their gossip. Some quickly stood up. A few bowed down on the ground before their masters. Terrified children ran to their mothers, who stared in silence at the landlord's son.

"Humaya! Gheet!" Jeevak called. "I see no workers in the paddies. Why did you disobey your master?"

Humaya hurried out and stood before Jeevak. "I did my best," he said.

"Your best is not good enough." Jeevak nodded to his servants, and they jumped down from the back of the truck. They ran out among the clusters of men and lashed at them with the whips. The men covered their heads and struggled to get to their feet, but the blows rained down on them so fast and so hard that they could not stand.

"No!" Gheet cried.

"If you beat them so severely, who will prepare for the harvest?" Humaya pleaded.

Jeevak shook his head and looked around him. Men, bleeding and screaming, lay all over the courtyard.

Humaya's eyes flashed. "If we lose the harvest, what will your father have to say? Another catastrophe will be your fault."

A look of panic crossed Jeevak's face. "Stop!" he ordered his servants. "Get back into the truck!"

As the servants pulled back, Jeevak ordered, "Tomorrow morning, every one of you will be back at work! Wounds will be no excuse. You brought them on yourselves. And there is to be no more talking about other landlords. And not one word about that teacher! I have spies of my own among you, so I will know. I will know! Break this rule, and the whips will be back—twice as many and for twice as long!"

No one uttered a word. Not so much as a moan.

"My eyes will be watching!" Jeevak threatened. "My ears will be listening! I will know."

That afternoon, Ajay sat alone with Sundar. "As you know, you are the son I have chosen to be the next landlord. Yet your brother Jeevak is the one who stopped the trouble and got the laborers back to work."

Sundar looked at his father and said nothing.

Ajay sighed. "Why must all my sons bring me so much trouble?"

"I cannot answer for my brothers," Sundar said. "But, with all respect, I think your methods bring the trouble to us."

"So now you are the expert? Now you are wise enough to teach me the job I have practiced for more years than you have lived?"

"No, Father. In most ways you are the expert. I have learned much from you and will surely learn much more. But times have changed, and—"

"Do not speak to me of changing times!"

"But I must. Because, like it or not, the times *have* changed. Even if you could rid the village of the teacher, another would come in his place. You think Jeevak can solve the problem with the workers by brandishing whips. But no matter how you beat the workers, someone will stand up to those whips."

"Stop it!" Ajay ordered. "I have heard enough from you!"

"No, you have not, Father. Because what you are doing is against the law."

"Ha! What do I care about words on a paper?"

"It is more than that. Yes, you have many influential friends. And yes, you wield great power. But sometime someone will come along who will find a magistrate who does not fear you. And then . . . Well, what then?"

❧

As the sun sank low, Jeevak strutted out to the veranda where his father sat alone eating a plate of cut mangos. "You will have no further trouble from the laborers," Jeevak announced. "I have taken care of everything."

Ajay picked up another piece of fruit and sucked it into his mouth. He looked at his juice-covered fingers. One by one, he licked them clean. "Sweet and juicy," he said. "Just the way I like them."

Jeevak scowled. "Did you hear what I said, Father?"

"Of course I heard. I am not deaf."

"Sundar did nothing to settle the problem. Once again, I am the one left to take care of it."

Ajay let his son simmer a bit as he picked up the last piece of mango and slowly ate it. After he had once again licked his fingers clean, he looked up at Jeevak and said, "Sit down, my son."

Jeevak sat, but his father stared at him in silence. Jeevak fidgeted and tried to look away, but he could not escape his father's gaze.

"I will not ask you how you handled the workers," Ajay finally said. "I do not want to know."

Jeevak sighed in exasperation. "I thought you sent for me to thank me for my good work. Obviously, you did not. So why did you send for me?"

"To talk to you about someone even more prone to trouble than you. Someone who, like yourself, can either cause us great difficulty or can come to our rescue. I need you to take me to see him first thing tomorrow."

Puran did not seem pleased to see Ajay Varghese stride up to his door. When the landlord introduced him to his second son, Puran nodded and stood uncomfortably.

"Do you have your daughter with you?" Ajay asked. "Did you bring Divena to me?"

Puran mumbled that he did not. That neighbors armed with clubs surrounded her grandmother's house. That as soon as he mentioned Divena's name, they battered him and all but broke his leg in two. He did not mention Shridula and her rocks.

"We have an agreement," Ajay said. "If you do not deliver your daughter to me, you will immediately become my bonded laborer. My slave."

"What?" Puran demanded. "I never agreed to any such thing."

"Oh, but you did. I have the paper with your signature to prove it."

Puran turned to Jeevak. "I tried to get her, and they all but killed me for my trouble. Your father never told me I would have to work for him, and he did not say—"

Ajay spread out his hands and smiled. "I am not an unfair person," he said. "If you cannot do it alone, I can supply you with a man to help you. He will have a club of his own. But you must lay out a plan to get your daughter that will not fail. Can you do that?"

"Yes," Puran said. "Yes, if I have that help you promise. Then I know I can get her for you."

"Fine," Ajay said.

"And the money?" Puran begged shamelessly.

"Of course. I made an agreement with you, did I not? Jeevak will come back tonight and bring the man."

20

July

"Thank you to all of you who copied the phrases you saw on signs in the village," Professor Chander Menon said to his class. "I wrote them out on cards, and I will hold them up one at a time. If you can read the phrase, speak it loudly. If you cannot read it, look carefully at the words and listen to the others. Ready? Here we go."

Bus stops here

Almost everyone could read this one. "Because we learned to read the bus schedule," Divena said.

Watches for sale cheap

Only a few attempted this one, so the professor read it to them. "If you ever want to buy a wristwatch, a place that displays this sign is not the place to make the purchase. Before too many days pass, your wristwatch would almost certainly stop running."

The class stared at him. "We are *Dalits*," Maya said. "How would we have money for a wristwatch?"

"When the time comes," the professor said. He held up the next card.

Keep out

Everyone knew what this phrase meant, though few could actually read the words. Some said, "Stay away." Others guessed, "Do not enter."

Toilets

"How many of you have a toilet at your house?" the professor asked. Not one person raised a hand. In fact, only Kilas had ever seen a flush toilet.

Watch your step

Fire Exit

No one knew what either of these meant.

Medical

Most everyone read this, although several read it as "hospital." The professor paused to write out that word as well.

Danger

Only a few knew this word, though everyone agreed it was an important one that they all should learn.

Sign up to vote

Everyone stared silently at this card. "Can you read it, Kilas?" Professor Menon asked.

"I can," Kilas said. "But I see no point in giving false hope."

"This is a most important sign for all of you to read and understand," the professor insisted. "Every one of you has the right to help choose the people who will be leaders, because they will be your leaders as well as leaders for members of the high caste. Every one of you has the right to vote for the person you believe will best represent the interests of *Dalits*."

"For our own village?" a woman in the front asked.

"Yes, but not only for your village," said the professor. "You can even vote for the prime minister. A *Dalit* vote counts every bit as much as a high caste vote."

Malik laughed out loud. "Everything changes," he said. "Everything except the plight of *Untouchables*."

"That is also changing," Professor Menon insisted. "Look at all of you, sitting here together, learning to read. Such a thing could not have happened in the days of your fathers."

"My grandmother used to belong to the landowner Varghese, in the next village," Divena said. "The landowners owned her family for three generations. She told me much about those days."

"But she got away?" asked a small woman hidden off to the side.

"She escaped when she was no older than I am now," Divena said. "But for several years before that she lived in the landlord's house. His daughter had her as a personal servant."

Kilas sat up straight and stared at Divena. "Your grandmother knows the landlord Varghese's house?"

"Back then, she did. She lived there."

"It must have been quite lovely," Kilas said. "Did she tell you about it?"

"Well . . . yes. She told me some."

Professor Menon cleared his throat. "We were saying you all have the right to vote."

"It sounds good," said Nagmani, a stringy-thin man so dark he looked to be almost black. "But you also warn us that the authorities like the high caste more than they like us."

"Especially the rich ones, like the landlords," Kilas interjected.

"Yes, especially the rich ones," Nagmani persisted. "So what are we to do when they will not let us vote? If they try to stop us by beating us? Or by doing any of these other things to us that you say they are not allowed to do?"

"Knock them in the head with a big piece of firewood," Kilas suggested.

"No, no!" Professor Menon warned. "If you use violence, you immediately lose your rights. Your power comes from unity. From banding together to pursue justice. Alone, you are a small voice easy to ignore, or even to punish. But together, you can be a great, forceful power."

"I still say, knock them in the head," Kilas said, though with a bit of a smile.

"It may sound strange to you, but many *Dalits* together, all practicing quiet resistance, will get you much further than an angry voice and a stick of wood. Think about it. Passive resistance is the way Mahatma Gandhi moved the will of India. And he got his way. Passive resistance is a more powerful force than violence."

Kilas shook his head doubtfully.

"Here is the truth," the professor said. "Any time *Dalits* fight the powerful upper castes, the upper castes will win. Your strength is in knowing your rights and then standing together in unity to claim them."

The class stared at the professor. Not one person looked convinced.

"For twelve years I lived in a bigger village," said a soft-spoken young man with exhausted eyes and a touch of gray in his hair. "I earned my living by riding a cycle-rickshaw. I carried people from where they were to wherever they wanted to go."

The man paused, but everyone sat silently and waited for him to continue.

"The rickshaw did not belong to me, of course. I had to pay one and a half *rupees* every day to rent it. Some days I earned six or seven *rupees*. Some days I earned fifty *paise*. Some days I earned nothing at all. Either way, I still had to pay one and a half *rupees* for rickshaw rent."

"The law does not guarantee you fair pay," Professor Menon said.

"We will still be *Dalits*," said a small woman who sat in front of Divena.

"Yes," the professor said. "When you go to a tea stall, you will still have to sit in separate seats and drink from separate cups. But you will be free to go to the tea stall, and you will be more likely to have the money to pay for tea."

"Come," Kilas said to Baka. "We have a long walk home." But his eyes were not on his wife. He watched Divena. She and Selvi had already headed down the road.

Baka talked about the class, about the monkeys she saw the last time she walked the road, about the first sign of clouds and her hope that they would finally bring rain and relief from the heat. But Kilas wasn't listening to her. His eyes stayed on Divena. She walked far enough ahead of them that he could just barely see her. Even limping on his crutch, he slowed his pace so they wouldn't catch up with Divena and Selvi.

". . . and that is what Jeba said tonight. Do you know who she is? That tiny woman who sat close to us?"

Up ahead, Kilas saw Divena and Selvi pause together. But only for a moment. Selvi turned toward a cluster of wood houses and Divena continued along the road.

"Kilas!" Baka said. "Are you listening to me?"

"You go on home," Kilas told her. "I will be along soon."

"What?" Baka stared at him. "What are you planning?"

"Nothing. I have many things on my mind tonight. Much to consider. I will be along soon."

"No," Baka protested. "I will slow down and walk with you. I will not talk anymore so you can consider the things in your mind."

"Go!" Kilas insisted.

Reluctantly, Baka went on without him.

Kilas limped along slowly so that his wife could get ahead. He could no longer see Divena. Fortunately, Baka walked fast. He followed as closely as he dared, but still he could not see Divena. He did see a small path that led off the main road. He decided to follow it.

Rough and uneven, the path proved to be a difficult one to maneuver in the dark with his crutch. A once-flooded trail, it had baked hard into cement-like ruts. But he quickly learned to manage his crutch, and hurried along as quickly as he could without tripping. As the path became rougher, he found it increasingly difficult to keep his footing and not stumble. Finally, up ahead, he caught sight of Divena.

Kilas rehearsed in his mind what he would say to her: *Do not be afraid. I only want to ask your help.*

Hopefully, that would put her mind at ease.

He would say: *I heard what you said in class about your grandmother living at Landlord Varghese's house. I want to ask you about that house. I am to do some work there, you see, and I thought I should know about the lay of the rooms.*

No, no! Divena would never believe that. Maybe if he said . . .

Up ahead, a soft lantern light appeared.

When Divena saw the dimmed lantern, she shivered with fear. She must get to her grandmother's hut! She started to run, but the men were ready for her. One lunged forward and grabbed her.

"No noise from you!" the man rumbled in a threatening whisper. Divena struggled and kicked, but he gripped her tightly from behind. When she tried to scream, he slapped his hand over her mouth, clamping down so hard she could barely breathe. Divena couldn't see who held her, but she did see the man holding the lantern. He was short and hunched, and his legs were crooked.

Divena's fear turned to fury. She raised her foot, and with all her strength stomped down, digging her heel into her captor's bare foot. He cried out and loosened his grip. Divena bit down hard on the fleshy edge of his hand. As the man bellowed in pain, she jerked out of his grasp and raced back up the path.

"Move, you fool!" Puran hissed to the hired *thag*. "She must not get away!"

The *thag* growled and lurched forward.

"Help me! Help me!" Divena screamed.

She stumbled ahead, but she could not outrun the burly thag. Once again, he grabbed her, this time crushing her head to his chest.

Divena never saw Kilas limp out onto the path. She didn't see him raise his heavy wooden crutch, aim the end over her head, and strike the *thag* between his eyes. All she knew was that the awful man suddenly let go of her and dropped to the ground.

But Puran saw it all. And while the other two stared at the *thag*, he backed away and scurried down the road.

"Get back!" Kilas called to Divena. "Move away!"

But Divena, stunned and confused, didn't move.

The *thag* pulled himself back up to his feet. "Wait until Landlord Varghese gets his hands on you!" he bellowed to her. "You will wish you had never been born!"

Kilas swung his crutch again and hit the *thag* in the chest. The blow knocked him backward. When the man managed to catch himself and lurch forward, Kilas raised his crutch a third time. But the *thag* was ready for him. He caught the end of the crutch and grabbed it away. Tossing it aside, he started after

Kilas . . . until a club of a stick caught him in the back of the head and knocked him to his knees.

"This is not my fault," the *thag* moaned. "Landlord Varghese sent me . . . to get . . . her."

"Shridula sent me to get *you*!" the potter stated. He raised his heavy stick and swung again. This time it knocked the *thag* to the ground. He lay facedown in the dirt.

The potter grunted and wiped the sweat from his eyes.

Kilas dropped to his knees. As he felt around on the ground for his crutch, the *thag* roused and tried to sit up. "I am not the one you want," he mumbled. "The landlord pays me to do his bidding."

The potter looked around. "Where is Divena?" he demanded.

She was nowhere to be seen. And neither was her father.

21

July

Heavy clouds drifted across the sky, blotting out the stars and shrouding the moon in mist. In her bushy shelter, off to the side of the path below where it met the road, Divena waited. Breathlessly she listened for footfalls. The wind picked up and noisily rustled the leaves in the trees. Up on the road, a man called out to someone who answered with a hearty laugh. A dog howled in the distance. Sounds Divena didn't usually hear seemed deafening this night. If her attacker left, how would she know?

Carefully, silently, Divena parted the brush and peered out into the darkness. She could barely make out the path. She pushed further forward and peered down toward her grandmother's hut. She could see nothing.

Should her attacker see her, she decided—or should she see her father—she would yell and scream for help at the top of her voice. Surely someone up on the road would hear her cries. Or maybe the potter would come back with his heavy stick.

But Divena saw nothing of the landlord's *thag*. Nothing of her father, either. Nothing at all in the dark night. The wind blew surprisingly cool. Divena shivered. She could smell the rain coming. Fresh and cool, the first rain of the season usually caused great rejoicing. But not for Divena. Not this night. After months of waiting, she dreaded the rain.

The night dragged on, yet Divena continued to wait. Weariness sapped her strength, but she dared not close her eyes.

As the night faded into a pasty-gray dawn, the *thag* recovered enough to get on his feet and limp up the path toward Divena's hiding place, mumbling bitterly all the way. As he passed by, so close Divena could have reached out and grabbed the hem of his *mundu*, he stumbled into a deep rut and fell flat. He lay in front of her, groaning and kicking at the hard ground, which only caused him more pain. When he finally managed to get himself up again, he stumbled past her, still mumbling under his breath.

With the dawn, the village awoke. Girls and women walked past Divena's hiding place carrying their empty water pots to the well. Jincy also hurried by, her water pot balanced on her head and her little son tied to her back. Divena almost called out to her, but what could Jincy do? She already had her hands full.

"Go! Go!" cried the little goat herder boy as he came up the path. His animals wanted to stop and eat everything they passed. "Move!" the herder ordered in his little-boy voice. The goats paid him no mind.

But Divena's father had not yet passed by. Could it be that he never went to her grandmother's hut at all? That her grandmother had slept peacefully all night and never knew anything might be amiss?

When the path finally emptied, Divena eased out of her hiding place. She straightened her *sari* and did her best to brush the brambles from her hair. Then she hurried for her grandmother's hut.

❧

As Divena approached, she saw smoke rising up from her grandmother's cook fire. That comforting sight of normalcy encouraged her. She came closer and saw Shridula hunched over the fire, stirring her pot, the same as she did every morning. Laughing out loud, Divena ran toward her.

But when her grandmother looked up, she gasped. "I see a rat!" she cried. "I see a rat! A rat!"

Divena froze.

"Then take a stick to it, old woman." Puran's voice sounded from inside her grandmother's hut. "Or grab up a handful of rocks and pelt it good. You do that so well."

Divena bolted back up the path. She ran all the way to the road, then on up the road toward the village. When she could run no more, she walked, gasping for breath. *Think!* she ordered herself. *Think of something!*

But she could not. Where could she possibly go for help? To Selvi? Selvi would already be on her way to the market, chattering and gossiping. Maybe she was already there spreading out her fruit before the early shoppers.

Divena hurried on along the road. She had passed all the way through the *Sudra* section before it hit her: this road would lead her directly past Landlord Varghese's house! Yet she could think of no other way. Panicked, she slipped off the road. But she found no place to hide. Nothing on either side but trampled brush. She moved forward, but more slowly.

Despite the clouds that hung heavy and dark, the day grew increasingly warm. Hot and sticky is how others described it. The village needed that first rain!

As Divena drew close to the landlord's veranda, a deep dread settled over her. She could not go back. She could not stay where she was. Yet what might lie ahead terrified her most of all.

Two women with huge baskets on their heads came up behind her. Might Divena blend in with them? She didn't get the opportunity to find out because the women were in such urgent conversation they never looked her way. As soon as Divena stepped over in their direction, they stopped talking and glared at her. Divena slowed her pace and let them go ahead.

"Hello!" called a man who had come up behind Divena on a motorbike. He pulled to a stop a bit ahead of her and adjusted the ropes that held a great load of chickens tied to the back by their feet. "Do you want a ride?" he called.

Divena had never seen such a motorbike—faded green and black, with all those chickens hanging on the back. She had at times been in danger of a motorbike running her down, but certainly she had never ridden on one. She looked at the small space between the back of the man and the front of the unhappy chickens. *No!* she decided. But then she spied the landlord's veranda up ahead. And—oh! She could see someone moving about on it!

"I . . . I . . . do not know," she stammered. "I am only going a short way."

"I will drop you wherever you wish," the man said. "Or you could jump off. As you can see, this motorbike does not go very fast."

Divena hesitated. But in the end, she squeezed herself between the restless chickens and the plump man.

As the motorbike jerked forward, Divena grabbed hold of the man's shirt. He sped up and she grabbed hold of him. Chicken feathers tickled Divena's back and made her itch, but she dared not let go of the driver long enough to scratch. With all her might, Divena wished to be out of sight of that horrid veranda. The moment that happened was the moment she would bid the driver farewell and go back to walking on her own two feet.

The motorbike putted up the road, then rounded a turn. Divena, clinging tightly to the driver, looked back. The landlord's veranda was no longer in sight.

"Excuse me," Divena said. "I would like to get off now."

The man drove on.

"Excuse me!" Divena gave the man's shirt a hard yank. "I want to get off!"

"What?" the man called back. "Get off here? But there is nothing around here."

"Yes, but . . . I know, but . . ." Divena stammered. "I must meet my friends."

"Where are they?" the man asked.

Divena had not anticipated the question. "In the forest," she blurted. "With the pepper vines."

"That is still up ahead," the man said. "I will let you off up there."

A wiggling chicken caught Divena with its beak and gave her a nasty scratch. "Hurry, please!" she begged.

The man sped up a bit. They may not have been going fast for a motorbike, but to Divena it seemed as though the trees blurred by. If it had been a woman driving, Divena would have wrapped her arms around the woman's middle. But not a man. No, not a strange man.

Trees, brush, paddies, people walking on the road—the motorbike zipped past them all. "There!" Divena called when she caught sight of the path she and Selvi had followed. "That is where my friends are!"

The man hit the brakes, and the chickens fluttered forward.

"I do not see anyone," the man said. But Divena pulled herself free and dashed for the shelter of the trees and pepper vines.

Chicken feathers everywhere! With a groan of disgust, Divena unwrapped the top part of her *sari* and shook it out. But when she wrapped it back around, her back and shoulders itched all the more.

Actually, Divena had never intended to go back to the pepper forest. But she couldn't think of anywhere else to go. And this way, if the motorbike man should decide to leave his chickens and come after her, she could easily slip in among the thick vines and hide. Perhaps she could make a shelter for herself and stay there for two days, until the next class met. She could arrive early and ask the professor's wife for help. Auntie Rani, that's what everyone called her. Auntie Rani had always been kind to her, and wise, too. She would know what to do.

The last time Divena had stepped into the forest, she had relished the coolness the trees afforded. But this day she stood alone and shivered. This day, instead of cool and welcoming, the pepper forest seemed gloomy and dank. No blue sky showed through the trees. No rays of sunshine lit her path. No Selvi chattered beside her. Hovering rather than sheltering, the trees loomed dark and threatening. But because she had no choice, Divena picked her steps carefully and moved along the path.

"Hello?"

Divena jumped and caught her breath at the sound of the unexpected greeting. Who could be behind her? Not Selvi. Slowly Divena turned around. A tall woman with a sharp chin and nose and bony arms smiled at her. It was Maya, the tall girl from the reading class.

"What are you doing here in our pepper grove?"

"Someone attacked me. A *thag,* I think." Words tumbled out of Divena's mouth. "The landlord in my village sent him to harm me. My father went to see my grandmother, too, but I know he did not have any good reason. He is so mean I worry for her. I do not know if he hurt her, or even if he ever left her house. But I am too afraid to go back because my grandmother warned me away with our signal."

Through her entire talk, Divena's eyes darted back up the pathway. She felt too humiliated to mention clinging to the man on the faded green and black motorbike who gave her a ride along with all his chickens.

For a long time, Maya stared hard into Divena's eyes. "How am I to know what you say is true?"

Divena covered her face and sobbed. "The landlord sent that *thag* to the village to lay in wait for me. I do not know why. He does not know me, and I do not know him. My wicked father went to my grandmother's house and was there all night. I do not want my poor grandmother alone with that angry man, but I do not know what to do. I cannot go back there. My grandmother warned me not to."

After thinking for a moment, Maya said in a gentler voice, "Follow me."

Maya padded quickly down the path, her bare feet soundless and sure. Divena rushed to keep up with her, padding more loudly and with steps much less certain. They followed the same path she and Selvi had followed, but Maya quickly passed the place where they had stopped. She hurried on, leading Divena deeper into the pepper forest.

As pepper vines grew thicker, the path grew more and more narrow. Divena looked up and searched in vain for any little bit of blue sky. All she could see were dark clouds.

"Where are you taking me?" Divena asked. She did her best to keep the anxiety from her voice.

"To a safe place," Maya assured her. She took a sharp turn onto an even narrower path—nothing more than a trail, actually. Divena would have missed it had she not been following Maya.

"Come," Maya urged. "We are almost there."

The farther they went, the thicker the trees and the darker the forest. It occurred to Divena that if she ever wanted to find her way out alone, it would be impossible.

"There it is," Maya announced.

Divena, puzzled, looked around to see nothing but more trees and more vines.

"Over there!" Maya pointed off to a hidden corner.

Yes, a small thatched-roof shelter made of sticks and mud stood back among the trees. Divena followed Maya around to the open back of the structure. Three walls, all solidly packed with dried mud. Only three walls with a straw roof and a mud floor. Although the wall facing the path had no window, the opposite wall had a nice one. But Divena did not look at the walls or the roof. She stared straight at the front wall. Over a box-like podium, someone had hung a long piece of rough wood. About a third of the way down, another piece of wood had been nailed across it. It looked very much like the faded gold picture she had seen so many times on the front of her grandmother's Holy Bible.

"Who lives here?" Divena whispered.

"It is the house of God," Maya said. "It is our church. You will be safe here."

"I must go, but I will be back as soon as I can," Maya had promised Divena. "When I come I will bring you *chapatis* and tea."

That's what Maya had said, but so much time had passed, and still Divena waited alone. Or maybe the wait hadn't been as long she thought. She found it hard to tell in the woods. Divena stood by the open back wall and stared out into the gathering dusk. Or perhaps dusk had not fallen at all. Perhaps it was only the rain clouds.

What if she would need to sleep in that church? Divena looked around the single room. Over in the corner she saw a stack of cloths piled up against the wall. To spread across the floor and sit on, no doubt. But they could also do for a bed.

Divena had just started to arrange the cloths when she stopped abruptly. She stood up straight and listened. Did she hear voices? Nothing but the wind, perhaps, blowing through the trees. *Please, please, God, let it be the wind!*

There, she heard it again! Definitely voices. Probably Maya with the tea and *chapatis*. Maybe she brought someone with her to help. Professor Menon, perhaps. Yes, and Auntie Rani. Just the person she wanted to see!

As the voices grew closer, Divena began to tremble. No, most definitely not Maya's voice. Not Uncle Professor and Auntie Rani, either. More likely, her father and that *thag* Landlord Varghese had hired had somehow followed her. Or maybe . . . maybe . . . Divena dove into pile of cloths, burrowed down, and covered her head.

Divena willed herself to stop trembling. She commanded her heart to stop pounding so hard. She heard footsteps—thumping ones and lightly plodding ones. Someone with shoes and someone with bare feet.

"What is this place?" The man's voice was gruff and unfamiliar.

"A shrine," said another man. Divena wasn't certain whether she recognized his voice or not.

"I do not see a god or goddess," said the first man.

A pause. Then the second man said, "The workers do their job. If this shrine keeps them satisfied, I say we forget it. You have enough problems already."

The first man mumbled something Divena could not understand. Already they were walking away.

Divena didn't move. Even after the footsteps faded into silence, she lay still, hardly daring to breathe. She felt safe, burrowed down in her nest of cloths. Protected. A profound weariness swept over her, and she closed her eyes.

"Divena? Where are you, Divena?"

Divena opened her eyes. Nothing but darkness. She couldn't figure out where she was, or why her *sari* seemed to be all over her head and face.

"Divena! It is me, Maya. Are you still here?"

Oh, yes. The pile of cloths. Cautiously, Divena pushed them aside and peeked out.

"Oh, Divena! I was so worried!" Maya exclaimed. "I am sorry I left you for such a long time, but I could not get back because—"

"Someone came," Divena said as she freed herself from the cloths.

"The landlord's overseer. That is why I could not get back to you. But Nagmani, that very dark man from our class—he walked along with the overseer. Somehow Nagmani managed to get him away."

"The overseer!" Divena gasped in alarm. "Will he be back?"

"No," Maya assured her.

"How can you be so certain?"

"Come outside. Just look at the heavy clouds," Maya said. "Soon the rains will start. The overseer will be far too busy to waste time down here."

Even as they watched, light rain began to splatter onto the dry ground. Then big drops fell, faster and faster. Divena and Maya hurried back inside the church, where the mud and thatch would keep them dry.

Divena ate her fill of *chapatis* and bananas, washing them down with tea.

"It is growing dark," Maya said. "I must go. I brought you a pot of water, and you still have the rest of the food. I will come back as soon as I can."

"Thank you," Divena said. "Thank you for everything."

She was safe, she was dry, and her stomach was filled. Everything would be all right . . . at least for a while.

22

July

Darkness fell quickly. Darkness total and complete. Not a star shone in the sky and no beam of moonlight broke through the clouds. Divena burrowed further into the pile of cloths and tried to sleep. But when she closed her eyes, she saw her grandmother. Her *ammama*, her wrinkled face etched in fear and anxiety. When Divena finally managed to fall into a restless sleep, she dreamed of the landlord's fearsome *thag*, shadowed by the hunchbacked form of her father. The two of them laughed at her. Mocked her. Called out, "I see a rat, I see a rat! *You* are the rat!"

Divena awoke screaming. The rest of the long night, she lay trembling in the pile of cloths. Trembling and weeping and worrying.

With the first gray of dawn, Divena pushed the cloths aside and stood up. No longer did she hear the patter of rain on the thatched roof. She moved to the open side and looked out. "Selvi," she whispered. "Oh, how I wish you were here with me!"

At full light, Maya came back bearing a small pot of rice with vegetables. A very dark man walked along beside her. Divena recognized him from class.

"My grandmother," Divena said. "I must go back to her."

"I know," said Maya. "That is why Nagmani has come. He will go with us."

"Not now, though," Nagmani said. "We will wait for the dark of the night. And we will not go on the road. Too many curious eyes watching."

"Tonight?" Divena asked eagerly.

"Tomorrow night," Maya said. "While the class is meeting. If anyone happens to be watching for you, their attention will be on the class."

All the next day Divena waited, but Maya didn't come. Finally at dusk, when she had all but given up hope, Maya walked in with Nagmani following behind.

"I did not hear you coming," Divena said.

"That is how you must learn to move, too," Nagmani told her. "With sure and silent steps."

Maya set out a dish of rice and two bananas.

"I am not hungry," Divena said. "I just want to go."

"Eat," Maya insisted. "It will be a long night."

Divena finished the food as quickly as she could. Nagmani and Maya were waiting outside, and Divena hurried to join them.

"I can see the moon," Divena gasped. The clouds had parted, allowing a thin beam of moonlight to shine through the trees.

"Follow closely after me," Nagmani warned. "And tread softly. The forest has ears."

Nagmani led the way down a narrow trail to a path that wound through the dark forest. He turned and crossed an expanse so clogged and overgrown it seemed that no one could have passed that way for many years. He scampered up impossible inclines, always careful to point out invisible footholds along the way. He ducked through walls of thick vines, and he sloshed through rivers of mud. Divena followed after him. Maya came along behind.

Off to one side, something made an unfamiliar rustling sound. Nagmani froze. Maya did the same. When Divena saw the looks on their faces, she froze, too. For many minutes no one moved. Finally, without a word, Nagmani began to edge forward. The others followed silently. Another turn and they stepped out into the open.

Divena looked around. Up ahead of her, she spied a public water spigot not far off the road. Beyond that stood a crudely constructed goat pen. Yes, she recognized her surroundings. Not many minutes along that road and they would pass Landlord Varghese's house, directly in front of its veranda. Divena tried to whisper a warning to Nagmani, but he waved for her to stay quiet.

Nagmani dropped down low and disappeared. Divena, perplexed, stared after him. Maya hiked up her *sari* and tied it around her waist, then she, too, dropped out of sight. Afraid to be left behind, Divena stumbled after Maya. She fell and hit the ground with a thud. Divena had landed face-to-face with the gaping end of a large water pipe, over three feet in diameter.

"Hurry!" Maya whispered from inside the pipe. "Keep to the middle."

Divena squinted into the pipe's black interior. With a prayer on her lips, she got down on her hands and knees and crawled into the darkness.

As Divena splashed through the remains of the night's rainstorm, she took comfort in the double splashing she heard echoing back from in front of her. "*Ammama*," she breathed. "I am coming."

The water pipe, long and filthy, did not reach high enough for Divena to stand up. It was so dark she could see nothing around her. Despite Maya's warning, she squeezed over against the side because she felt safer there. When she crawled through a thick spider web, she forced herself to swallow her terrified scream. But she fell back, swatting frantically at the spider that dropped down on her. She dare not delay for long, though. Not at the risk of getting left behind and lost in the maze of pipes. Divena listened for the sound of splashing in front of her, and tried to ignore the frightening scratches and squeals of unseen creatures.

At long last, a pale beam of moonlight signaled she was nearing the end of the pipe.

Divena stepped out to see Maya in front of her. One look and Divena covered her mouth to muffle a giggle. What a sight! Maya's hair hung loose and undone, plastered into a wicked shape. Her face, splotched with mud, and her tangled *sari* were a worse mess than Divena had ever seen.

"Do not be so quick to laugh," Maya scolded. "You should see yourself."

Divena did her best to quickly straighten up. She raked her fingers through her mud-stiffened hair and worked it into a fresh lopsided braid. She pulled and tugged at her hopelessly filthy *sari*, then dipped the edge of it into a puddle of rainwater and wiped her face. She also splashed water over the worst of the mud spots that stained the front of her clothes. But instead of getting her clothes cleaner, she only succeeded in smearing the mud into bigger stains.

"Which house belongs to your grandmother?" Nagmani whispered.

Divena looked around. They stood in the open field. Yes, she recognized the place. They were behind the potter's work shed. "There," she breathed, pointing off to one side to her grandmother's garden plot.

"I will go alone and see who might be there," Nagmani whispered.

"No!" Divena protested. She tried to run after him, but Maya held her back.

Shridula awakened with a gasp. Nagmani slipped his hand over her mouth. "Shhhh, listen to me," he whispered.

With an unexpected burst of strength, the old woman shoved him away. "Who are you?" she demanded.

Divena rushed up behind Nagmani and grabbed hold of her grandmother's arm. "It is all right, *Ammama*. He will not hurt you. Is *Appa* gone?"

"Divena!" Shridula gasped. "God be praised!" But even as she spoke, she tossed a suspicious glare Nagmani's way.

"These are my friends, *Ammama*," Divena explained. "They protected me and hid me. But I had to come back and see that you were safe."

Shridula pulled herself up on her sleeping mat. "That wicked Puran finally left, but only after I agreed to cook for him. I told him you had run away. I told him you vowed to never come back."

"Did he believe you?"

"Who can say? Probably not. Puran trusts no one. Liars always think everyone else lies as well."

Divena ran her fingers over the crevices of the old woman's face. Perhaps it was only because the moonlight cast deep shadows, but her grandmother looked terribly thin and drawn. "You are not well, *Ammama*," she whispered.

"I am old. I have lived a hard life."

Divena wrapped her arms around her grandmother. "Do not say that! Please! I will not leave you again."

Shridula pushed Divena away. "Nonsense! You must go. Puran will be back."

"But you—"

"He does not want me. He wants you. Already he has sold you to Landlord Varghese. He told me as much. But he will not get the money until he turns you over to that wretched man."

"Why? What does the landlord want of me?"

"I warned you, Divena. I told you gossipers have ears. They also have flapping mouths. Oh, if only you had not gone to that class. If only you had never spoken to everyone about it!"

"I do not understand."

"Go back to your hiding place, my blessing," Shridula said. "Go far away and do not come back. Please. Please, my love. Go now!"

"You could come with me to the—"

"No! Do not tell me where. I do not want to know."

Trembling, Divena took her grandmother's hands in hers. Hot tears ran down her face and fell onto Shridula's twisted fingers. "When my father leaves, I will come back," Divena whispered. "When the landlord no longer—"

"Your father means nothing to anyone," Shridula said. "But Landlord Varghese is the most powerful man in this village. He will never give up. He wants you, and he will never, ever give up until he gets what he wants."

Divena buried her head in her grandmother's lap and wept.

"Every day I will pray to God to watch over you," Shridula said. "You are a blessing, now and forever. God will protect you."

Gently Maya pulled at Divena's shoulders. "We must leave. Quickly, before the dawn breaks."

"Go!" Shridula said. "Go now, my blessing, and do not come back."

With the dawn came the rain. Great sheets of water poured from the heavens. A flood roared through the drainpipe, drowning rats, washing spiders away, and clearing out every other living thing. But not Divena. And not Maya and Nagmani. They had already made it through and were safely in the pepper forest, protected from the deluge by a thick canopy of trees.

When they got back to the church, someone had loosened the rope that held the rolled-up back wall and lowered it down. Though no shoes sat outside, the cloths had been spread across the floor. A dozen men and women, and as many children, sat together, all praying out loud.

Dripping wet and filthy, the three slipped inside. Divena tried to sit at the back, but Maya urged her up to the front.

Maya folded her hands, bowed her head, and squeezed her eyes shut. "Thank you, Lord God Jesus for leading us safely back." Her voice joined the jumble of prayers throughout the room. "Thank you for keeping old Grandmother safe from those who would harm her."

"Greater is He who is in you than he who is in the world," Nagmani recited behind them.

Divena folded her hands, the same way Maya did. She, too, bowed her head and squeezed her eyes shut. "Walk with my *Ammama*," she whispered. "When she can walk no more, please God, carry her. Please carry her to some place safe where her stomach will be full, and she will be sheltered from the sun and rain."

23

August

As soon as Sundar sat down at the table, a servant rushed over with his breakfast: a boiled egg, *idli* cakes with lentils, and an array of fruit. Ramesh had already begun to eat his usual corn flakes and bananas with cream.

"What is Father on about this morning?" Sundar asked as he sopped at the lentils with the *idli*.

Ramesh made a face. "You have to ask?"

"Dinish Desai again?"

Ramesh rolled his eyes and lifted his spoon to his mouth. No one else in the family used a spoon and knife and fork. No one they knew did. But Ramesh refused to eat with his fingers the way Indians had always done.

"Such a rampage for that same old complaint?" Sundar made a concession and reached for Ramesh's knife to crack his egg. But he quickly handed it back in favor of a swift smack on the table with his efficient fingers.

"You know Father," Ramesh said.

"He only need give a little bit," Sundar said. "Just to agree to let Desai take care of his own land and laborers as he sees fit. Then Father could concentrate on seeing that his own laborers take care of the rice in our paddies—which are right now drowning, by the way."

"All he needs to do is tend to his own business," Ramesh said.

"Both of you, eat your breakfast!" ordered Hanita Varghese. It was a command, but coming from their mother, neither Sundar nor Ramesh paid it any mind.

"Such a pleasant surprise, Mother," Sundar said.

"Why are you so late at breakfast?" Hanita asked him. "Your father and Jeevak ate an hour ago and are already at work."

Ramesh reached for the box of cornflakes and poured himself another bowl. "And you have been waiting until we eat? Please, Mother! You do not need to sit by until all the men are finished eating before you can eat. When did someone set that silly rule? Two thousand years ago? Three thousand?"

"I will wait." Hanita sat down away from the table and opened a book.

"Well," Ramesh said sarcastically, "we would not want to be arrested by the breakfast police, would we?"

Sundar had expected to go out to inspect the rice paddies with his father, to see what damage the hard rain might have done. But when he caught up with his father, he found Ajay Varghese in a foul mood. He didn't want to talk about anything but "that weakling landlord and the havoc he is causing in the entire area."

"Do not think that I do not agree with you, Father," Sundar said. "That is, not with your goal. What causes me anguish is your approach."

"Are you going to start up again criticizing the way I live my life?" Ajay demanded. "Because if you are, I will not stay and listen."

"It's just that I worry, Father. If we continue to operate outside of the law, the time will come when—"

"My son, my son," Ajay interrupted. "Why must you always be so dramatic? All I want is a temperate approach. Ramesh says Americans have a saying: *Do not throw the baby out with the bathwater*. What that means is—"

"I know what it means. I also know that your 'approach' is making enemies between two neighboring villages. It is also causing us to neglect our real business, which is protecting the rice in the paddies until the harvest. And that is still a month away."

"I will go to see Dinish Desai one more time," Ajay said. "I need you to drive me in the truck."

Sundar closed his eyes and sighed. "Please, Father—"

"Either you go with me or I will ask Jeevak."

Sundar lowered his head into his hands and rubbed his temples. "I will go. But only this one last time."

❧

"Please, Father, do not holler and scold the man," Sundar said as he drove the truck up the road. "Be friendly and calm, and do not argue."

"I do not know what you are talking about." Ajay looked genuinely puzzled. "I am always friendly and calm, and I never argue—unless someone forces me into it, of course. But then it is not my fault."

"Yes," Sundar sighed. "Of course not."

As soon as Sundar stopped the truck in front of Dinish Desai's house, the landlord's young son called out, "Hey! You want to play soccer? I have been practicing. I hardly ever fall down anymore."

"Not today," Sundar called back with a smile. "We came to see your father. But keep up with your footwork."

The child smiled. "I will!" He grabbed up the soccer ball and ran toward the house calling, "*Appa! Appa!* Two men are here to see you!"

"What did he mean by that?" Ajay asked his son.

Sundar shrugged. "Soccer. Every boy around the world plays the game."

When Dinish Desai saw who the two men were, his smile faded. "Go and play!" he ordered his son, who had followed him back. To Ajay he said, "What do you want this time? More commands about how I should conduct my own business on my own land?"

Ajay balled his fists and clenched his jaw.

"No, no," Sundar called. "My father only wants to talk about how we can better work together."

"I do not need you to speak for me!" Ajay grumbled. But when landlord Desai grudgingly invited them to his veranda, Ajay nodded his acceptance.

"If you have come to lecture me, I will warn you right now, I am in no mood to listen," Dinish Desai said.

"No, no lectures," said Sundar. "We only wish to discuss our common difficulties and concerns."

"Especially the difficulty of that teacher," Ajay said.

Landlord Desai threw his arms wide. "I, too, long for the old days," he said. "Do you think I do not? My father and grandfather ruled like kings. What it will be like when my son grows up and takes over, I cannot imagine."

"Far worse than it is today if you refuse to restrain your workers," Ajay snapped. "You are making trouble for every landlord in Kerala. In fact, for every man of high birth, landlord or not!"

"But that is precisely my point, Varghese. If my laborers do their work, I cannot stop them from going to their class. If I were to do as you wish—beat them and punish them and force the professor away—it would only bring out the authorities. And they have the law on their side."

"Today you allow them to meet on the edge of your land," Ajay insisted. "What will you do tomorrow? Sit together with them in the tea shop? Share a cup and a plate of lamb curry with them? Pshaw! You would never find me doing that! I would put the workers in their place, and order that teacher back to his schoolhouse or university or wherever he came from."

Dinish Desai heaved an exasperated sigh. "You talk about me making trouble for everyone of upper caste birth? That is exactly what will happen because—"

"Because you are afraid of your laborers! They talk big and they act big and you . . . you . . . you roll over like a beaten dog!"

"Now, see here! You cannot come to my house and talk to me that way! If I am to throw anyone out, it will be you!"

"Stop!" Sundar ordered. "Father, if you insist on fighting everyone and demanding that everything be done your way, you will end up with enemies on all sides. And you, Dinish Desai, if you refuse to draw a line on the ground and set a boundary, no one will ever respect you or listen to anything you say. What does it matter if the workers learn to read the signs at the bus stop and over the shops?"

"It matters because it will not stop there," Ajay insisted.

"What will really matter is that our workers might discover that they do not need us nearly as much as we need them,"

Sundar said. "The angrier we make them and the more cheated they feel, the sooner that will happen."

❧

"You betrayed me, Sundar," Ajay accused as he stomped away from Landlord Desai's house.

"We can talk about it on our way home."

Ajay, seething, positioned himself on the truck's seat as far away from his son as possible. "You made me look like a fool!"

Sundar started the truck, turned it around, and headed for home. "You said your piece, and I said mine. You are angry because I do not agree with you."

When they reached the house, Ajay got out, slammed the truck door, and stalked to the veranda. There he found Brahmin Rama and his sons waiting for him. Ajay rolled his eyes and mumbled under his breath. He didn't even try to make a show of civility.

Brahmin Rama sat cross-legged on his own mat, his spotless white *mundu* tucked around his legs in such a way that the gold *kara* shone even on so cloudy a day. He used that *kara* to display his family's wealth and power. A loose tunic covered the old man's bony upper body, and his soft, translucent hands lay folded in his lap.

"I have never eaten meat nor have I drunk alcohol," Brahmin Rama said. "I have never eaten ginger or onion or any vegetable grown in the ground. Even at my advanced age, I can assure you that my mind is as clean as my clothes."

"Yes, yes," Ajay said impatiently. "But you must excuse me. This has been a most tiring day."

"With my own eyes, I saw Mahatma Gandhi." Brahmin Rama continued as though he had not heard the landlord.

"Yet I refused to touch his feet. Why? Because the Great Soul was only a *Vaisya* and I am a *Brahmin*."

Ajay rolled his eyes. "I am in no mood to sit with you as you recite your spiritual meanderings."

"Then let us talk of something more interesting to you," said the Brahmin's first son, Vrispati. "The ripping apart of the social order passed down by the gods, perhaps. *Harijans* doing the work that rightfully belongs to upper castes."

"I have no idea what you are talking about," Ajay snapped.

"*Untouchables* who are told they can learn to read in English. And if they can learn to read, that they can take seats in the university that rightfully belong to those of the upper caste. And if they can take university seats, they can take the jobs that also rightfully belong to the upper castes. This includes government jobs. And if they take government jobs, they will run for political office and sit in Parliament. And if they sit in Parliament, they will make laws that favor themselves and punish us."

"They already have made such laws," said Brahmin Rama's second son, Satpathi. "University seats are now reserved for their kind. Government jobs are set aside for them. Money they did not earn is doled out to give them houses never intended for . . . their kind."

Ajay sat down and leaned closer so that he could listen more carefully.

"Then their coarse, dark-skinned daughters will marry our fine, fair-skinned sons," Brahmin Rama said. "And that, Landlord Varghese, will bring about the destruction of India."

Ajay pulled a handkerchief from his pocket and mopped his face. "I am not the one to whom you should be talking," he said. "Dinish Desai is the one causing all the trouble."

"I am still the spiritual leader of this village," said Brahmin Rama. "And I am well acquainted with the *Brahmin* who is the spiritual leader of Landlord Dinish Desai's village."

"Yes, yes," Ajay said impatiently, "but about our problem—"

"As spiritual leaders, it is in our power to *outcaste* anyone who attempts religious or social reform."

Sundar had been listening from the side. But now he, too, leaned in close.

"The classes are not on his land," Ajay said. "And he is not actually doing any of the teaching. Even if he were, it is lawful. Schools for *Harijans* are everywhere. It may, as you say, steal away some of our economic power and give it to *Harijans*, but still the law might support them."

"Also social or religious reform," Brahmin Rama repeated.

"Dinish Desai is a Hindu," Ajay said.

"He is, but not all who live in his settlement are."

Sweat broke out on Sundar's face, and his hands trembled.

"They mock our gods and goddesses," Brahmin Vrispati said. "They drink offerings to a foreign god."

Ajay blinked back his confusion.

"On Dinish Desai's own land stands a Christian church."

"Not a Christian church like your church," Brahmin Rama hastened to assure Ajay. "Not just a benign place of beauty built on Christian property. No, this is a wild place, dedicated to pulling Hindus away from their beliefs and making them into Christians."

For once in his life, Ajay Varghese sat speechless.

"Unless a penalty is attached to an act of transgression, men will not keep to their rightful classes, and our entire social system will break down. Laws of caste must be enforced. And so must the laws of the gods."

24

August

Malik sloshed through the largest of Landlord Dinish Desai's muddy rice paddies tugging at weeds that seemed to have sprung up overnight. He looked hopefully up at the sky. Nothing but blue. No rain today. It felt as if the summer heat had returned, determined to burn away the monsoon rains that should be falling.

"Hurry with those weeds!" the overseer called to Malik. "The cleaner the paddy, the easier the harvest will be."

Malik had specifically asked to work in the pepper groves. Not because he thought that work any easier, but because he worried when he wasn't able to keep his eyes out for the church. Not that it really mattered. At least that's what he told himself. The mud building had been carefully set back, hidden from the path. Besides, Nagmani worked in the groves. He had a special knack for diverting attention and steering curious eyes away. And now that Divena no longer stayed there, the situation did not seem nearly so precarious.

"You! Malik!" the overseer called. "I have a special task for you."

Malik pulled his *chaddar* off his head and mopped his perspiring face.

"Go out to the far field and give it a full inspection. The landlord suspects someone may be living there."

"That field where nothing grows?" Malik asked in surprise.

"That is the one. Look it over in detail." When Malik didn't move, the overseer said, "Now! Landlord Desai says you are to be back before dark."

"I cannot get to that field except along the road," Malik protested.

"Along the road, then. Off with you!"

Malik shaded his eyes and gazed across the steamy paddy. "Where is the water boy? I have not seen him all morning. My throat is parched."

"Never mind the water boy," the overseer said. "Your job is to get out to that field and give it a thorough inspection."

Malik wrapped his *chaddar* back around his head, into a turban and hesitantly turned toward the road.

"At that speed, you have no chance of making it back before dark," the overseer called after him. "Run!"

Loping, then walking, then loping, then walking, Malik managed to make good time. But as the sun rose higher and higher, and the temperature soared, Malik gave up the loping and walked. He searched the ground for a rain puddle. Anything to quench his burning thirst. Now and then he spied a ditch lined with thick mud, the closest thing he ever saw to water. Imagine! So great a rainstorm not five days earlier, yet not a drop of water to be found.

By the time Malik approached the field, the sun shone well past its zenith. He had decided he would beg the next person he saw for a drink. Not out of their cup, of course. He had reached high caste territory. He would ask the person to pour a bit of water into his hand. Only enough to relieve his parched mouth. But he saw no one. Everyone seemed to have been scorched back into their houses.

When he arrived at the field, Malik saw that it had not changed from the way it had always been—barren and rocky and totally unfit for either cultivation or habitation. But of course the landlord already knew that. The overseer did, too.

Malik began to feel faint. He tried to spit on the end of his *chaddar* so he could wipe the bit of moisture over his face, but his mouth had gone completely dry. Maybe if he sat for a few moments and rested, he thought. Only long enough to catch his breath. Already he would have to run part of the way back if he hoped to arrive before dusk.

He dropped down and lay back on the rocky ground, but the sun beat down on him mercilessly. That would never do. Malik felt as though he were a dressed goat speared onto a spit, slowly being turned over the fire. He had no choice but to make his way back as quickly as he could, in any way he could manage.

Malik stepped out of the field. But before he could turn to his right to go back, he saw a wondrous sight. A well. And on the side, a small metal cup. He wanted to ask permission to take a drink, but he could see no one to ask. Not a man or a woman in sight.

"Thank you, God!" Malik panted. "Thank you, thank you, thank you!"

He leapt for the well and grabbed up the cup. He dipped the bucket and filled the cup to its brim. Then he gulped the water down so fast he almost choked. So, so good! He filled the cup again, and drank that down, too. For the third time, he filled the cup. That's when they came. A swarm of men, all with clubs and rocks, all bellowing at him. "How dare you pollute our well!" they cried. "How dare you touch your filthy lips to our cup!"

Malik tried to explain about the overseer and the landlord, about the rocky field and the path with no puddles. But before he could get the words out, a club smacked him across his face. He couldn't speak with his mouth full of pieces of teeth.

"Let that be a lesson to you!" someone yelled. "A lesson to all of your kind!"

A second crushing blow knocked Malik back against the well. He covered his face with his arms. Another blow knocked him to the ground. Malik closed his eyes and begged God to take him quickly to heaven.

❧

As tiny Aswati played her carved flute and Udeep beat out the rhythm on a handmade *ghatam* drum, Divena stood up in the church, closed her eyes, and crooned the song Professor Menon had taught them:

> What a friend we have in Jesus,
> All our sins and griefs to bear.
> What a privilege to carry,
> Everything to God in prayer!

The clutch of worshippers didn't realize that drops of light rain had begun to fall. But Sundar did. From his hiding place in the shadows of the trees, he felt those first welcome drops. So nice after such a sweltering day!

> Have we trials and temptations?
> Is there trouble anywhere?
> We should never be discouraged,
> Take it to the Lord in prayer.

The professor had told them what the words of the song meant, though none found it easy to remember. In fact, only

Divena had managed to memorize all the English words. Of course, her grandmother had already taught her a good deal of English, though she did not mention that to the others. She didn't want anyone to know in case it might get her grandmother into trouble.

Sundar eased forward so he could better see the girl who sang like an angel. He could not remember having seen her before. Surely, if he had, he would never have forgotten her. He certainly couldn't now, not even if he tried.

When the song ended, Nagmani stood up. "Professor Menon is not here to teach us this evening," he said. "But we can still sing. We can talk about Jesus God who loves *outcastes*. And we can pray. That is what Divena's song said. Take our problems . . ."

Sundar almost gasped out loud. Could that lovely girl truly be Divena? The one his father wanted as a slave for Jeevak?

"I thank you, Jesus God, that I am no longer a hated *Dalit*. Now I am a *Dalit* that the true God loves. Now I am a real person."

"Thank you, Jeba," Nagmani said. "Anyone else?"

"I thank Jesus that I am learning how to read," said a small woman. She spoke in little more than a whisper and never looked up from the floor. "My prayer is for my children, that they will learn to read, too. That they will not grow up working for the landlord."

"Thank you, Rupali," said Nagmani. "Anyone else?"

"You are all my friends. I thank Jesus God for you."

"Thank you, Nisha," Nagmani said. "I think this would be a good time for us to pray together."

Everyone bowed low, some all the way to the floor, and squeezed their eyes tightly closed. They had all started murmuring their prayers out loud when they were interrupted by a call from outside. "Help us! Hurry! Help us!"

"Kilas?" Nagmani said. He rushed to the open back of the church. The others scrambled after him.

Even though Kilas had struggled along the path through the trees, not far from Sundar's hiding place, his cry shocked Sundar as much as anyone. He didn't dare show himself, but he craned his neck to see what could be happening.

"It is Malik!" Kilas cried out. "Come and see what they did to him!"

Nagmani and Udeep helped Kilas and Baka carry Malik into the church. "Wa . . . ter," Malik gasped. Jeba rushed to pour him a cup, but when she got back with it, Malik shut his lips and turned his head away.

"We were on our way here from our village when we found him," Kilas said. "Crumpled and beaten and broken, the same as this."

"By the well," Baka added. "Near the *Brahmin* section of the village."

"What could he possibly be doing there?" Aswati asked. "Did he run away?"

"Landlord," Malik mumbled. "Made me go. No water."

"Malik," Nagmani said. "Who did this to you?"

"Waiting for me. Already there . . . waiting."

"Do you not see?" Kilas demanded. "The landlord set him up. He sent him out on a hot day with no water. Poor Malik could do nothing but go to the well where those men lay in wait for him."

"We should send for the professor," Divena said. "He will know what to do."

"We know what to do," said Nagmani. "Tonight we will care for Malik. Tomorrow we will take him to the police station and demand justice for him."

"No, no!" cried Rupali. "The police will beat us, too!"

"It is easy to jump out with clubs and beat one person who is weakened and alone," Divena said. "But it will not be so easy when it is all of us together."

"Yes," Maya agreed. "And not only us, but all the others from the class who are sure to join us."

"Tomorrow we will go to see the superintendent of police!" Nagmani said. "If the landlord tells us to stop, we will ignore him and go anyway. We will leave early in the morning and walk along the road. If the landlord tries to beat us, we will have witnesses. Everyone on the road will see, and those who are not on the road will soon hear all about it."

"We know our rights, and we will go!" Udeep exclaimed.

"I will care for Malik here tonight," said Divena. "Bring us water, and I will care for him."

Sundar wanted to run out and offer to help. He wanted to cry, "I have money! Tell me what you need and I will get it for you!" He wanted to say, "My truck is parked off the road, not far away in a tamarind grove. I will take him to the medical clinic." He wanted to say, "I had nothing to do with those who beat Malik, but I am upper caste, and I am so sorry. I am so, so sorry!"

But he did none of those things. Instead, Sundar slunk further back into the shadows and waited. When he thought it safe, he crept away.

25

August

First, Divena filled a cup with water, then she poured the rest into the bowl in front of her. She soaked a blood-stained cloth in the bowl and gently dabbed it over Malik's wounded face: his lips, cut and battered. His eyes blackened—one swollen shut and the other nothing but a puffy slit. Three of his front teeth were gone and of two others, nothing remained but jagged stumps. Still, he did breathe easily. And for most of the night, he had slept.

The bones in Malik's fingers were broken and his arms badly bruised. Divena had placed his arms across his chest, which seemed to give him a bit of relief.

With a groan, Malik opened his slit of an eye and tried to move his mouth. Divena raised his head and put the cup of water to his lips.

"You are safe now," she said softly. "No one will hurt you here."

"Sit," Malik murmured.

Carefully, tenderly, Divena raised him up so that he half-sat, propped against the wall. "I dwank . . . dwank their . . .

wader." Malik struggled painfully to form each word despite his missing teeth and swollen lips.

"The water is not theirs," Divena said. "God sent it for all of us. The sin is theirs, not yours."

In the morning, the others arrived together, twenty-two of them. All from the professor's class.

"Look!" Baka exclaimed. "A gift from God, sitting on the ground outside the door." She held an armload of fresh fruit—mangos and bananas, even a ripe pineapple.

"From God, yes, but who left it?" Divena asked.

"It is a mystery," Kilas said. "But a wonderfully delicious mystery!" He took a knife from the waist of his *mundu* and cut first into a mango, then started on the pineapple.

Divena crushed a bit of mango in her fingers and held it to Malik's lips. He licked it in with his tongue and did his best to smile, so Divena gave him another bite.

Twenty-two people gathered outside the church. Although Divena recognized all of them, she didn't know each one by name. Twenty-two people, but no Selvi. How Divena missed her old friend. Well, why would she come? Selvi didn't work for Landlord Desai. But then, neither did Kilas or Baka, and they both came.

"I think we should tell the professor not to come anymore," said Udeep. "We should stop the class."

"No!" cried Rupali. "The class is the only thing that brings us hope."

"And trouble," Udeep said. He looked at Malik. "Just look at what it did for him."

"Anyway, if we stop the class now, all we have accomplished will be for nothing," Divena pleaded. "Do you not see? If we quit, we will be giving the landlord exactly what he wants."

"Our choice is a dangerous one," Nagmani said. "To learn to read has always been dangerous for us, yet we have persisted. Some have given up, but we have not."

"Talk and threats," Udeep said. "That is all we have endured. Up until now. But now . . . well, look at Malik!"

"Not everyone has to go to the superintendent of police with us," Nagmani said. "Anyone who wishes to stay behind, step back to the door. We will not think any less of you."

Udeep stepped back. "I wish you well," he said.

Tiny Aswati hung her head and stepped back, too, and also the woman beside her. But no one else.

"It is decided, then. The rest of us will leave immediately, before the overseer realizes we are not at work in the paddies," Nagmani said.

"What about Malik?" asked Divena.

"I will . . . go, too," Malik mumbled, lisping through swollen lips and broken teeth. "If you helf me . . . I will go."

Nagmani nodded. "It is best," he said. "You will be the proof of our accusation. You can testify to what happened. I will help you."

"And I," said Kilas. "Walk with us if you can, Malik. If you cannot, we will carry you."

"If the overseer looks for you, we will make up excuses," Udeep told the group.

Aswati nodded. "And we will pray for you, too. Every minute until you return, we will pray."

Nagmani removed his *chaddar* and wrapped Malik's arms into a double sling. Although in great pain, Malik stifled his cries as they prepared him for the journey. But when Nagmani and Kilas lifted the battered man to his feet—though they were most careful and gentle—Malik groaned and swayed. The two men gripped him tightly between them.

A bit more steady on his feet, Malik mumbled, "Good. We will go."

What a sight they were, twenty-one shabby *Dalit* workers, men and women walking together, pulling along one badly beaten man who could barely manage to put one foot before the next, supported on one side by a limping man on a crutch. The group shuffled along in silence, punctuated by an occasional groan from Malik.

Jeet made his way forward and said to Kilas, "Let me share your burden."

"He is no burden to me," Kilas answered.

"Nor to me," Jeet told him. "When you tire, I will gladly take your place beside Malik."

Women with water pots on their heads stopped along the road to gape at the procession. Men on their way to market, or to conduct business, stepped aside and stared. Men of high caste set their teeth on edge and glared at the group that could be nothing but *Untouchables*. People of low caste trembled, though they couldn't say why. They knew instinctively that something momentous was about to happen.

The group of *Dalits* stopped to let a yellow-turbaned man drive his herd of water buffalo across the road in front of them. Beggars set their cups aside when they saw the throng approaching, and mothers pulled their children close. Whenever a cow blocked the marchers' way, the *Dalits* eased into a single line and walked around it.

Divena looked neither to the left nor the right. She did not want to risk seeing a familiar face. Since this wasn't her village, she did not think it likely. Still, her father had claimed to live and work in this very place. And, as everyone knew, village gossip could be fearsomely effective.

As the group drew nearer to the office of the superintendent of police, their pace lagged. Confident faces wilted. One after another, jaws firm with assurance and resolve were replaced by brows wrinkled with worry.

"We know our rights," Nagmani reminded the people. "Truth is on our side!"

"Together we are extraordinary," Baka added. "The law walks with us!"

"And great power, too," Maya said. "We have the power of unity!"

Divena, who walked along at the front of the group beside Maya, raised her head high and quickened her pace. "Not too fast!" Nagmani said. "Poor Malik's strength is fading fast."

As the group neared the simple stone block building that served as the village police station, Divena and Maya looked around them uncertainly. Their footsteps slowed, then stopped. Nagmani and Kilas, still supporting the sagging Malik, made their way up to the front. "Come," Nagmani called. "We must stay together."

Two monkeys digging in the courtyard dirt turned to stare at the crowd that walked toward them. Both monkeys screeched out a warning, and when no one stopped, they shrieked their displeasure and scampered to the trees.

Nagmani and Kilas led the others through the courtyard and up to the front door. "Open it, Jeet," Nagmani said to the man beside him.

With more than a little foreboding, Jeet turned the knob and pushed the door open. Nagmani and Kilas, half-carrying Malik between them, made their way through. No one followed.

"Come on," Divena said to Maya. "We have come this far. There is no turning back." The two grabbed hands and pushed through the doorway. Jeet followed them, then a couple of the women. Then more and more people, until all twenty-one of them stood crowded together in the single small room.

A tall policeman with a bushy moustache held out his arms to stop the intruders. "What is the meaning of this!" he exclaimed. "Why are the likes of you barging in here? You have no business with us!"

"We have a crime to report," Nagmani said. "This man received a severe beaten for doing nothing more than drinking water from a public well. We want the men who did it brought to justice."

The policeman stared in disbelief. Then he burst out laughing. "Perhaps in the future your friend will take more care in where he chooses to get his water!"

"This happened at a public well, built along a public road with public funds," Kilas insisted. "Anyone can legally drink there."

The policeman looked Malik up and down. "Obviously not anyone," he said with a smirk. A police inspector, short and stout, came from the back room. When he saw the situation, he broke into a hearty laugh.

"Anyone can drink there," Kilas repeated. "That is the law. Surely you, being a policeman, know that."

The tall policeman's smirk melted into a frown. "Take your friend home and put him to bed. That is where he belongs."

"We have come to see justice done," Nagmani said. "Our friend can identify the men who beat him."

Kilas looked from the tall policeman to the short police inspector. "If neither of you can help us, we wish to talk to the superintendent of police," he said.

"He is not here," stated the police inspector.

"Then we will wait for him," Nagmani answered.

The police inspector eased back through the door. The tall policeman with the bushy moustache stood uneasily as twenty-one resolute faces—one battered and swollen—stared intently at him. No one spoke. In the silence, the whir of the overhead fan seemed deafening.

As the clock on the wall ticked off passing seconds, the policeman shifted his weight from one foot to the other and glanced back at the closed door. He took a deep breath and opened his mouth to speak. But Malik peered at him through his slit of an eye, and the policeman closed his mouth.

"Who are they?" the superintendent of police demanded of the police inspector.

"I do not know. *Harijans*, for sure. Some men and some women. Must be two dozen of them, maybe more. And they dragged that beaten man along with them."

"Can he identify his attackers?"

"They say he can."

The superintendent of police heaved an irritated sigh. "My guess is that this has something to do with that professor who insists on coming in and stirring up trouble. Could these people be Dinish Desai's laborers?"

The police inspector shrugged.

"What is the name of that other landlord who is so up in arms? The one over in the next village?"

"Ajay Varghese," the police inspector said.

"Yes, that is the one."

The superintendent of police stood up and opened the door a crack. But he quickly closed it again. "They fill up the entire room! We have got to get them out of here."

Although the fan whirred overhead, the crowded room grew hotter and hotter as the sun heated the building's tin roof. Nagmani and Jeet laid Malik down on the floor. Divena knelt beside him and fanned him with the edge of her *sari*. One by one, other women also sat down, and soon the men did the same. They showed not the least sign of leaving. With them before him, and with the sound of voices on the other side of the door, the tall, moustached policeman had no choice but to stand and wait.

When the door finally opened, the police inspector stepped back into the room. "The superintendent of police says you are all to leave these premises at once," he announced.

The *Dalits* scrambled to their feet. Kilas allowed Jeet to take his place beside Malik for a bit, so Jeet and Nagmani lifted him back up.

"With respect," Kilas said to the police inspector, "we came to see the superintendent of police, not you."

"Now, see here!" the police inspector said. "You do not dictate what happens in this office."

"Nor do you," Kilas said. "The law does that. And the law says everyone has the right to drink from a public well, caste and *outcaste* alike. It also says that when a person or persons deliberately harm another, for no lawful reason at all, the injured person has a right to restitution."

Both policemen stared at Kilas, the tall policeman with his mouth hanging open.

The door behind them swung wide. "What is the trouble here?" the superintendent of police demanded.

"Our friend took a drink at a public well—"

"Yes, yes!" the superintendent said. "I heard your complaints. A most unfortunate incident, I agree. But situations do arise. And in villages such as this, tradition holds sway, as regrettable as that might be. I will see that inquiries are made into this matter and—"

"Why would inquiries be necessary?" Kilas asked. "You can see for yourself the injuries inflicted on our friend. And he is ready to identify his attackers."

"Yes, but can anyone verify his version of the event? If not, it is one side's story against another."

"You need only look at him and you can see!" Nagmani exclaimed.

"Leave your names, all of you, and I will be certain to personally look into the matter on your behalf."

Divena shrank back. Leave her name? Most assuredly they would turn her over to Landlord Varghese. Baka rubbed her hand across the scar on her cheek, and she, too, stepped back. Slowly Malik shook his wounded head.

"No names?" the superintendent of police asked in mock surprise. "Well, then." To the two policemen he said, "Turn off the lights and the fan. It is time to close the police station for the day." To the silent crowd before him, he said, "I will look into your complaint." Then he turned and disappeared into the back room.

The tall policeman with the moustache turned off the fan and the lights. The police inspector opened the door to the courtyard and the *Dalits* obediently filed out. Only Nagmani and Jeet were left holding Malik. Malik mumbled something to them, and they, too, turned and left.

The police inspector shut the door with a bang and threw the bolt into place.

In the back room, the superintendent of police cradled his telephone receiver on his shoulder. "Yes, Mr. Varghese," he said. "I thought you should know . . . Yes, I already talked to Dinish Desai, and he said the same thing as you. In fact, he so appreciated my handling of this difficult situation that he insisted on bringing me a reward. Yes, I understand. Where there is law, there are loopholes. Always . . . Why, thank you, Mr. Varghese! That is most generous of you. Most generous, indeed. With the cooperation both you and Mr. Desai have shown, I think we can forget that this most unfortunate ordeal ever happened."

26

August

Blinding sheets of rain turned the road into a river. Everyone scattered for the refuge of their homes, or huts, or lean-tos, or thrown-together shelters of sticks and sheets of plastic. The ground, which at first had swallowed up every bit of rain, had become so engorged with the deluge that it could not hold another drop.

At the Varghese house, rain pounded down on the roof and rattled the windows.

"The paddies need this," Sundar said as he stared out at the storm. "As long as it does not beat the rice off the stalks."

"As long as it does not last so long that the rice molds," Jeevak added.

"The monsoon season started so late this year. I think it will be fine," Sundar said. "At least the paddies are clear of weeds. As soon as the rains stop and the fields dry out a bit, we can start the harvest."

"And a great harvest it will be, too!" Ajay announced as he strode into the room. "Wife, tell the cook to roast a tender mutton tonight. I feel like celebrating."

In amazement, Sundar turned to look at his father. Jeevak laughed out loud and shook his head. Ramesh sighed in resignation and laid his book on the table.

A look of concern crossed Hanita's face. "Are you quite all right, Husband?"

"What is wrong with all of you?" Ajay exclaimed with a hearty laugh. "Am I the only one who knows how to celebrate success?"

Sundar turned back to the window.

"Come, come! That fool landlord Dinish Desai got himself caught in his own trap, yet even his bumbling worked out for our good. It cost me a bit for the superintendent of police's gift, but what does that matter? Those *Harijans* have been put in their place, and we can rest easy."

"Whatever are you talking about, Father?" Ramesh asked. "Has that teacher who so annoyed you finally stopped his reading classes?"

"Not yet, but he will," Ajay assured his son. "Very soon, he will."

Ajay had Ramesh's attention. Jeevak, too, looked at him in anticipation. Hanita, who had been busily sorting through a stack of *saris*, pushed the silk garments aside and sat down, ready to hear.

Ajay, relishing the chance to be the center of attention, smiled broadly. "What is so interesting about the rain, Sundar? Have you never before seen it fall? Come over and join us. I have a good story to share on this rainy day. Come and sit right here beside me. I want you to hear."

Sundar's stomach rolled and his head pounded, but Ajay gave him no choice. He took the only empty chair—next to his gloating father.

"Landlord Dinish Desai thinks himself to be an extremely smart man," Ajay began. "I pushed him hard, then harder, then harder still. He had to do something to regain control of his laborers." Ajay winked and jabbed Sundar with his elbow. "I told you I should go out there, my son. A very good idea it was, too. Did I not tell you? Your father always knows what is best. Remember that."

Ajay leaned back and laughed heartily.

"Are you going to tell us the story, or are you not?" Jeevak asked with a sigh of irritation.

"Patience, patience," Ajay said. "This story is worth the wait." He laughed again. "Well, landlord Desai did something, all right. He took advantage of that hot day last week to set up one of those workers of his who attends the professor's class. Saw to it that the poor fellow had no choice but to drink from a new government community well, built right next to the village's *Brahmin* houses. Some other workers, ones faithful to the landlord, armed themselves with clubs and hid in the brush. When that dupe worker drank from the well, the others rushed him and beat his face in."

Ajay laughed heartily, and Jeevak joined in.

"A government community well?" Sundar asked. "But those are intended for the use of all castes."

"Well, that may be what government officials say," Ajay answered, "especially when they want votes, but anyone with so much as half a brain knows that a well next to *Brahmin* land is only meant to be used by the unpolluted castes."

"Even *Harijans* know that," Jeevak added with a laugh. "And they have less than half a brain!"

Ajay laughed all the harder. "Less than half a brain!" he slapped his leg and laughed some more. "Good, Jeevak. Good!"

Sundar looked in disgust from his father to his brother.

"Well," Hanita said, and she turned back to her stack of *saris*.

Ramesh smiled a tight smile. "Did they kill him?"

"No, no," Ajay said. He pulled out his handkerchief and wiped his eyes. "Better than that. A whole crowd of disgruntled *Harijans* dragged the poor fool to the police station and tried to file a charge against the landlord's men! Can you imagine such a spectacle?"

"The police should have arrested the lot of them," Jeevak said. "It would have served them right."

"Or handed around thick clubs and gone after them as payment for such insolence," Ajay said. "That is what the police in this village would have done."

The rain thundered down with renewed vengeance. Sundar got up and stared out the window at the downpour. "Some *Harijans* do not give up easily," he said.

"No, they do not," Ramesh said bitterly. "Some of them sat for the last engineering exam, and one passed it."

"Cheated, no doubt," Ajay said.

"He got my seat at the university."

"Probably had a father who worked in the Gulf States," Ajay said. "Those types send so much money home. Probably bribed the officials."

Sundar, still staring out at the blur of rain, asked, "How much of a bribe did you give the policeman, Father?"

All the mirth disappeared from Ajay's face. "A gift of appreciation. That is all," he said. "A gift from a man of high birth to an official who does his job well. Nothing more than that. If you hope to be the next landlord, make certain you understand the difference between a gift of appreciation and a bribe."

Sundar strode to the front door, shoved it open, and hurried out into the rain.

Divena stared out at the driving rain. "Do not leave now," Maya said. "You are so small and skinny, the water might wash you away."

"But my grandmother," Divena said. "She will worry about me. And I am worried about her."

"The neighbors will look in on her," Maya said. "Maybe tomorrow will be a better day."

Divena shook her head. "Or maybe it will be worse."

Nagmani and Udeep pushed their way into the church, both soaking wet, their hair dripping. Aswati and Jeba came right behind them. Divena gasped in surprise. "A meeting today? In all this rain?"

"Because of all this rain!" Udeep said. "No one can work in the pepper groves, so we can sing out loudly and clap our hands and stomp our feet. No one will hear us."

"We cannot work, so we will praise God!" Jeba laughed.

Maya grabbed up the pile of cloths and mats and quickly spread them across the dirt floor. Several men followed, then more women. Children came, too, laughing as they splashed through the rivers of water.

By the time everyone settled themselves, thirty-two people sat crowded inside the building. Rainwater trickled through the thatched roof, but what did that matter? Everyone already sat in soaking-wet clothes. The children pushed together, bunched up under the trickles. As the leaks grew into little waterfalls, they nudged each other and giggled.

Aswati pulled her flute out from inside her *sari*. "Sing the professor's song for us, Divena," she urged. "The part about trials and temptations."

Divena stood up, and the room grew silent. To the trill of the flute and steady beat of the rain, she sang:

> Have we trials and temptations?
> Is there trouble anywhere?

We should never be discouraged,
Take it to the Lord in prayer.

Sundar had nowhere to go, but he could not abide his father's voice one more minute. Brag, brag, brag! He sounded like a fat old peacock who continued to gobble and crow long after all the peahens in the world had stuffed their fingers in their ears to stop the racket.

A whole crowd of disgruntled *Harijans*, his father had said. *Would I recognize any of them?* Sundar wondered. *Might* she *be one of the crowd?*

For a fleeting moment it occurred to Sundar to drive out to the pepper grove and see if everyone was all right. He rubbed his burning eyes and shook his head. What a foolish thought! It wasn't his father's land. It wasn't even his village. What a foolish, foolish thought!

Divena had finished the song and everyone had begun to pray fervently when Kilas limped into the church. He ran his hand over his face, wiping away water and mud. Everyone stopped in mid-prayer and turned to stare.

Kilas looked around in confusion. "I did not know you would be meeting today," he said. "I came with a message for Divena. Selvi sent me."

Divena gasped and jumped to her feet. "*Ammama!*" she cried. "Is she all right?"

"Selvi says she feared you might hear about your grandmother asking for you and decide to go to her. But Selvi wants you to know that you must not. She says she fears it is a trick."

"But if *Amamma* is asking for me!" Divena cried.

"Selvi says you should leave here as soon as you can. She says you should go to another village much farther away. She says . . . She says . . ."

"What?" Divena demanded. "What does she say?"

"Selvi says you should forget about *Dalits* and be a television woman. That you should run far away and find a television man who will marry you."

As one, all eyes turned from Kilas to Divena.

"What does that mean?"

"I do not know," Kilas said. "I gave you all of her message."

Divena slumped to the floor, buried her face in her hands, and sobbed.

"What has gotten into you, boy?" Ajay demanded when he found Sundar out by the garden. "Look at you! The mud is halfway up your legs!"

It was not, of course. It only reached to his ankles.

"Get yourself into the house and clean up. Have you lost your mind?"

Sundar pushed his dripping hair back out of his eyes. "Perhaps I have," he said. "Or perhaps I have finally found it."

Ajay grunted in disgust. "We try to sit together as a family. I tell the cook to roast mutton as a great treat. And what do you do? You walk outside in the pouring rain and stand in the mud like a crazy man. Your mother is in the house right now wringing her hands and wailing over you."

Sundar sighed. "I am sorry, Father. I did not mean to distress her. Or any of you."

Ajay took a deep breath and smiled. "Did I sound as though I was scolding you? I am sorry. I suppose I lost myself in my pleasure at having a problem buried behind us."

When Sundar didn't respond, he said, "I need you, my son. When you are landlord, you will make our land more profitable than it has ever been. And you will care for me in my old age."

Still Sundar said nothing.

"Come inside, now. Put on dry clothes and sit at the table with us. You will have first choice from the roasted mutton platter. Even before me. Come inside where you belong. Come, Sundar, and take your rightful place with your family."

27

August

Let the rain pour down. Let the road flood into a river. Divena refused to stay hidden away while her grandmother cried for her. After all, she could not stay in hiding forever.

Divena slogged her way through the pepper grove and splashed up onto the road. No drainpipes to pass through this day. Every one of them would be a rushing torrent. Divena self-consciously lifted her *sari* up to her knees and tied it in place. A disgusting display, she knew, but what did it matter? No one had business pressing enough to take them out on such a day. No one except her.

Stepping cautiously, choosing with great care where she planted her feet, Divena managed to pick her way along the road without being washed away. When she passed a cart that had rolled over onto its side, she whispered a prayer for protection. At the sight of a family cowering together under a torn piece of plastic stretched between two sapling trees, she whispered a prayer for safety and warmth. She also prayed for her grandmother: That the old woman might be safe inside her house. That she would stay dry. That she would have food and water.

Divena resisted the temptation to run. *Patience!* she told herself. *God will protect Ammama*. Softly Divena began to sing,

> What a friend we have in Jesus,
> All our sins and griefs to bear . . .

All the way through the village, she whispered her song. She sang as she approached Landlord Varghese's veranda, and she kept on singing as she splashed past the upper caste homes of her village.

> What a privilege to carry
> Everything to God in prayer!

Dear God, protect my Ammama. Protect me, too, and keep me safe in this flood. As soon as she said *amen*, she started her song from the beginning and sang it again. All the way through. Every verse.

❧

Sundar paced back and forth across the great room in his father's house. Back and forth, back and forth. Savory fragrances came from the kitchen, but he had no interest in food. Not even in roast mutton, usually his favorite. He simply had no appetite.

Come inside where you belong, his father had said to him. *Come and take your rightful place with your family*. The more Sundar went over it in his mind, the more his father's words disturbed him. In simple fact, Sundar did not feel in the least as though he belonged in this house. It did not seem his rightful place at all.

Ramesh had gone to his room to study. Jeevak and Ajay sat together, engrossed in some television show. Hanita had retired to her room. And Sundar paced. And paced. And paced. Jeevak hooted something from in front of the television, and Ajay roared with laughter. Sundar stopped pacing. He grabbed the truck key off the nail by the veranda door and silently eased out of the house.

"*Ammama*?" Divena whispered as she pushed the door open. "Are you all right?"

The old woman lay on her sleeping mat in the middle of the floor, carefully positioned so that none of the roof leaks dripped directly on her.

Shridula struggled to sit up. "Divena? Is that you?"

In the darkness of the hut, it took a minute for Divena's eyes to adjust. She bent down to kiss her grandmother's cheek, but when Divena saw the old woman more closely, she gasped in spite of herself. How had her grandmother gotten so much thinner? She looked like a skeleton with skin stretched over it.

"*Ammama!*" Divena cried. "Do you have any food? Do you have water?"

"I do not want any," Shridula wheezed. "I only want to see you, my blessing. I only want to hold your hand one more time."

"Do not talk that way!" Divena swiped at the tears she could not hold back.

When Divena reached for the water pot standing next to Shridula, it amazed her to find it half full. And a dish of mashed rice also sat beside Shridula's sleeping mat.

"Your friend Selvi," Shridula said. "She comes by every day. Perhaps she is not such a bad girl, after all. Even if she does watch that television box and laugh like a horse."

In spite of herself, Divena smiled through her tears. She took the dish and lifted a bite to the old woman's lips. Shridula turned her head away.

"Please, *Ammama*," Divena begged. "Just a small bite."

But Shridula would not. So Divena lay down beside her grandmother and forced herself not to cry.

Sundar knew exactly where he intended to go. But he had no idea what he would do once he got there.

The truck managed fine on the flooded, partially paved road. But long before he reached the mud path that led through the pepper grove, Sundar pulled off the road and parked the truck so that its tires would not mire down in the gooey mud. He splashed along the road watching for the path. When he found it, he turned down and slogged on through the narrow river of mud. Only days before, it was all dry dirt.

When Sundar first heard the soft babble of voices, he thought it most likely to be a group of laborers. But that made no sense. Who would be out working in such conditions? Even his father's laborers sat idle this day. If Ajay Varghese couldn't find anything for the workers to do, no one could.

Sundar slowed his pace. No, he couldn't be hearing workers. The voices were all mumbling at once, like a mob of people. A peaceful mob, though. Not angry. And a small mob. Very small. It wasn't until he got all the way to the church that he understood the sound he heard: fervent prayer.

Even up close, Sundar couldn't see inside the church. The back wall had been lowered to keep the rain from pouring in. But if he took great care, he could glance into the window at the far side without attracting attention. Of course, he couldn't really see any specific person.

Outside the window, huddled in forested shadows and soaking wet, Sundar listened to the voices inside. To prayers for poor beaten Malik. To prayers for the reading class, and also for the professor and his wife. To prayers for Divena.

Divena!

"Guide her footsteps through the rain and the flood," someone said.

"Protect her from the cruel landlord." That one really hurt.

"Watch over her grandmother. Please do not let her die."

Divena rested her hand on her sleeping grandmother's chest to feel her breathing. Sometimes her breath came in quick, ragged pants, other times it gasped along in slow wheezes. Worst were the frightening gaps between, when Divena could hear no breath at all.

"Please, *Ammama*, get well," Divena breathed. "Please! What would I do without you?"

But her grandmother slept on, and her sleep seemed peaceful. Divena shivered, soaking wet and exhausted. She took hold of Shridula's hand and fell asleep beside her.

How many hours she slept, Divena had no idea. But at the sound of her name, she awoke with a start. "I am here, *Ammama*," she said.

But Shridula had not called to her. Shridula still slept soundly.

"Divena! What are you doing here?" Selvi, hands on her hips, stared at her friend.

"I had to come," Divena explained. "To check on my grandmother."

"I warned you to stay away!" Selvi scolded. "Did Kilas not give you my message?"

"He told me, but I had to come, anyway." Divena disentangled herself from her grandmother's grasp and moved away. "Oh, Selvi, I am so afraid. I have only been away a short time and look at how she has withered."

"She refuses to eat or drink," Selvi said. "I think she is tired of living."

"It is all my fault! I never should have left her. I should have stayed and cared for her."

"Do you think she would be better off if she saw you carried away by that devil who calls himself your father?"

Divena sank back down onto the sleeping mat. Shridula still slept. "Now that you are here, I will run and fetch Mahima," she told Selvi.

Selvi avoided her friend's eyes. "Mahima has already been here. She said her prayers and chanted her *mantras* and cooked up some herbs, but your grandmother turned her face away and refused to drink the medicine. Mahima said she would add the charge to your bill."

"The doctor, then," Divena insisted. "In the next village. He knows real medicine. I will go and beg him to come."

"He will not," Selvi said. "Not unless you give him a large payment. And what do you have to pay him with?"

By the time Sundar stopped the truck in front of his father's veranda, the sky had faded to black. Every window in the house was shrouded in darkness. Sundar felt his way across the veranda and stumbled into the strangely silent house.

No television. Sundar thought. *The electricity must be out again.*

A fire burned in the kitchen oven, and a lone candle glowed on the table. Sundar picked up the candleholder, but he didn't move. He was in no mood to go to the room he shared in rainy weather with Jeevak. In no mood to answer questions or listen to his brother harangue him.

"Is that you, Sundar?" his mother called. "Are you hungry?"

But Sundar didn't even want to talk to her. So he took the candle and walked to the closed-up back of the house, to the room where his grandfather and grandmother used to live when he was a young child.

Sundar set the candleholder on the small table beside his grandparents' old bed. As a little boy, he used to take naps there, always on his Grandmother Sheeba Esther's side of the bed. She would tell him stories and call him Sundar Samuel and remind him to listen for God's voice.

A heavy layer of dust lay over everything in the room. Sundar pulled the sheet off the bed and gave it good shaking. Then he lay down.

"God never said anything to me, Grandmother," Sundar whispered. "All my life I listened, just as you told me to, but God never said one word to me."

Somewhere up the path, a car horn blared. Divena sat up and listened. It wasn't on the road, she felt certain of that. She wouldn't have been able to hear it so clearly from way up there. Another long blast. Divena stepped outside to look. At first all she could see were curious children running to and fro. But then a black car pulled up and stopped right in front of Shridula's hut.

Panic seized Divena. Could it be the police? Or perhaps the landlord? She didn't know anyone with a car. Surely her grandmother did not. Divena dashed back inside before the stranger could see her and she peeked back out through a crack beside the door.

A man got out of the car and walked toward the house. He carried a strange black purse. Divena couldn't run. The house had only one door, and the man stood right out in front. Nor did she have any place to hide. The house had only the one small room.

"Miss Divena?" the man called. "Are you at home?"

Trembling, Divena opened the door, but only a crack.

"Miss Divena? I have come to see your grandmother. I am a doctor."

Divena swung the door wide. "Yes, my grandmother," she said. "She is very ill."

The doctor stepped inside. He knelt down by Shridula and opened his purse. It was filled with tiny tools. The doctor asked Shridula to open her eyes, and he shined a small light into them. He picked up her hands and examined them, first one and then the other. He felt her wrists, and he used a funny metal tube to listen to her heart. With gentle hands, he prodded her chest, and then her arms and legs. When he pressed on her abdomen, Shridula cried out in pain. "I am sorry," the doctor said. "I do not mean to hurt you."

The doctor looked up at Divena. "When did she have malaria?" he asked.

"Not so long ago," Divena said. "Not even half a year."

"Was she very sick?"

Divena nodded. "Very sick."

The doctor glanced down at Shridula. "Please," he said to Divena, "can we step outside for a moment?"

Outside bustled with curious neighbors. But they were respectful. They stayed back and let the doctor talk to Divena alone.

"Your grandmother's eyes are yellow," the doctor said in a soft voice. "So is her skin. That tells me that her liver is badly damaged. I am sorry, but I can do nothing to make her well."

Divena caught her breath and moaned.

"Your grandmother is dying," the doctor said. "I can give her something to make her comfortable, but that is all I can do. If you would like, I will stay here with you and watch over her."

Divena covered her face and sobbed. "You must not," she wept. "I have no money to pay you."

"Do not worry yourself about that," the doctor said. "I am here to care for your grandmother as long as you need me. Your bill has already been paid."

Divena stared incredulously. "What? Paid by who?"

"You need not worry over it," the doctor said. "You have no debt. Come, let us sit with your grandmother."

When Divena and the doctor stepped back inside, Shridula's eyes were wide open. Divena dropped down beside her grandmother and grasped the weary old hands in her young ones.

"Wipe your eyes, my blessing," Shridula said. "I am at peace. Go and find your freedom."

With Divena holding her grandmother's hands and speaking of her love for her *Ammama*, Shridula breathed her last.

28

September

For three entire weeks, rain poured down. No laborers worked in the paddies or the pepper groves. Village markets were all but closed; only farmers with canopies over their truck backs continued to sell. No one ventured outside except the poor souls who had no choice. A little boy, a son of Divena's neighbor Chitra, wandered out of the yard and slid headfirst into the flooded ditch. Chitra's screams brought neighbors running. They barely managed to pull the little one out before the water swept him away.

For three weeks, Professor Chander Menon and his wife held no classes. The road from the city to the village remained impassible, and the field where the class met was transformed into a muddy pond.

For three weeks, Landlords Dinish Desai and Ajay Varghese believed their problems lay behind them, washed away with the monsoon flood. Each chortled privately over his success. Each believed himself to be the better man, wholly responsible for the victory. But then the rain stopped. Soon the sun broke through the clouds. No longer a running river, the road had dried into a muddy track of muck. As the two landlords watched the water recede from their lands, they shouted orders to their overseers: "Enough loafing! Get everyone back to work!"

All over the village, life resumed. Selvi's father hastily cut down the herbs and wild onions he had gathered in the spring and Selvi had hung from the ceiling to dry. At her father's insistence, Selvi laid them in her basket and headed back to the still-soggy market.

After her grandmother's passing, Divena could no longer bear to stay in *Ammama's* hut. "Come and live with me," Selvi pleaded. "We can be like sisters. We can plan our futures together."

Divena went to Selvi's house, but after three days she could no longer bear her friend's constant chatter. So she slogged her way back to the church. She sought solace in the familiar pile of cloths, damp and dirty though they were. She yearned for the solitude of long walks in the pepper grove interspersed with church meetings. It gave her hope. And she had friends there who gave her love.

Never again would Divena's life be the same. She knew that. But for better or for worse, she could now claim her life as her own.

As soon as roads were passable, even before the field at the edge of Dinish Desai's land reemerged from the water, Professor Menon drove out to the church to check on everyone. An onslaught of frustration awaited him.

"The landlord tried to frighten us away from coming to your class by having his *thags* beat poor Malik," Udeep told him.

"Yes," the professor said. "I heard about that most horrible attack. Unforgivable! Absolutely unforgivable!"

"We tried to claim our rights," Nagmani told the professor. "We went to the police and took Malik with us to give witness."

"We remembered what you said about the power of unity," Maya added, "so we all went together."

"The police tried to push us away, but we demanded to see the superintendent of police," Nagmani continued. "We crowded into the police station and refused to leave until he listened to us."

The professor nodded but made no reply.

"The police chief could see for himself what had happened to Malik. Even so, he told us that unless we had a witness, he could do nothing about it."

"He tried to get us to give our names," Divena said. "But we were too smart for that trick."

"We tried to stand up for Malik, but we failed," Nagmani said. "We can get no justice. Unity holds no power for us."

"You were extremely brave," Professor Menon said. "Wise, too, in many of the things you did. Justice does come, but not easily. Unity does bring power, but not every time. Sit with me. Let us talk."

For a long while, the group kept Professor Menon busy listening. Such frustration! People had not spoken of it—not even among themselves.

"Force and power!" Jeet exclaimed. "That is the way of the high caste. Well, I say violence begets violence! We have sticks and clubs of our own. We, too, can lie in wait!"

"No, no!" the professor warned. "If you turn to violence, the landlords have won. The authorities will immediately beat you down. The high castes have the money and they have the power. Which means they have the greater influence."

"What do we have?" Nagmani asked bitterly. "Nothing. We have nothing!"

"You have *achama*," the professor said. "You have the power of nonviolence."

Nagmani pursed his lips and squinted his eyes. "*Achama*? What good does that do us?"

"Plenty of good," Professor Menon said. "Consider Mahatma Gandhi. How did he fight back? With nonviolent resistance. He did not attack with sticks and clubs, but neither did he give in to his oppressors. In his struggle against Britain's unfair salt tax, for instance, he walked to the sea in protest. So many others joined him along the way that by the time they reached the sea, they numbered in the thousands and the authorities were forced to pay attention."

"But they could have killed him," Udeep said.

Professor Menon nodded. "Yes, they could have. But they did not. You must consider carefully: How important is this struggle to you? How much are you willing to risk?"

After a moment's silence, Divena said, "Everything. I am willing to risk everything. Otherwise, where will any of us ever be?"

"And where will our children be?" Jeba said.

"And who will be the nextht one beaten?" Malik lisped through the jagged edges of his remaining teeth.

The next day, as they worked together in the rice paddy, Nagmani asked Jeet, "When does the landlord need us most of all?"

"I do not know," Jeet said. "Harvest, I suppose."

Nagmani ran his hand along the bent stalks, hanging heavy with rice ready for the harvest. "I say we go back to the superintendent of police. If he refuses to see us, then we will go on to the head of the *gram panchayats*. If he is no help, we will go to the magistrate of the district court. If the magistrate will not see us, we will sit and wait until he does. We will sit and wait until we get justice."

"Yes!" Jeet said. "If it takes too long, we will not be here to harvest the landlord's rice."

A mournful look fell over Nagmani's face. "Poor Master Landlord! Without us, he may have to watch his entire crop wither in his paddies."

Every person who attended the reading class agreed to gather for the march to the police station. "You do not need to go," Maya told Divena. "This is not your fight."

"It is a fight for all of us," Divena said. "I most certainly will go."

Kilas and Baka came, too. But not Selvi.

Word spread quickly. By the time the group had assembled at the end of the path where it intersected with the main road, instead of two dozen workers, forty-two *Dalits* showed up.

"You are our leader, Nagmani," Maya said. "You walk in front."

"You, too, Kilas," Divena added. "You are the one who knows the law."

"And you, Malik," Nagmani said. "We need you."

A joyful sense of hope washed over the group as they stepped out onto the road. A pleasant breeze blew, and many of the women had brought filled water pots along with them. Other travelers on the road stepped aside to gawk at the strangely joyful procession.

"Where are you going?" called a man walking toward them, a huge basket of fresh-baked bread balanced on his head.

"We are marching to the sea!" Nagmani answered with a laugh.

"Like Gandhi in our fathers' day?" the bread man asked.

"Yes! And we will be equally successful."

The man turned around and joined them.

Much chattering accompanied the trek. A good deal of laughter floated over the growing crowd. Now and then, someone broke into song, and others joined in, accompanied by the rhythmic slap of their bare feet on the muddy road.

Word traveled more quickly than the *Dalits*' feet. When the tall policeman with the bushy moustache informed the superintendent of police that a crowd of *Dalits* were headed their way, the superintendent grabbed his hat and ordered, "Go home and lock the door behind you. This police station will remain closed and locked up tight until those *Dalits* are gone!"

When the group reached the police station, they found it dark and the door locked.

"Come!" Nagmani called. "We will go on to see the chairman of the *gram panchayats*! The *sarpanch*."

"Can we rest first?" Jeba called out.

"No time," Nagmani said. "We must keep moving."

Kilas looked up at the sky. "The sun is directly overhead," he said. "We have time for a short rest. Give us all a break so we can hand around the water jugs and refresh ourselves."

"And ease our hungry stomachs with bites of bread!" the bread man announced as he took the basket off his head. "There is enough for everyone . . . as long as no one takes too much."

As the assembly approached a line of small shops, their number continued to grow. One after another, people passing on the road called out, "Where are all of you going?"

"To see the *sarpanch* of the *gram panchayat* to ask for justice!" someone in the group would answer. Then someone else would call out, "Come along with us!"

A young man with a serious face fell in step with Nagmani and asked the same question: "Where are you going?"

Nagmani gave him the same answer: "We are *Dalits* going to see the *sarpanch* of the *gram panchayat* to ask for justice."

"I, too, want justice," the young man said, "but the *sarpanch* cannot help you. The *gram panchayat* only makes decisions about repairs on the road and where to put health clinics and village schools. It does not involve itself in justice for *Dalits*."

Kilas pondered this. "I do believe he is right," he said to Nagmani. "We should go straight to the district magistrate. We still have time to get there before the building is locked for the night."

Word quickly passed back through the crowd. "We are going directly to the district magistrate. Yes, to the district magistrate!"

Three women heading home with filled water pots on their heads slipped in beside Baka. Two men, who had been doing nothing but sitting along the roadside, shrugged and stepped in beside Udeep. Four laborers at work in a rice paddy laid down their tools and ran over to join the growing throng.

Even a man driving a bullock cart joined them, moving into place at the rear of the long procession. A fortunate addition, too, for Malik, whose injuries had not yet healed, had begun to grow weary. The driver called out for him to climb up and ride in the back of his cart. A woman soon expecting her first child joined Malik, and so did an old man who walked with a cane and had more and more trouble keeping up. Kilas, though he limped badly, refused to ride.

As the temperature rose, so did the humidity. Clouds of tiny flies swarmed around everyone's heads and buzzed their eyes.

Divena, groaning, swatted at the flies. "Do you suppose it is much farther?" she asked Maya.

"Not much farther." Maya fanned the pests away with the edge of her *sari*. "Look up ahead. We have almost reached the first places of business."

The voices that at first had chattered and laughed so enthusiastically gradually faded away. No longer did anyone sing. An open mouth presented too great an invitation to the pesky flies.

Kilas turned around and shouted, "We are almost there! The district magistrate's office is around the bend and off to the left." Although he spoke with a great deal of confidence, Kilas had never actually been to the district magistrate's office. He knew nothing but what the professor had told him. Even so, as his message carried back from person to person to person, the mood grew even more solemn.

"My children will be all alone this night," Jeba said to Divena.

Divena reached out and touched Jeba's brown arm. "But because of you, they will have a future," she said.

"Look!" Maya called as they rounded the bend.

"The District Court," Kilas announced. "That is where the great magistrate has his office."

Fine and large, the structure sat back off the road, surrounded by a carpet of beautifully trimmed grass and shaded by two huge banyan trees. Across the front of the building grew a fence of trimmed hibiscus bushes, their flowers of pink and yellow and red battered and a bit scraggly after the rains. Even so, they presented a magnificent sight.

❧

"Whoever you are, you cannot simply walk into the District Court and expect to see the magistrate!" a policeman called down from the top of the stairs. "He is a busy man. Leave your names, and I will pass them along to him."

"We have a legitimate complaint," Nagmani replied. "The police in our village will not listen to us. We have walked a long way to see the district magistrate."

"He has no time today!" the policeman said. "Go back to your homes."

Jeet pushed his way forward. "Now, see here—" he began.

Nagmani shot Jeet a warning look. "We will wait," Nagmani told the policeman.

The policeman stared out at the immense crowd. Surely it numbered one hundred. Possibly many more. "All of you will wait? Impossible! We only have one small waiting room."

"In that case, we will wait outside," Nagmani said. "On the grass."

"Absolutely not! The law says—"

"The law says we have the right to be heard by the magistrate," Kilas replied. "We will wait here until he sees us."

❧

"Look at them!" the magistrate raged. From his upstairs window he could see the entire crowd. *Dalits*, *Dalits*, everywhere. Under the banyan trees. On the road. They practically covered the whole of the well-trimmed lawn. "This cannot continue! Drive the lot of them away."

"How?" the policeman asked. "They know that the law gives them the right to be heard."

"Well, then, let them sit there until they roast in the sun!"

"Sir," the policeman said. "How will you get out of the building tonight without facing them?"

"Well, I will simply . . . I will just . . ."

"There are so many of them and only a few of us."

"Scare them away! Or starve them, I do not care."

The policeman shook his head. "They do not look afraid to me. And how will it look to have the lawn littered with starving *Dalits* who are doing nothing more than demanding their lawful right to be heard?"

"Why do you insist on siding with these *outcastes*!" the magistrate yelled as he strode back into his office and slammed the door.

As the sun sank low, many of the *Dalits* began to settle themselves down for the night. Even worse, local women brought water and food for the protesters. A farmer, on his way home from the local market, stopped his truck and handed out his unsold produce.

"They will never leave!" the magistrate complained. "Go get their leader and bring him to me. I will see him, but no one else."

When the policeman carried the magistrate's message outside, Nagmani stepped forward. "We have no single leader," he said. "One person alone cannot fully state our complaints."

With a sigh and a groan, the magistrate relented. "A few people, then. Two or three. No more than four."

Nagmani nodded his agreement. He would go. And Kilas, who knew more about the law than any of the others. And Malik, of course. "And you, Divena," Nagmani said. "You are a free woman. Also, you are the only woman who can really read. Please, come inside with us."

❧

Never before had Divena seen such a sight as the inside of that building. The magistrate's office especially amazed her. A beautiful wood desk and chair took up most of one side. More chairs stood in a line under the window, which was covered in regal elegance by richly woven silk drapes. Oh, and the magistrate had a telephone of his own, right on his desk.

Kilas, shifting nervously from his bad leg to his good leg, told the magistrate about Landlord Dinish Desai and the ambush of Malik at the well. "By law, it is a public well," he emphasized. Kilas pulled Malik forward and pointed to his face.

"My teef are gone," Malik lisped. He pushed his lips aside to show the jagged remains. "My lipth are thtill thwolen, and my armth are badly hurt."

"Most unfortunate," the magistrate said. "But this is a matter for the police in your village, not for me."

"The village police refused to see us," Kilas said.

The magistrate shook his head. "You are the landlord's workers. Work it out with him."

"I am not," Divena said.

"What?"

"I am not one of the landlord's workers. And I also have suffered."

The magistrate leaned back in his soft chair, frowned, and rubbed his temples. "It will take time to work this out," he said.

"We will wait," Nagmani assured him. "We are quite comfortable on the grass. Unfortunately, no sanitary facilities are nearby, but we will manage."

"You will need to provide us with food and water, of course," Kilas said. "Our friend here is still weak, and so are some of the older men in our group. Oh, and one woman is soon to give birth—"

The magistrate looked with frustrated disdain at the disheveled *Dalits* standing before him. "Can you identify your attackers?" he asked Malik.

"Yeth," Malik lisped.

The magistrate leaned back in his chair. "What exactly is it you want from me?"

"Justice," Kilas said.

"An apology for what wath done to me," Malik said. "And money to pay a doctor to fikth my armth and teeth."

The magistrate nodded. "I think we can arrange that. I will talk to the landlord."

"One more thing," Kilas said. "The majority of the people out on the grass are Landlord Desai's bonded laborers. But according to Article 23 of the Indian Constitution, bonded labor has been illegal since 1976. Fourteen years ago."

"Well, that is another subject entirely," the magistrate said. "If money is owed to Mr. Desai, it must be repaid."

"Yes," said Kilas. "But repaid legally. With any extra charges duly accounted for. And at a fair rate of interest."

The magistrate waved his hand dismissively. "That is a subject for another time!"

"No, it is not," Nagmani insisted. "An apology and restitution for our friend here is only the first part of our demand. The second part is our freedom. If Landlord Desai wants us to work for him, if he wants us to harvest his rice crop and later on, his pepper crop, he will have to pay each of us a fair wage. In return, we will pay him fair rent to live in his settlement. If he does not agree, we will find work in another field."

"When you call to talk to Landlord Desai, be sure to tell him that, will you?" Kilas asked. "We will be waiting outside for your answer."

❧

"Ridiculous!" Dinish Desai shouted into his telephone. "Apology and restitution? I will do no such thing! And as for my runaway laborers, I would beat the lot of them if I did not need them whole for the harvest."

The magistrate told him the second half of the workers' demands.

"What?" Desai roared. "Hire them? Pay them wages? I will not! Throw the lot of them in jail, then we will see what they have to say!"

The magistrate informed the landowner that, in such a case, his rice paddies might well go unharvested.

Dinish Desai had much more to say, but the magistrate cut him off. "Tonight!" he said. "I want this dispute settled tonight!"

❧

Early the next morning, the *Dalits* had just begun to discuss who would go for water and where they might find food, when Landlord Desai's truck came up the road. In front of the magistrate's office, it slowed down and the driver crept past the encampment. Because he had no choice, he parked up the road. Dinish Desai and the four men who had beaten Malik had to walk through the encampment to get to the front door. Two policemen hurried out, prepared to beat down any violence. But not one of the *Dalits* moved. Not one yelled or scolded. Everyone simply stared.

The landlord and his men entered the magistrate's office, and the door closed. The window, however, did not. The crowd on the grass stared at that open window in absolute silence. "Because you cannot or will not control your workers, Desai!" The magistrate's angry voice echoed down to the *Dalits*. And after a while: "This is how things are today. The law does not change to suit you!" The crowd moved in closer, but for a long time they could hear only words and snatches of thoughts. Then: "No, I will not! I refuse to risk my position for you!"

An hour or so after the magistrate's door closed, it opened again. The magistrate stepped out, and the landlord followed him. Then came the landlord's men, all with their heads bowed low.

"Will the beaten man please step forward?" the magistrate said.

Malik stood and stepped up to the porch.

The magistrate nudged Dinish Desai, and Desai elbowed the man next to him.

The four men who had done the beating knelt down. "I am sorry for what I did to you," the first man said. "It was wrong, and I apologize."

"I also apologize," said the second man. "Thank you for not requiring the right to beat my face in."

The third bowed low. "I am most sorry," he said. "Please forgive me for doing this to you."

"I also apologize for my cruel actions," said the fourth. "May the gods be merciful to you and allow you to heal well."

After a moment's silence, the magistrate again nudged Desai.

"I have given money to the magistrate to pay the doctor for your care," Dinish Desai said. "From this day, you who have worked for me are free men and women. I would like to have you continue to work in my paddies and pepper groves. As you know, my rice is ready for harvest. Please, come back to your homes. I will write up a legal contract for each of you."

29

September

"The heat of summer is behind us," Divena assured Maya as they tied the chopped rice stalks into bundles. "I like this time of the year."

Shading her eyes, Maya looked up at the sunny sky. "The monsoon rains did not last long enough," she said. "I keep waiting for another storm to blow through. A really violent torrent that will sweep in and wash all the rice away."

Divena laughed. "You worry too much."

"You know as well as I do that the worst storms hit at the end of the season."

Divena stood up, settled her hands on her hips, and laughed out loud. "Why, Maya, I do believe you still fear the gods and goddesses."

Maya made a face.

"You worry that they will punish us because we did not keep to our place! Tell the truth, now. Is that what you think?"

"I am a Christian, not a Hindu," Maya said. "Get down here and help me tie this bundle."

Divena knelt back down, gripped the bundled rice stalks, and held them tightly. But she couldn't stop sniggering. "Here we are, tying dry sheaves on a dry ground in a dry rice paddy," she teased. "Even so, you worry that the gods will send a flood and wash us away, or will send some other disaster even more horrible. My, but you like to worry!"

Ajay Varghese and his son Sundar stood up in the bed of the truck and gazed out at their workers. The men chopped the rice stalks, the same as they had done for generations. The women followed along behind and tied the sheaves into bundles, the same as they had always done.

"I am glad this will all be yours," Ajay said with a sigh. "Everything looks the same, but nothing truly is. Who can say what next year will bring, or the year after that?"

"So what if Dinish Desai now pays his laborers?" Sundar said. "From what I hear, his harvest is coming along fine, but so is ours."

Ajay stared at his son. "Since when have you taken so keen an interest in Landlord Desai's harvest?"

"Since the magistrate forced him to obey the law." One look at his father's face, and Sundar quickly added, "It has been the law most of my life, Father. I am surprised the *Harijans* waited this long to claim their rights."

"*Harijans*! Huh!" Ajay sneered. "They are still *Untouchables*, and *Untouchables* are meant to do our work."

Sundar shook his head. "I cannot understand you, Father. All this business about pollution and uncleanliness. All this *karma* and *dharma* talk. You pride yourself on being a Christian. A modern man all ready to march into the twenty-first century. Why do you continue to hold on to those old-fashioned Hindu prejudices and fears?"

"Some change is good and some change is bad," Ajay said. "Next you will tell me we should release all our workers, then pay them to come back to us and do what they are already obligated to do for no pay."

"It makes no difference what I think and it makes no difference what you think," Sundar said. "That is what happened to Dinish Desai, and in time it is certain to happen to us."

Ajay clenched his jaw and glowered at his son.

Sundar shook his head and climbed down off the truck bed.

"Where will it end, I ask you?" Ajay called after him. "Where will all this end?"

After their evening meal, Ramesh, as usual, went to his room to study, and Jeevak, as usual, turned on the television. Ajay sat on the couch beside his son. "Come and watch with us," he called to Sundar. "You will like this show. It is about science."

"I am going out for a while," Sundar said. He reached for the truck key.

"Again?" Ajay demanded. "Where do you go every evening?"

"To see a girl, I hope," Jeevak smirked. "Maybe you will finally get married, older brother, so I can at last have a chance for a wife before I am too old to care."

"Of course Sundar is not going to see a girl," Hanita called from the side room. "He is a good boy. He will accept the girl his family finds for him—when we find him the right one."

Sundar left before his family had a chance to ask any more questions. He started the truck and headed toward the next village, and the path through the pepper grove.

More than a month had passed since Professor Chander Menon and his wife last held a class for the workers. Not since the downpours of early August. They would not start again until the end of the rice harvest. Still, Uncle and Auntie sometimes came to the church in the pepper grove to sing and pray with the people. Sometimes they stayed to answer questions.

Sundar had just edged in to his favorite place in the shadows of the trees, behind the open back wall. The professor and some workers were there, deep in a discussion.

"You say India is a democracy," Jeet said. "But how can that be? We walked for two days, we ran great risks and had to threaten the landlord's livelihood in order to get one single law enforced one single time. Yet the upper castes need only make a telephone call and hold out a bag of money, and they immediately get whatever they want. How is that a democracy?"

"You are right," the professor said. "India is not truly a democracy. We are independent from Britain, yes, but a large part of our population is not independent. We cannot truly be a democracy until we as a people determine to finally relinquish the restraints of caste."

Sundar did not hear the rest of the questions, or the prayer that followed. He liked these people, but he could never make himself known to them. They would look at his caste, at his landlord father, and they would despise him.

Sundar sneaked away and drove back home.

"Humaya!" Jeevak called out the truck window. Even before Sundar had a chance to apply the brakes, Jeevak jerked the door open and stepped out. "What kind of a lazy overseer are you? Sundar and I were at the upper paddy, and the harvest has not even been started up there!"

"We do not have enough workers," Humaya said.

"What are you talking about?" Sundar demanded. He got out of the truck and stepped over next to his brother. "We have plenty enough workers to have the lower paddies finished and the upper ones well under way."

Humaya pulled the *chaddar* off his head and mopped his face. He stepped back and shifted his weight from one foot to the other. "Not now," he said. "Some of our workers are gone."

"Gone?" Sundar exclaimed. "What do you mean *gone*?"

"I mean they are no longer here." Humaya folded his *chaddar* and carefully rewrapped it around his head. "The landlord in the next village needed more workers because some of his left before the harvest, and some of our laborers went over to his land to work."

"But . . . they cannot do that!" Jeevak exclaimed. "They belong to us! Send a couple of the strongest men to drag them back."

"Our strongest men are the ones who left first," Humaya said.

As Jeevak sputtered in frustration, Sundar demanded, "What is going on?"

Humaya looked down at the ground and nudged at a dirt clod with his toe. "They declared themselves free and went to work for that other landlord," he said, "because that landlord offered to pay them."

Jeevak growled and raised his fist to swing at the overseer. Sundar grabbed his brother's arm and forced him into the truck. "Get the harvesting finished, Humaya!" Sundar ordered as he started the truck. "Any way you can! My father will hold you responsible."

"I will kill that Dinish Desai!" Ajay bellowed when Jeevak told him what the overseer had said.

"And I will help you," Jeevak promised.

"Find me a club! I will beat that traitor to death in front of his workers! We will see what they have to say about freedom then."

"Stop it!" Sundar ordered.

Ajay turned on his eldest son. "What would you have me do, Sundar? Hand over my workers to that snake, Desai? Or perhaps you think I should bid against him for laborers for the harvest. Bid to pay *my own laborers!*"

"It is just that if you act now, while you are so angry, you—"

"He probably has those other two of my workers as well. Not that it matters so much. A lame man and a scarred woman. Who wants them, anyway?"

In the most conciliatory tone he could manage, Sundar began, "Father, please, let us consider—"

Jeevak started to laugh. But Ajay cut both of them short. "And that other one, too! The daughter of that no-good wastrel, Puran. Dinish Desai probably has her hidden away somewhere as well!"

The reference to Divena caught Sundar off guard. He did not dare look at his father. He did not dare move at all.

"Well, I will show him!" Ajay's eyes flashed with rage. "I will pay him back, pound for pound!"

In spite of everything, dinner passed with amazing calm. Jovial, almost.

"How goes the harvest, my sons?" Ajay Varghese asked as he scooped up a huge bite of curried chicken and rice.

"Quite well," Sundar said before Jeevak could answer. "The lower paddies are finished. The yield is always best there, of course. But with no signs of more rain, the others should come in soon."

"Excellent, excellent!" To his wife, Ajay said, "I have a hunger for a nice fruit this evening, my dear. Something fine and extravagant. Pineapple, perhaps?"

Hanita stared at him. "We have no pineapple."

"Perhaps I shall take the truck and go out in search of one," he said. "The fresh air will be good for me."

Sundar pushed his chair back. "I will drive you."

"Never mind. I quite enjoy taking the truck out alone now and then. Especially in the evening when few others are out on the road."

"Well," Hanita said with a sigh, "it is a strange craving, Husband. But at least it will take your mind off of—" She caught herself in time, but barely.

With jerks and stalls, Ajay managed to start the truck and drive it around to the supply shed.

"It is not that we landlords take such advantage of our workers," he said to himself. "But on the other hand, we do not need to teach them all our tricks, either."

It took Ajay a long time to find everything he needed—the metal can and all. It surprised him to discover how little he actually knew about the operation of his own land. Were his servants to leave . . . well, such a thing would be unthinkable. Absolutely unthinkable!

"I am not helpless, though," he said. "Not in the least!"

His laborers had always been happy, Ajay reasoned. They bowed when they saw him. They didn't have to, as in bygone days. No, they did so willingly, out of respect and affection for him.

"Except for that girl Jeevak laid his eyes on," Ajay said. "Laid his *hands* on! Jeevak can be such a difficult one."

Still, Ajay admitted silently, he could have handled that unfortunate episode better. A lighter punishment for the girl and her husband would still have gotten the message across. More like Sundar and less like Jeevak. That's what he should aim to be from now on.

Slowly, carefully, Ajay drove down the road to the next village and on toward Dinish Desai's settlement. Part of the time, he kept the truck's lights turned off. He didn't need them with the moon so bright. Anyway, he always felt it wise not to attract any more attention than necessary. And he really didn't know the road this far out. He had been out to Desai's land only twice before.

"Of course, Sundar drove both of those times," Ajay said. "But if I cannot drive my own truck, what am I?"

Ajay drove past a paddy he felt certain belonged to Landlord Desai. It was already harvested and already cleaned.

"Sure, the front one looks good," Ajay said. "But what about your back paddies, Mr. Landlord Desai?"

Ajay, laughing, turned off the road before he got to Desai's house and parked the truck in a grove of trees. He pulled out the metal can he had put in the back. By the light of the moon, he picked his way down the path toward Desai's storehouse.

"He needs to learn," Ajay muttered. "And how can he learn if no one teaches him? He needs to hurt so he knows how it feels when he hurts others." Ajay managed to follow a bit of a trail. "And my workers, too. They also must learn."

Stacks of hay left over from the spring harvest stood tall around the storehouse. Yes! Could it be more perfect? No houses, only a full storage shed and haystacks. Ajay did his best to keep from chortling out loud as he poured gasoline from the metal container around the storehouse. Not all the gasoline, though. A bit remained in the container. He poured that over the closest haystacks. Just in case the hay had not had time to dry thoroughly enough.

Then Ajay Varghese lit a match and threw it onto the haystack. When he heard the whoosh, he picked up the can and ran back to his truck.

30

September

Each night, as the sun set, Divena spread out the cloths for her bed and lay down before it grew too dark for her to see. Maya had shown her where the candle stubs were tucked away in the front corner of the church, but Divena refused to use them. Candles cost money. Why would she burn a candle when she could as easily go to sleep when the sun set and get up when it rose at dawn? She lay down at sunset, but she did not necessarily go to sleep. Many nights she lay awake and listened to the comforting sounds of the night.

But not this night. This night something seemed amiss. The mice that crept about in the dark—usually in silence—scurried and scratched in a most disconcerting way. Divena slipped out of the pile of cloths and rolled the back wall up far enough to allow her to step outside.

How could the moon have disappeared? Why had all the stars vanished? All day long, not a cloud had drifted across the clear sky.

Then she smelled the smoke. Fire!

Divena ran from the church and up the path. Before she reached the road, she ran headlong into Maya, who was running down to her.

"Everything is burning!" Maya screamed. "Our houses and the fields, they are all on fire! Everything!"

She grabbed Divena's hand and pulled her forward.

Always, fire was the dread of summer. The sun burned so hot that the whole world seemed to turn into dry tinder. Should one house catch fire, within minutes, the whole village could be burning. With wells low and ponds so dry, there was no way to stop a fire once it started.

But summer had passed. And even though the monsoon season was short, the rains had poured down heavily. Nothing could be called tinder dry. Water filled the wells, and ponds brimmed to overflowing.

When Divena and Maya got to the settlement, they found everyone huddled together, watching in horror as the flames destroyed everything they knew. Some moaned. Many wept. Terrified children shrieked and clung to their mothers' skirts.

"It is the will of the gods," a worker cried out. One after another they took up his fatalistic lament.

So very sad. Another disaster to be endured. Everyone stared helplessly.

"If we had only had a bit of gold," a woman next to Divena wailed. "We could have put it in a pot of water and sprinkled it over our houses, and it would have kept the fire away from us."

"If I had a bit of gold, I would be far away from here," Jeet mumbled.

As the sun rose dusky red, shrouded in smoke, it revealed a hopeless landscape. Nothing remained but smoldering ruins. The huts were piles of ashes.

"When the cinders cool, we can sift through and look for what is left," Jeba said hopefully.

But the woman beside her shook her head. "We can look, but we will find nothing. Because nothing is left."

"Even if we did find a pot or a bowl, whose pot or bowl will it be?" another woman asked. "Whose ashes are whose?"

"All our work for nothing," Maya mourned. "The storage shed is gone, and all the rice inside it."

When Dinish Desai arrived in his truck, everyone stepped aside to make room for him to pass.

"How did this happen?" he demanded. "Who is at fault?"

The overseer bowed his head. "An act of God," he said.

Landlord Desai glared out at the distraught workers. "Who of you saw the fire start? Speak up, now! Someone must have seen something!"

"The haystacks caught fire first," Jeet proclaimed. "I saw them go up in flames. Then the fire spread to the storehouse, then to everything else."

"Yes, everything," the woman behind him agreed. "Everything!"

"What will we eat?" a man called out. "We have nothing left."

In exasperation, Landlord Desai glared around at the workers. "That is no longer my concern!" he said. "The law says you do not belong to me, so I bear no responsibility for you."

"But we have nothing to eat!" Jeba cried.

"You have your rights!" Dinish Desai climbed back into his truck. "Look to them to feed you!"

"Of course, I do not take pleasure in the misfortune of another," Ajay Varghese said after his servant delivered the news. "Yet I cannot help but believe that by his own recklessness, Dinish Desai brought this tragedy on himself. Life follows a proper order. Disrupt that order, and disaster is sure to follow."

Sundar sat in the great room with his brothers and his father. He did not, however, join in the talk, which quickly grew more and more boisterous and sarcastic.

"We will be gracious, of course," Ajay said. "We will allow our laborers to return to us without penalty."

"That is actually quite good, Father," Jeevak said. "Because our harvest is not yet finished. It should be, but it is not."

"Soon, soon!" Ajay declared. "And when our rice is in, it will be like gold. For with Landlord Desai's storehouse destroyed, both his village and ours will be vying to buy it."

Sundar stared at his father. "How do you know his storehouse is destroyed?"

Ajay blanched. "Well . . . the servant said so, of course."

"No, he did not."

"Desai's land burned. His storehouse is on his land, is it not?"

"The servant said the laborers' *settlement* burned. He did not mention the storehouse."

"Well . . ." Ajay, flustered, looked to Jeevak, but Jeevak said nothing. "Well, I . . . I figured the storehouse must be gone." Recovering himself, Ajay added in a conciliatory tone, "But perhaps I am wrong. By God's grace, I *may* be wrong and Dinish Desai's storehouse still stands."

Sundar, holding his gaze steady on his father, said nothing.

"Come, come!" Ajay insisted. "Dinish Desai's trials are not our concern. Let us forget about him and consider our own fortunate futures!"

All day, Dinish Desai's workers waited for the smoldering ashes to cool. No one ate, because no one had anything to eat. Only a few had water pots, which meant the group had a scarce supply of drinking water. As the afternoon waned, one person after another picked up a stick and ventured barefoot into the still-steaming ash bed to poke around in search of something useful. They found a few unbroken bowls and fewer pots. A belt buckle. The charred sole from a man's shoe. A broken mirror. A few scattered coins.

"A cloud of smoke is coming toward us," a young boy cried in terror. "I think it is another fire!"

Everyone ran to look.

"That is not smoke," Nagmani said. "It is dust."

Jeet swung up to the lowest limb of a tamarind tree. With the agility of a monkey, he scrambled on up to the higher branches.

"What do you see?" the overseer called up to him.

"Bullock carts. And people!" Jeet exclaimed in disbelief. "A whole line of carts and people along the road. It looks like a train, and it seems to be coming this way."

"Not a single person at work in this paddy!" Ajay exclaimed to Sundar. "Where could everyone be?"

"Perhaps they have not yet gotten to this one," Sundar said. "I will drive on to the lower paddy. Jeevak is down there."

But before they reached the halfway point, they met Jeevak coming up the road. "Everyone is gone!" he said. "I have been bellowing for Humaya, but I cannot even find him!"

"Drive on to the settlement," Ajay ordered.

Jeevak jumped up into the truck bed, and Sundar drove down between the fences. "Not one worker in any paddy!" Ajay exclaimed. "Not even on the road!"

When they got to the settlement, Sundar called to a woman filling her water pot at the well. "You! Where is everyone?"

"Gone," the woman said.

"Gone!" Ajay bellowed. "Gone where?"

"In the next village, a terrible fire burned—"

"I know all about the fire," Ajay interrupted impatiently. "I do not care about that. What I want to know is, why has my harvest stopped?"

The woman bowed her head. "Some of us are still here, but we cannot work alone. We cannot bundle rice that has not yet been chopped."

Shaking with frustration, Ajay roared, "*Where . . . are . . . my . . . workers?*"

The woman fell to her knees. "Gone. They all went to help those who were burned out."

The "whole train" Jeet had seen from the treetop turned off the road and made its way down the path to the burned-out settlement.

"As soon as we saw the smoke, we knew what happened to you," Humaya called out. "We brought you food!"

Food. Yes. Great amounts of food. Ajay Varghese's baskets and bowls overflowed with Ajay Varghese's rice and fruit, all piled high in the back of Ajay Varghese's bullock carts.

"Who sent you to us?" Nagmani asked.

"The God your class worships," Humaya said. "He sent us."

As the distraught workers stared in disbelief, an old woman from among Landlord Varghese's workers pushed her way forward.

"Step back, old woman," Gheet said. Not with an unkind tone of voice, but with a definite one.

But the old woman, ignoring him, continued to push forward.

"You heard what he told you," Jeet said. "Do not interrupt us." The woman tried to talk, but Jeet shouted her down. "Can you not hear? I said, do not bother us now!"

Divena pushed past Jeet and touched the old woman's arm. "What is it you have to say, old grandmother?"

The old woman opened her hand.

"It is nothing but a filthy piece of cloth!" Jeet said in disgust. "This woman has spent too many years working in the hot sun!"

"All of us have spent too many years working in the hot sun," Maya snapped. "Let her speak."

"You lost so much," the old woman said. "And some of you are our friends. Maybe all of you would be our friends if we knew you."

Jeet and Gheet exchanged glances of exasperation.

"We have saved some money for the time when we grow too old to work. Money for our children, so they can learn to read in English the way city children do."

With her calloused fingers, stiff and bent, the old woman struggled to untie the knot in the dirty cloth. Jeet sighed impatiently, but the others pushed forward, and stood on tiptoes, in an effort to see.

Slowly, painfully, the old woman picked at the knot until she finally worked it loose. Carefully she unfolded the cloth. Then she took Divena's hand and laid the dirty cloth in it.

"*Rupee* coins!" Divena gasped in amazement.

"Twenty-two of them," the old woman said. "We give it all to you to buy food for your little ones. To build your houses again. To bring your reading classes to us. We want to be free like you."

31

September

From the front, where children sat crammed together, all the way to the back, where men and older boys stood outside and listened in, the little church overflowed. Men even leaned through the window, and older boys peered down from their perches on tree limbs.

To the haunting melody of Aswati's flute and the beat of Udeep's *ghatam*, Divena sang:

> Vazhiyum sathyavumaayavane,
> Nin thirunaamam vaazhthunnu.
> (Father and God your kingdom come,
> Your will be done forever, on earth as it is in heaven.)

Hands clapped along. Voices joined in, singing loud and strong.

But Divena stood in front of them all, singing in a voice of blessed hope. Throughout the room, men and women squeezed their eyes shut so as to better hear the melodious words.

Enthralled, Sundar Varghese eased out of the shadows and moved up behind the church. He paused for a moment, then stepped out of his shoes and in through the open wall. Only the men in the back saw him, but their mouths fell open. They gaped at the pale man dressed in expensive clothes and holding his fancy shoes. None of the men knew his identity, but they all knew for certain that he was not one of them.

> Manujanaay bhoovil avatharichu,
> Mahiyil jeevan balikazhichu,
> Thiruninavum divya bhojyavamaay,
> Ee ulkathin jeevanaay.
> (Lord of Israel, God who reigns forever,
> You are the way, the truth, the life, born as a human.
> You are a loving God.
> You give us eternal life.)

Sundar edged forward through the men at the back of the packed church. One by one, they stared, and each one nudged the one next to him. Each did his best to move away and let the stranger through, but the packed crowd made it impossible.

Sundar squeezed his way to the side wall and pressed in against it. The tall man in front of him turned around to stare. The man's nose was splayed flat, his scarred lips were thick. He nodded to Sundar, and when he smiled his crooked smile, Sundar saw nothing where his front teeth should be—except for a couple of jagged edges.

Divena sang,

> Vazhiyum sathyavumaayavane.
> (Your will be done on earth as it is in heaven, forevermore.)

When Divena finished, Professor Chander Menon stepped up to the front. "Some of you have come today to thank the God of Heaven for sparing your lives," he said. "A worthy prayer indeed, for although the fire roared through the settlement at night when you were all preparing to sleep, not one person lost his life. Not even an injury—aside from a few scorched fingers and toes."

People smiled and nodded.

"Others of you have come to ask God why He would allow a fire to destroy everything you owned. Especially a fire of such suspicious origin."

A few grumbled in agreement, but most listened silently.

"We have talked about your rights," the professor said. "Many of you joined together to demand those rights on behalf of one unfortunate man among you."

It wasn't until this moment, when he turned to acknowledge Malik, that Professor Menon saw Sundar. He recognized him immediately. A few others, who also turned to smile at Malik, stared at the light-skinned man. But most couldn't see him.

"I am happy to report that the district magistrate sent word that you need not come back to his office. He is already working to settle this—in his words—this 'unfortunate situation.'" The professor smiled broadly. "Look at what you have accomplished! My congratulations to all of you."

"But how will the magistrate settle it?" Jeet called out. "However the fire started, an apology will not be enough to set this right."

"No!" Udeep agreed, and a chorus of voices joined in.

Professor Menon raised his hands. "A fine of ten thousand *rupees* has been levied against each of the two landlords involved—Landlord Dinish Desai and Landlord Ajay Varghese."

A roar rose up through the room.

"For the fire?" Sundar gasped.

"No," the professor said. "For illegally and intentionally holding bonded laborers. For denying them their rights under the Indian Constitution. Some of the fine will be kept by the magistrate's office. That is unavoidable. But the remainder will be divided among all of you."

The room erupted in cheers.

The professor, smiling, waited several minutes. Again he raised his hands and called for silence. "You are all invited to come to the classes, which, with the help of my wife, I will be restarting in two days. We will talk about the ways you might use the settlement money. To go out and drink and gamble may sound tempting after all you have been through, but if you do that, the money will soon be gone and you will once again be destitute. We will talk about owning land of your own that you can work as you choose—to raise rice or tea, or start a mango grove, perhaps. Or maybe start a dairy. Or even to open a shop of some sort."

Everyone fell silent.

"I do not know how to do any of those things," Rupali said.

"But you can learn. Every one of the things I mentioned, and many more besides, other *Dalits* in other villages are doing successfully. Someone taught them. Now many of them are willing to teach you."

"Is it possible?" one woman murmured to another.

"Land of my own. Imagine!" exclaimed a man to anyone around him who would listen. "Of course, after working for the landlord, I already know all about planting and harvesting rice crops. I also know . . ."

"A whole new life for my children!" Jeba exclaimed to other mothers. "School! Can you imagine my little ones actually attending school?"

". . . only drank and gambled because I saw no hope for tomorrow," the man with protruding front teeth said defensively. Those around him called out their agreement. "But now, with such an opportunity . . . well, that is a different matter. Yes, an entirely different matter!"

Children got up and ran back to find their mothers. "Can I go to school, *Amma?* Can I? Can I?"

If Professor Menon had more to say, he wisely gave up trying. He looked at his wife, but she sat in the middle of a group of eager women, deep in conversation. He smiled at one person and then another, all the while weaving his way toward the back. Clutches of men, all talking at the same time, left the church together. Women huddled and talked, then gathered up their children and they, too, left, chattering as they made their way to the road. Divena talked excitedly with Maya and Baka. "Even if I am not included, I am so happy for all of you," she said.

Sundar, grateful that everyone had lost interest in him, eased across the room as unobtrusively as possible, and edged out the back. But a short way away, Professor Menon waited for him.

"I did nothing wrong," Sundar insisted. "I know nothing of the fire, or of the magistrate. I simply—"

"No, no," the professor laughed. "I merely wanted to welcome you to our group this evening."

"I knew nothing about any of this," Sundar said again. "I expected the church meeting to progress like every other time."

"Ah ha," Professor Menon said. "So you have been with us before."

"No!" Sundar said. "That is, not really. Not inside."

"I am not able to come as often as I would like, either," the professor said.

For several minutes, the two walked in silence. But then Sundar stopped abruptly. "Do you know who I am?"

"Yes," the professor said. "I do not imagine many of the others do, however. Some, certainly, because they were your father's laborers."

"Were?"

"If your father wishes to have them work for him, he will now have to pay whatever wage they ask."

"Or?"

"Or he will have to find other *Dalits* to do his work. They prefer the name *Dalits* to *Harijans*, by the way. Although I think most of all they would prefer to simply be called people."

"My father could hire *Sudras*," Sundar said.

"Yes, that is another option, of course. *Sudras* would expect considerably higher wages, however."

"I know nothing of my father's involvement in all of this!" Sundar insisted again.

"Why, neither do I," Professor Menon said. "Neither do I."

"That is to say, the fire and everything. As far as I know, my father went out to look for a pineapple to refresh us after our supper."

"I see," the professor said. "And did he find a pineapple?"

"No," Sundar murmured. "He did not."

They had walked up the path all the way to the road. Sundar said, "That is my truck over there."

The professor nodded. "Well. This is farewell, then. I do hope you will come and see us again."

"I am not so certain everyone would be pleased by my presence."

Professor Menon smiled. "You might be surprised. You might be very surprised indeed."

Sundar nodded and climbed into his truck. Professor Menon started back down the path, but then Sundar threw the truck door open. "Professor!" he called as he jumped out. "Wait! My family is Christian," Sundar said. "Ask any of them, and they will tell you."

Again, the professor nodded.

"But I do not feel like one of them. Like one of my family, that is. I never have." Sundar wiped at his eyes and slowly shook his head. "I know the people at the church are all *Har . . . Dalits*. Except you and your wife, of course. But I feel more comfortable there than I ever feel at home. Which is why I keep coming back, I suppose. Those people do not know me at all. I only know them because of what I hear in their prayers. Even so, I feel closer to them than I feel to anyone in my family."

"That is how it is when you come from the darkness into the light," the professor said.

Sundar took a handkerchief from his pocket and wiped at his eyes. "Long ago, when I was very small, my grandmother told me that one day I would hear God's voice speaking to me."

Professor Menon put his hand on Sundar's shoulder. "Perhaps this is that day."

32

September

Stay at home, Father," Sundar pleaded. "Too much has happened too quickly. I will hire workers to finish the harvest and take charge of the threshing. You stay here."

"Yes, yes!" Hanita agreed. "You are in no condition to face the workers, Husband."

Ajay Varghese jumped to his feet. "All of you, stop treating me like a troubled child! I already have my own workers, and I intend to see to it that they do their job!"

"The magistrate made his decision," Sundar reminded him.

Ajay laughed. "You have much to learn, my son! All a decision does is placate the losers. Put a thousand *rupees* in his pocket, and that magistrate will manage to lose those orders. As for the workers, they require far less. An extra bag of rice, and they will grovel before me as they always have before."

"Father, I—"

"No! Do not talk. Listen for a change. All of you, be quiet and listen to me! I do not want to hear any more about India changing, or what century is just around the corner. I know what is mine, and I know what I have to do to keep it. I refuse to hear anything else!"

Sundar and Jeevak exchanged glances.

"What is my overseer doing about this?" Ajay demanded. "Bring Humaya to me. I will have him get out the whips, if I must. Even the branding iron, to mark those who are mine. I never should have given up that practice. Whatever it takes, I want my workers in the paddies *right now*!"

"Humaya left with the others," Jeevak said. "You have no workers!"

Ajay stared at his second son. "What?"

"It is true," Sundar said.

"Then bring Crispin to me. He is young, but I will give him the chance to be in charge."

"Do you not remember, Father?" Sundar said. "Crispin was among the first to leave."

Ajay stared from one son to the other. "Who is left to work my harvest?"

"Many are gone," Sundar said. "And the ones who remain refuse to work until we write out contracts with them and pay them, the same as Dinish Desai is being forced to do."

"Never!" Ajay sputtered in frustrated fury. "I will not do it. I will not!"

Hanita laid her hand on her husband's arm. "No, Husband, you will not. That is why you must stop fighting and let Sundar do it his way."

Jeet and Udeep and Nagmani were among the men who signed contracts to harvest the Varghese paddies. Kilas did, too. Humaya signed a contract to work as overseer, but Gheet would not come back. In the line of women waiting to sign contracts, Sundar saw others he recognized: Aswati and Jeba, Nisha and Rupali. They kept their eyes down, for which Sundar felt an overwhelming gratitude. He could not bring himself to look them in their eyes.

Divena did not come.

"Treat the workers right," Sundar warned Jeevak. "And stay far away from the women. I am the new landlord, and I am not my father."

When the district magistrate finally admitted Dinish Desai to his office, the landlord wasted no time on formalities. "I throw myself on your mercy," he said. "My storehouse is gone, and my entire rice harvest with it. As my labor settlement is also completely destroyed, I have nothing to attract laborers to work my pepper groves."

The magistrate listened, but he fiddled impatiently.

"I have nothing left," Landlord Desai said. "I cannot pay the ten thousand *rupees* you levied against me."

The magistrate nodded. "It is indeed a dilemma," he said. "What a tragedy that you spent so much time and energy circumventing the law."

"Please, sir," Dinish Desai begged. "Perhaps I am guilty of negligence in my oversight. For that I am truly sorry. But the fact remains, I cannot pay so large a fine." He paused. "However, even in my poverty, I brought a gift for you." The landlord slipped an envelope from his pocket and slid it across the magistrate's desk. "Please, sir, I cannot pay the fine you levied against me."

"I see. Well. If you do not have the money, you do not have the money."

"Thank you, sir," Dinish Desai said. He heaved a sigh of relief. "I always knew you to be a wise and fair man."

"I shall revise my judgment to better fit your circumstances," the magistrate said.

"You are most gracious. I shall not forget this."

"No, I am sure you will not." The magistrate took the envelope and put it in his desk drawer. "Fortunately for you, you have a large parcel of empty land. It only needs to be cleared of the ashes. In lieu of the fine, you will give that land to your former workers so that they can build houses for themselves. Whether or not they choose to work your pepper vines is completely up to them."

"What?! No, please—"

"Should certain of them decide they have no wish to ever lay eyes on you again, they will be free to sell their portion of the land."

"Magistrate! Sir!" Desai begged. "You cannot mean that!"

"I most certainly do. Now, if you will excuse me, I have a full calendar today."

But when the magistrate returned from his noon meal, he was most unhappy to be greeted by Ajay Varghese and his third son, Ramesh. The magistrate sighed loudly, shot a scathing look at his assistant, and reluctantly allowed the landlord to follow him into his office.

"Sir," Ajay Varghese began, "I only request a small amount of your time."

The magistrate rolled his eyes.

"I understand the pressure on you to deal with this *Harijan* situation that has been brewing ever since Dinish Desai so unwisely allowed a teacher to conduct reading classes for them on his land."

"Please, Varghese, come to the point."

"I humbly request that you rethink the ten-thousand-*rupee* fine against me. Because of a misunderstanding over their status as workers, many of my laborers—all of them my debtors, I should add—have left my employ. And with my rice harvest not yet complete! My sons and I must hastily find new workers and make out contracts with them, which will cost us far more than we expected. In addition, much of my rice crop was badly damaged by the heat. I simply cannot afford to pay that fine."

"Sell something," the magistrate said. "Your wife's jewelry, perhaps?"

"My rice harvest is not yet in," Ajay Varghese repeated. "Yet it must feed not only my village, but the neighboring village as well."

"Since your neighbor happened to be burned out and his harvest destroyed."

"Unfortunately," Ajay said. "Most unfortunately."

"Yes," the magistrate said dryly. "I can see how deeply you feel for him."

"Oh, I do! I most certainly do!" Ajay insisted. "And also for your position in all of this, sir. In fact, in appreciation of your efforts, I brought you a small gift." Ajay took an envelope from his shirt pocket and laid it down on the desk.

The magistrate heaved a weary sigh. "Come, come, Varghese. What is it you ask of me?"

"Please, sir, rethink that fine you levied against me."

The magistrate shut his eyes and caressed his throbbing temples. When he looked back up at Ajay, his face had softened. "Your words have touched me," he said as he reached for the envelope and pushed it into his drawer.

"Thank you, sir!" Ajay said with a bow. "I knew you to be a sensible man."

"While I cannot see my way clear to reduce the amount of your fine, I do appreciate what you said about your rice needing to feed two villages because of the fire that destroyed so much of Dinish Desai's land. Your concern over his misfortune moved me. So I will add the condition that you divide your rice crop evenly between yourself and him."

"What?!" Ajay struggled to control himself. "I am worse off than I was before I came to see you! Before I came here in person and rewarded you with a gift!"

"Not at all," the magistrate said. "In consideration of your visit, I will drop the matter of the fire. I will not look further into the cause of that strange event that occurred so soon after the monsoon rains, while the air remained cool and the hay fresh."

Ajay opened his mouth to speak, but he could think of nothing to say that wouldn't get him deeper into trouble.

"Good of you to come by," the magistrate said as he turned his attention back to a pile of papers on his desk.

Ajay Varghese made no move to leave. "But . . ." he began. "The thing is . . ."

Without looking up, the magistrate waved him away. "Good-bye, Varghese. Be off with you."

For most of a week, Divena seldom saw anyone. She made a cook pit off to the side of the church building, and there she prepared her own rice. She found two nice stones to throw into the fire so that she could fry *chapatis*. Her water pots she filled from a nearby pond. She had brought along the Holy Bible that belonged to her grandmother's father, and to pass the time, she read it. She also read a book called *Pilgrim's Progress* that the professor lent her. Divena found it a difficult book to read, but she enjoyed the challenge. And every day she walked up the path among the pepper vines and wondered what would become of her.

One morning when she went out to start her cooking fire, she found a huge papaya lying beside it. Another morning she found a whole pineapple. Who left them, she had no idea. But that did not keep her from enjoying the delicious fruit.

On Sunday, however, the church filled up. Some people came early, but most didn't arrive until the afternoon. They had to walk all the way from Landlord Varghese's settlement.

"The rice harvest is almost finished," Maya told Divena. "I do not know what I will do then, but whatever it is, I will do it with money!"

"Did you hear the newth?" Malik announced. "Landlord Dethai ith giving the old thettlement land to uth! When the harvetht ith over, we can build our own houtheth on it."

"Or we can pay someone else to build it," Jeba laughed.

For that one day, no one seemed to be in a hurry. Everyone lingered, talking and laughing together. They paused for a breath of air, then they talked some more.

Udeep had just started to beat out a rhythm on his *ghatam* drum when Sundar stepped through the door. As one, every person turned to stare. Sundar didn't sit down. He simply stood beside the open back.

Looking straight at Sundar, Nagmani said, "Welcome to the house of the Lord. Welcome, everyone."

Later in the afternoon, after their worship time ended, the newly freed men and women talked about the future. "This is a church, yes, but it does not have to be *only* a church," Kilas said. "The professor could hold his classes here. Outside when the weather is nice, inside when the rains come."

"It could serve as a schoolhouse for the children, too," Jeba suggested. "Someday. If a teacher should ever come to us."

"If other *Dalits* are willing to teach us things, they could do it right here," Aswati said. "Maybe we could work together to grow cashew nuts on our land. If we knew how. If we had any cashew nut trees."

"Strangers could wander in and demand shelter from you, and no one would ask questions."

Divena gasped. She recognized that voice! With great dread, she slowly turned around. There he was, her father. Stony-faced, he stared in through the window, straight at her.

"Any stranger at all, with any story, could come and live among you." Puran laughed out loud. "Strangers can come, but then they can suddenly be gone. And no one will know where to look for them. Or when they might be back."

Divena covered her face and wept.

Sundar, with Jeet and Nagmani behind him, ran out the back and around to the window, but Puran had already slipped away.

"You cannot stay here," Maya told Divena. "It is not safe."

"Nowhere is safe for me," Divena cried.

"You need a good place to hide," Nagmani said. "Maybe we can put up a lean-to deep in the pepper groves."

"No, no!" Maya insisted. "She must not be out there all alone. And it must be some place more secret than that. Where her father would never think to look."

"Maybe you could go live with Kilas and Baka," Jeet offered.

"Only a few of us must know the place," Aswati said, looking around suspiciously. "Only the ones she trusts most."

"I cannot hide forever," Divena protested.

"No, no. Not forever," Maya said. "Only until the danger is past. Only until your father stops searching for you."

"He said he would never give up," Divena wailed, "and I know him. He never will."

"Well, you cannot stay here," Maya said. "Even if we all stay with you, it simply is not safe."

They talked and argued until long after the sun had set, but still no one had come up with a workable plan.

Sundar, who had stayed off to the side, cleared his throat. "I know the perfect hiding place," he said. "A place your father will never look. Nor will my father."

Divena wiped her eyes and looked up at him.

"Where?" Maya demanded.

"In my father's labor settlement."

❧

Divena, eyes wide, sat stiffly in the front seat of Sundar's truck. She squeezed herself as tightly against the door as she could manage. She had ridden in bullock carts. She rode between the chickens and the heavy man on the back of a faded green and black motorbike that one time. A few times she and Selvi rode to class in the back of the farmer's truck. But never before had she sat on the front seat of a truck. With a man, no less. A man of high caste!

Divena turned to check the back window, just to make certain the others were still behind her. Malik, Nagmani, and Udeep sat on one side in the truck bed, and on the other side were Maya, Aswati, and Jeba.

"It is better that you ride up here," Sundar said. "You will not be so easily seen."

Yes. He was right, of course. Divena relaxed—but not much.

"I come from a Christian family," Sundar told her. "Saint Thomas Christians is what they call us. It is not a flattering term. Because so many of us dress western instead of Indian, is why. Even more, because so many of our number offend others by dancing and smoking and drinking alcohol." Sundar cleared his throat. He hastened to say, "Not me, of course. I do eat meat, but that is allowed for Christians. I do not want to offend Hindus, though. We are all Indians together."

The speed of the truck made Divena's head spin round and round. She gripped the door handle.

"Do not pull on that or the door will open," Sundar cautioned.

Divena turned around to check the back of the truck again.

"Your friends are still there," Sundar said gently. "You need not worry. You are perfectly safe."

33

October

Day after day, week after week, Sundar found an increasing number of reasons to make his way out to the rice paddies. Diligence to see the harvest completed, he told himself. Certainly Humaya had been overseer long enough to require little supervision, yet Sundar insisted that the prudent approach must be to personally follow the progress of the laborers. Even though they knew the routine perfectly well. Even though they had proven themselves to be good, steady workers.

The men chopped the rice stalks, and the women followed along behind to tie the stalks into bundles. As the day progressed, the women gathered up the tied bundles and carried them on their heads to the storage shed where Malik and Nagmani stacked the shocks to dry.

As Sundar checked the women's progress for the third time since dawn, Jeevak made an exaggerated point of shading his eyes and gazing up at the sky, then pointing out the straight-up position of the sun. "I have never known you to pay such close attention to the gathering of rice bundles, Brother," he said to Sundar. "Is this a new interest of yours?"

Sundar flushed crimson. Jeba and Rupali, who had just arrived with bundles and were in the process of lifting them off their heads, kept their eyes averted.

"Perhaps I am required to pay closer attention because the women are such an on-going interest of yours," Sundar replied. "Brother."

Sundar and Jeevak glared at each other. Jeba and Rupali hurried away. Malik and Nagmani grabbed up the bundles, the same as they had done for days. Only this time, both gave the cut rice their undivided attention.

"I would suggest that the men doing the chopping need more supervision than do the women carrying the rice bundles," Sundar said.

Jeevak glowered, but his brother held his ground.

"Work faster!" Jeevak called out to Malik and Nagmani as he hurried away.

After he had gone, Nagmani murmured to Sundar, "Divena is safe inside. The women are watching over her."

When the harvest ended, so did the workers' contracts with the Varghese family. Many of Dinish Desai's former laborers left the Varghese area in order to claim places of their own on Desai's burned-out land, and to set about putting together their own new settlement. Many of Ajay Varghese's old laborers came back to him, but every one of them demanded a new contract. Ajay had no choice but to comply because the land had to be prepared for the winter crop. Divena didn't know these people, and they didn't know her. She stayed close to her hut and did her best to avoid unnecessary contact.

For many weeks, Divena didn't go back to the church. It frightened her to walk along the open road. And though Sundar Varghese offered to drive her in his truck, she refused. She knew it would not be right.

So although it surprised Divena the day she saw Maya walk up to her door, it also brought her much joy.

"Are you working here?" Divena asked.

"No," Maya said. "I only came to see you."

"Why? Is something wrong?"

Maya laughed. "No, nothing. I only wanted to ask you to come and see us at the church. We miss you."

"I do not dare. My father—"

"Nagmani and Jeet will walk with us," Maya said. "They are waiting in the courtyard, over near the well. You will be perfectly safe."

"I do not know—"

"Do come!" Maya said. "So much is happening now. It is an important time for all of us. And for you, too, of course, because you are a part of us."

Divena had to admit, it did feel wonderful to be outside. It seemed as though she had been locked away for a year. To breathe in the fresh, cool air of fall brought a spring to her steps and a smile to her lips.

"Many of the houses at the new settlement are almost finished," Maya said. "Oh, and do you remember Aswati's idea about us growing a grove of cashew nut trees? That is exactly what we plan to do. All of us working together, you see, to . . ."

Divena listened, but not fully. She had to force herself not to leap up into the air and sing at the top of her voice.

"Auntie Rani brought a *Dalit* woman from another village to talk to us about growing cashew nut trees and to answer our questions. In her village, they have groves of cashew trees as well as mango trees. The women are going to help us grow the cashew trees and harvest the nuts and everything. After a while we will also have mangos, but not right away. The woman who came told us how to get mango seeds at the market and make them sprout quickly by . . ."

Divena tried to see herself in a house of her own, surrounded by cashew nut trees and mango trees. She sucked in a deep breath. She could almost smell the mango blossoms. Oh, and the ripe fruit, too. Like the mango Selvi brought for *Ammama*. The one they did *not* offer to the goddess. How good it tasted! Cashew nuts and mangos, all she wanted. All her own.

". . . to move the church to the new settlement, because most of us are Christians, anyway. It will be a perfect place to start the school—for the children during the day and for adults in the evening. We have to wait on that, though, because . . ."

Divena tried to picture herself with children of her own. Three little ones, two boys and a girl. She and the children, all laughing together. Her teaching the children to read out of *Ammama*'s father's Bible. She would tell them the whole story of her family, starting with poor little Ashish, who dared to drink from the wrong well, of her grandmother Shridula, who was forced to live at the landlord's house but escaped. Of the old missionary Miss Abigail, who wore a blue lace dress. Of . . .

"Divena? Divena!" Maya said. "Are you even listening to me?"

"Uh . . . yes. Yes, of course." Divena shook the silly visions out of her head. "It all sounds wonderful, Maya. Every bit of it."

Well, not all of it. Not the part where her never-to-be children disappeared from her dream. Not the part where her father forever prowled through the shadows—watching, watching, watching. Not the part that left no place anywhere for Divena.

When they got to the church, Jeet and Nagmani excused themselves and headed back up the path. Houses half built, they explained. Land still needing to be cleared. Vegetable gardens to plant.

Divena followed Maya inside. To her surprise, the only ones there were Uncle Professor and Auntie Rani. Divena searched their faces for signs of bad news. Not a death in the family. It could not be that. Divena had no family left to die.

Uncle Professor smiled broadly, and Auntie Rani actually clapped her hands. The news could not be too bad.

Because Divena felt obligated to say something, she ventured, "Maya told me about the new settlement. What great good news."

"Yes," the professor said. "A blessing none of us could have foreseen."

"Even a school for the children," Auntie Rani bubbled. "Did Maya tell you that?"

Divena smiled. "Jeba must be especially pleased."

The professor cleared his throat. "Divena, have you given any thought to your future?"

Divena willed her lips not to tremble. "I have tried," she said.

"You are an intelligent young woman. Both Auntie and I could see that immediately."

"We knew you could already read," Auntie Rani said. "From the very first, we knew that."

"You are resourceful, too," the professor added. "That is an important quality. You think for yourself, but always with utmost kindness toward others. Both are characteristics to be treasured."

"And you are beautiful to look at," Auntie Rani said with a big grin.

Divena had no idea how to respond to such kind comments, so she looked silently from one to the other.

"You would make a fine wife, Divena," Uncle Professor said.

"A wonderful wife!" Auntie Rani agreed. "And a wonderful mother, too."

Divena looked questioningly at Maya, but her friend only grinned back at her.

"I am sorry, Uncle and Auntie," Divena said. "But I do not understand. I know I am of an age to marry, but my grandmother could not leave me money for a dowry. And my father . . . well, you know about my father."

"Not every man asks for a dowry," the professor said.

Divena shook her head. "I will not marry a man who is a drunkard or a gambler. Or one who is too old to work anymore."

"How about a young man who works hard? A man who admires you very much? Who cares a great deal for you?"

Another trick, Divena thought. Probably from her father. With fear fast building into panic, she looked from the window to the open back wall. But her father wasn't there. Sundar was. Sundar Varghese. The landlord's son.

Divena stared at him, then at Maya and Uncle Professor and Auntie Rani. Then back at Sundar again.

"Sundar asked us to approach you on his behalf," the professor said. "If it were possible, I would ask your grandmother for permission. Unfortunately, that is not possible."

"Surely she is watching from heaven," Auntie Rani said.

Uncle Professor asked, "Divena, will you consent to marry Sundar Varghese?"

It must be another dream. Surely a wonderful delusion. Another of her silly imaginings. Soon someone would call for her to pay attention, and she would wake up. She would never tell anyone about this dream, though. She would not dare do that.

"Divena?" Sundar said. "Will you marry me?"

"I . . . I . . . cannot," Divena whispered. "I am a *Dalit*. I am *Untouchable*."

"Not in the eyes of God," Sundar said. "Not in my eyes, either."

Divena couldn't speak. She didn't want to. To talk would awaken her from her dream.

"Caste is Hindu, Divena," Sundar said. "It is not Christian. We are Christians, you and I. Why should we be bound with Hindu fetters?"

"Your father would see me dead," Divena said. "Your father would find you and have you killed, too."

"I may as well be dead to him already," Sundar said. "We will leave here. We will go to the city where no one knows us and caste is not as important."

"If you marry me, you will become like me," Divena whispered. "You, too, will be an *outcaste*."

"I do not care. I am ashamed of my caste. Castes are not for Christians. God has neither *Brahmins* nor *Untouchables*."

Tears flooded Divena's eyes and ran down her cheeks.

"So much you have learned!" Sundar said. "Well, I can learn, too. I do not need to bob my head gently as my family does. I can learn to bounce it as you do. I will say *Dalit* instead of *Harijan*. When we go to a tea shop, I will decline the glass cups and take my tea in a clay cup. I know I will make thoughtless upper caste mistakes, but you can correct me."

"You inherited wealth from your father," Divena said. "I inherited nothing but debt. Your father—"

"I ask nothing of my father. I will leave his house and his land and his money with a smile on my face, and I will never look back."

Divena could not trust herself to speak.

"I can speak English. I know how to read and write in English and Hindi and Malayalam, and also how to keep accounting books straight," Sundar said. "Surely I will be able to find a job in the city. If I cannot, I will work outside the city in a rice field. I certainly know how to do that."

A smile crossed Divena's face.

"I know it will not be easy," Sundar said. "But I will be beside you."

Divena's smile faded. "What if you change your mind? What if we go to the city and you leave me?"

Sundar got down on his knees and lifted his arms to heaven. "As God is my witness, Divena, I will never leave you. If you marry me, I will stay by your side until we go to heaven."

Suddenly Divena's legs felt as though they no longer had bones in them. She sank to the floor, covered her face, and wept.

34

November

As the sun sank low in the sky, and the shadows of the pepper groves grew long and dark, Auntie Rani moved to the front of the little church and lit a row of candles that had been set along the edges of the wooden cross. They cast a soft glow over Divena, who sat on the floor in front of the cross, her head bowed. She wore a magnificent red and yellow silk *sari*, and her beautifully oiled hair framed a radiant face. The *sari*, a wedding gift from Uncle Professor Menon and Auntie Rani, had to be the finest thing ever to touch Divena's skin. On her arms, gold bangles sparkled, a wedding gift from Sundar.

Sundar Varghese sat beside her, dressed in new trousers and a silk shirt. He, too, had his head bowed.

Professor Menon looked out at the assembled guests. "This evening you will witness a wedding like none you have ever seen before," he said. "No feast will follow, though I know you have not come for the food."

A smattering of giggles twittered around the room.

"You know these two as Sundar Varghese and Divena," the professor said. "That is who they were this morning. But this afternoon I had the blessed privilege of baptizing them. To symbolize their complete break with the past, they have taken new names. Christian names. A big step for Divena, to be sure, for she comes from a wonderful line of 'Blessings.' The names they chose carry on this tradition."

Murmurs. Smiles.

"I am pleased to introduce to you Baruch, whose name means 'greatly blessed.'" Professor Menon put his hand on Sundar's shoulder. "And Anna, whose name means 'blessed with grace.'" Here he gently touched Divena's shoulder.

"Baruch Sundar," the professor said, "do you understand that if you marry Anna Divena you will lose your caste standing?"

"Yes," Baruch Sundar said in a voice loud and firm. "And I gladly bid it farewell in order to spend the rest of my life with Anna Divena. She will be my partner. My heart and my spirit."

The room grew quiet. The only sound was the persistent buzz of mosquitoes.

"Marriages are arranged by parents and relatives," Professor Menon said. "That is the way of India. But here this evening you will witness something different. You will see a love marriage."

An audible sigh rose up in the room. Or was it a gasp?

"Anna Divena has no appropriate parent to make a marriage arrangement for her. According to the law books, if a girl is not married by her parents soon after puberty she may choose her own husband. She can have a *svayamvara* marriage—a marriage of self-choice. But here today we have an especially exceptional marriage. Not only does Baruch Sundar have parents who would gladly choose for him—yea, who *demand* to choose for him—but he is the one who chose Anna Divena for himself. He chose romantic love."

Not a sound broke the stillness of the room. Even the mosquitoes fell quiet. Romantic love was the stuff of storybooks. The forbidden subject of the most daring cinema movies. Romantic love was impossible love.

"As surprising as this might be, it pales in the light of the other matter that makes this marriage so unique. Never before have I known a member of an upper caste who, simply for the sake of love, gave up his standing and all the privileges of caste. Never have I known one to willingly become *Untouchable*."

Baruch Sundar flushed crimson. Tears filled Anna Divena's eyes and spilled down her cheeks.

"The love of God drew them to the church, and to faith. You accepted them with love and made them your own. And here they found each other."

The wedding had none of the ceremonies the Varghese family would have demanded for their first son. Yet simple and short as it was, it bound Anna Divena and Baruch Sundar together in the eyes of God.

At the end of the ceremony, Professor Chander Menon held up a plate of torn *chapatis*. "In remembrance of Christ, who left his high heavenly home to become one of us and make a way for our salvation," he said. Baruch Sundar took a piece, and then Anna Divena took one off the same *Untouchable* plate. They both ate.

Professor Menon picked up a clay cup and held it high. "In remembrance of Christ, whose blood was shed for us." He handed the cup to Anna Divena first, and she drank from it. Then he handed the same clay cup to Baruch Sundar, high caste *Kshatriya* son of a powerful landlord. The entire group held their collective breaths. Without a moment's hesitation, Baruch Sundar lifted the cup to his lips and drank. The group uttered a united gasp.

Unthinkable. Impossible. Yet it had to be true. They had seen it with their own eyes. The man of so very high birth had put his lips on an *Untouchable* cup. Not only that, but he did it directly after an *Untouchable* had drunk from it!

"In the name of the Father, the Son, and the Holy Spirit," the professor said. "In Christ, there is no rich nor poor, no male nor female, no slave nor free. In Christ, there is no caste. All of us are one in Him."

Although no one served a fancy wedding feast, everyone did receive a special treat. Maya and Auntie Rani handed around dishes of sweet *payasam* pudding. Such a delicious delicacy! Raisins and cardamom and pistachio nuts, and . . . what brought the dish that distinct flavor?

"Saffron," Auntie Rani said. "To celebrate this special day, I flavored the pudding with saffron."

Saffron, the royal spice. The flavor of high caste. *Dalits* were not allowed to use saffron. Everyone ate their royal pudding with special delight. They smacked their lips and licked their fingers. When the pudding was gone, they ran their fingers around the edges to get the last bites and licked them again. They smiled wicked smiles and licked their bowls clean.

No difference in Christ. No caste. No *Untouchables*.

Afterward, the group hung garlands of marigolds around the new couple's necks, each one offered with a tearful prayer for God's blessings and protection. But Anna Divena and Baruch Sundar could not linger. The professor and his wife rushed them to their jeep. They must get to Cochin in time for the midnight train to the great city of Chennai. They absolutely must be away by the time Ajay Varghese read the letter from his son.

"I feel as though I am giving up on my sister," Anna Divena said sadly. "Now she has no one."

"Do you think you are the only one who cares about her?" Professor Menon asked. "God gave your sister her beautiful voice. Surely he will allow her to use it to be a blessing and encouragement to others."

"Could that be true?" Anna Divena asked.

"It could be," Auntie Rani said.

❧

The railway platform bustled with men, with families, with bony stray dogs that howled out their hunger. And also with child beggars. "A *rupee*? Ten *paise*?" the ragged children called as they pushed their way between travelers, expertly dodging kicks and swats. "A piece of bread? A *chapati*? Please, a *rupee*? Just ten *paise*?"

Baruch Sundar pulled out a handful of coins and handed them around. In a flash, a cloud of tattered children swarmed the new couple, clinging to them and yelling until a policeman came by and swatted them away. "Put your purse away," he scolded Baruch Sundar. "Do not encourage these rascals."

Eager to get away, Baruch Sundar whispered to Anna Divena, "We have first-class tickets. Follow behind me and let me do all the talking."

Yes. She understood. If she opened her mouth, if she bobbed her head too emphatically, she would give away her caste. Suddenly there might be no more room in first class. She might find herself squeezed into the steaming hot cattle-car conditions of third class. Yes, she understood perfectly.

A turbaned Sikh and his turbaned son pushed up behind them. A dark-skinned *Dalit* pressed in from one side and a woman laden with packages from the other. In the crush of the crowded railway platform, one could not possibly concern oneself with the unwelcome touch of the lower classes.

"Two in first class!" Baruch Sundar called out.

Anna Divena stared wide-eyed at everything. At the skeletal bodies of the abandoned children who swarmed the platform, at the sweating porter who so effortlessly threw their two bags up onto his shoulders, at the tea vendors with their urns and their clay cups that could be broken after one use and tossed out on the tracks. She followed her husband into a small compartment, only big enough for the two of them and their bags. Baruch Sundar pulled down the window blinds and sat back with a sigh.

"Do you think your father has read the letter you left him?" Anna Divena asked.

Her husband reached over and touched her arm. "Do not worry," he said. "The train is ready to leave."

"No!" Ajay Varghese roared. "No, no, no!"

Ramesh hurried out of his room, still rubbing sleep from his eyes. Hanita sprang from her bed and came running.

"What is it?" Hanita asked. "More trouble from the magistrate? At this hour?"

"Jeevak!" Ajay bellowed. "Jeevak, bring me the truck! We must leave immediately for the railway station in Cochin. Hurry, Jeevak. Now!"

Ajay Varghese had been watching television when his servant handed him the envelope. "Who is it from?" Ajay had asked without taking his eyes from the screen.

"I do not know," his servant said. "Someone knocked at the door, but when I answered, no one was there. Only this envelope for you."

At first Ajay set it aside, intending to wait until the show ended. But his curiosity got the best of him. A *familiar hand*, he had thought as he glanced at the writing.

Now Ajay stood shaking, his face flushed a purplish red.

"Husband, what is it? What is it?" Hanita's hands flew to her face. "Whatever happened?"

"Your son left us." Ajay struggled to speak. "He married a . . . a *Harijan*. Now he is gone."

Hanita burst into tears. "You must stop him! You must get him and bring him back!"

"It is too late to stop him. But I fully intend to get him. And when I do, I will break his neck in two! I trusted that boy. I promised him everything I have. And what does he give me in return? Humiliation! He disgraced the name of Varghese."

"Was he married by a priest?" Hanita cried. "If not, we can have the marriage undone. Sundar was not of sound mind, Husband. No, he obviously was not. He could not possibly have understood what he was doing."

"What does he think?" Ajay ranted. "That if he finds a comely girl, he need only say a few words and the practices of thousands of years will disappear? That caste is nothing more than an old barbed wire fence to be yanked down and trampled underfoot? No! To change one's caste is to fly in the face of nature. To fly in the face of God Himself!"

Jeevak rushed in with Ramesh behind him. "Ramesh told me what happened. I am sorry, Father, but you are too late. The train is scheduled to leave for Cochin at midnight. It is already past that hour. I can drive you there, but what good will it do? Sundar is already gone."

Hanita covered her face and moaned.

"You mean he married that Divena girl who was supposed to be mine?" Jeevak exclaimed. "He cheated me once again?

You signed a contract with her father! You cannot let that crippled, old, broken-down creep get the best of you!"

"He will not," Ajay vowed. "At first dawn, you go to his hovel and pull him out of his sleep. Take him to the settlement, toss him into the worst of the huts, and lock the door. He will labor for me until his fingers are raw and his back broken."

"He will not stay," Ramesh said. "Everyone knows the law now."

"Yes, the law. But for once it will help us. Remind Puran I have his signed agreement, Jeevak. With a kick and a punch, let him know that at any time I can take it to the magistrate and prove that the wretch tried to sell his daughter to me."

"My son, my son!" Hanita wailed.

"Your son is now a *Harijan*," Jeevak said. "An *Untouchable*!"

Ajay, stunned to hear the situation spoken so bluntly, stumbled backward and sank down onto the couch.

". . . all this and more happening in the cities," said the announcer on the television. "It is a new day for our country. A new day for India."

The train rounded a sharp turn, jolting Anna Divena out of her slumber. Quietly she reached over her husband to raise the window shade. The golden light of the rising sun cast a long shadow over the train rails. Birds, freshly awakened from their night's rest, sailed overhead.

Anna Divena smiled and arranged her mussed hair. Then she smoothed out the skirt of her *sari*. Such a gorgeous garment! Oh, if only her grandmother could see it. If only she could know!

Baruch Sundar opened his eyes and stretched.

"It is a new day," Anna Divena said.

Baruch Sundar smiled. "For us, it is a new life."

"You are not sorry, are you?" Anna Divena asked anxiously. "I mean, about . . . everything?"

Baruch Sundar grasped her hand and held it tightly in both of his. "Never. Today is the day we start planning for better days to come."

Anna Divena looked out the window. So much land rushing past, and not a bit of it familiar to her. So many people awakening to begin what to them was another normal day. Both those people and their days were strange and unknown to Anna Divena. Strange, unknown, and amazing.

"Someday, a long time from now, we will tell our children that my great-great-grandfather Virat the *chamar* had to tie a cup over his mouth and a broom to his back in order to visit your great-great-great-grandfather the landowner in his part of the village," Anna Divena said. "What do you suppose they will think? Will they believe us?"

"I think they will find it most difficult to believe," Baruch Sundar said. "I pray they will."

Anna Divena considered for a moment. "Imagine what our own great-great-grandchildren might think. Perhaps they will not be able to understand any of it at all. Perhaps by that time, India will no longer know the meaning of caste."

Epilogue

1995

Baruch Sundar watched as his three-year-old son, Daniel Harpreet, carefully stacked his wooden blocks higher and higher. "Look at that," Baruch said. "I think that boy might grow up to be an engineer, just like his Uncle Ramesh."

Ramesh laughed out loud. "I hope he does not have to take his exam three times before he passes!"

The two brothers sat in silence and watched the child build his tower. The higher it grew, the more it leaned to the side.

"It has been a long time," Baruch Sundar finally said. "What of Father?"

Ramesh bobbed his head gently. "He cannot change. Life has been a disappointment for him. You left, then I did." Ramesh wrinkled his brow. "These days Mother spends most of her time in her room. Jeevak's wife does not like her. And Father—I do believe his only pleasure is to make certain Puran's life is miserable. He takes all his frustrations out on that little man. Works him hard. Too hard. Berates him constantly and punishes him for everything." Ramesh shrugged. "But who am I to say? Perhaps it is right. *Karma* and all."

"They are village people of the old India," Baruch Sundar said. "With them, everything is about caste, money and power, and the futility of life."

"Did you know that Father lost much of his land?" Ramesh asked. "Forced settlements to workers, mostly, and fines to the authorities. And Jeevak's gambling, of course."

"If only . . ." Baruch Sundar began. He stopped and shook his head. "I send letters, but every one comes back to me unopened. I telephone, but as soon as Father hears my voice, he hangs up."

"He is a stubborn man."

Tiny Joanna Nivedita toddled in, clinging to the skirt of a tall, lovely young woman. Baruch Sundar grabbed his baby daughter up and swung her high. Joanna shrieked with delight. "Meet your niece," Baruch Sundar said to his brother.

Even as Ramesh smiled, his eyes turned back to the young woman. "Oh!" Baruch Sundar said. "You have not met Tanaya. She is Anna Divena's sister."

Ramesh looked from the girl to his brother, then back to Tanaya. "Oh . . . I see." He looked back at the young woman's blind eyes. "That is . . . Well . . . I thought she was . . ." He flushed red and shut his mouth.

Tanaya turned toward him with a teasing smile. "I am pleased to meet you, too, Ramesh."

"Tea!" Anna Divena announced as she stepped into the room. She passed around the cups—steamed strong, creamy, and fragrant—then a plate of biscuits. When everyone was served, she settled herself between her sister and her husband.

"Tanaya was Baruch's wedding gift to me," she said, beaming. "It took Professor and Auntie Rani more than a year, but they found her, just as Baruch asked them to."

Little Daniel stood up and scowled at his leaning block tower. "Not good!" he pronounced, and he kicked it over. Joanna giggled and clapped her little hands.

"Would it not be wonderful if we could solve our problems so easily?" Ramesh asked with a laugh. "If all of India could?"

Baruch grabbed his son and pulled the child to him. As Daniel squirmed, Joanna climbed onto her father's lap. "Here it is, right in my grasp," Baruch Sundar said as he hugged his children. "New hope for a new India."

Afterword

Welcome to India!

The "Blessings in India" trilogy is fiction. Sort of. What I mean is that while the stories and characters are fictitious, the situations in which they live and move and suffer definitely are not.

Today, India enjoys a robust economy spurred by growing industries and a developing middle class. With a population that will soon surpass that of China, it is on the fast track to becoming the most populous country in the world. No wonder India has grabbed the attention of the West. It is indeed a land to be reckoned with.

Even so, much of the world knows little about India. We Westerners see it as mysterious and otherworldly. A land of cheap labor. The place where our phone calls for technical help are answered by sometimes difficult-to-understand technicians.

In truth, India is a country of amazing contrasts: A land with a soaring number of millionaires whose extravagant homes tower above huge slums and countless beggars. A nuclear powerhouse where traffic-jammed city streets are clogged with bullock carts and water buffalo and impossibly laden motorbikes and wandering sacred cows. A democracy scarred with the tragic burden of caste, the country's social order for more than three thousand years.

Untouchable is the name by which a huge segment of Indian society was known for thousands of years. *Outcastes*—oppressed and trodden under the feet of people of caste, doomed by *karma* and supposedly forgotten sins of a past existence to suffer the indignities and oppression heaped upon them. Polluted ones—trapped in a never-ending wheel of life and death and rebirth.

Mahatma Gandhi called them *Harijans*, which meant "Children of the god *Vishnu*," or more simply, "Children of God." Many Indians, mostly upper caste, still use that term. But the *outcastes* themselves hated the name. Children of God? That certainly is not what Hinduism teaches. And in no way does it reflect the way they are treated. Instead, they adopted their own term: *Dalits*. The name doesn't refer to a status or condition at all, but rather to a position. Derived from *Sanskrit*, the word means "crushed, broken, or downtrodden." It is a terrifyingly accurate reflection of the desperate condition of a people who are still today forced to endure social, religious, economic, and political oppression.

Of India's almost 1.1 billion people, approximately 300 million are *Dalits*. And their situation is still bleak. Many continue to be denied the most basic of human rights—including the use of public wells. Many in the upper castes still consider them backward and inferior. Many of their women are abused and sold into prostitution. Almost three-quarters of all *Dalits* live below the poverty line. Only a small percentage of *Dalit* women can read and write. Millions of *Dalit* children still work as child laborers.

The vast majority of twenty-first century slavery is attributed to debt bondage, the fate suffered by generations of Divena's family, ever since her great-grandfather—as a five-year-old child—chanced upon a well on an unexpectedly hot day. The practice has been officially outlawed in India since 1976. That's the good news. The bad news is that many legitimate debt bondage complaints are ignored by the government on the grounds that the problem "no longer exists in India." Yet as recently as the year 2000, Human Rights Watch estimated that forty million men, women, and children were enslaved as bonded laborers. A huge difference between that number and the Indian government's estimate of less than three hundred thousand. Most victims who suffer debt bondage fall outside the Hindu caste system. They are *outcastes*. *Untouchables*. *Dalits*.

But, as deeply entrenched as the caste system is in India, it is finally beginning to show major cracks. Not because of an enlightened commitment from the upper castes, unfortunately—although there most certainly are some high caste people dedicated to seeing the system change. Mostly, though, it is happening because the *Dalits* themselves are rising up and demanding change. More are insisting that adequate education be provided for their children. More are claiming their legal rights, and are finding a resonant, collective voice to do so.

Also, millions of Indians are becoming Christians. Often in the past, conversion was seen simply as a way to escape the discrimination and exploitation of untouchability. Searching for a way of escape is certainly understandable. One must be truly convinced of the truth of reincarnation, and the debt he or she owes for past sins, to quietly bow down and accept so crushing a fate. The thing is, for thousands of years, much horribly oppressive effort has gone into reinforcing this belief.

Can you imagine, then, the joy of a *Dalit* who discovers the truth that all humans are created in the image of God? That sin is universal, but so are God's love and grace?

Indian communities are being transformed. As more and more villages change, as more and more *Dalits* speak out and join together to act as a unified force, we will see an even greater movement toward a restructured society. And through God's grace, His people will lead the way. They will refuse to tolerate caste distinction in their churches as well as in their social lives. They will speak out against the crushing burden of marriage dowries, which is essentially the buying of a husband. They will rail against the prejudices that tolerate—even encourage—the killing of baby girls and the abuse of women. They will champion education for all—girls as well as boys, women as well as men.

Perhaps then Anna Divena's dream will come true. Perhaps the day truly will come when a generation of Indian children will hear stories of oppression under the caste system and will shake their heads in disbelief. "No!" they will exclaim. "That has to be fiction!"

Glossary of Terms

Achama: Malayalam for grandmother (father's mother)

Ahimsa: A Buddhist and Hindu doctrine promoting nonviolence toward all living beings.

Amma: Malayalam for mother

Ammama: Malayalam for grandmother (mother's mother)

Appa: Malayalam for father

Betel nut: A chew made of nuts and tobacco wrapped in the leaves of the betel plant

Brahma: Creator god of the Hindu "trinity." The other two gods are Vishnu, the preserver, and Shiva, the destroyer. (Not to be confused with *Brahmin*. See below.)

Brahmin: The highest and most honored of the *varnas*, or castes, in Indian society. Brahmins are the Hindu priests and spiritual leaders. They put great and minute emphasis on ritual purity, and are forbidden from doing any manual labor. They make up approximately five percent of India's population. (Not to be confused with the god *Brahma*. See above.)

Caste: Traditional Hindu society is divided into four main *varnas*, or hierarchical groups known as castes: Brahmins (5 percent), Kshatriyas (5 percent), Vaishyas (5 percent), and Sudras (50 percent). Below this fourfold caste structure are the *outcastes*—now called *Dalits*—an oppressed people forced in all ways to occupy the lowest positions of this social order (25 percent). Also outside the caste system are the "tribals," the indigenous Indian peoples. Technically, Christians and Muslims are also outside the system, since caste is really part of the Hindu religious philosophy, though in actuality most *outcaste* Christians and Muslims remain mired in its oppression. These and people of other nationalities and religions make up the other 10 percent of the population. Each caste has its own group of occupations associated with it.

Chaddar: A long strip of cloth, half the size of a *mundu* (see below), worn by men as a shawl or turban.

Chamar: One of the many *Untouchable* occupational sub-castes, this one being that of leather tanners.

Chapati: Round, flat-baked bread, similar to unsweetened pancakes or tortillas.

Chennai: The capital city of the Indian state of Tamil Nadu, Chennai (formerly known as Madras) is located on the Bay of Bengal. Chennai is the fifth most populous city in India.

Civit cat: A cunning-looking little animal, with a catlike body, long legs, a long tail, and a masked face resembling a raccoon or weasel. It is not really a cat at all, but is more closely related to a mongoose.

Cows, sacred: In India, "Mother Cow" is respected and looked after. Every one is considered sacred, and to harm a cow is a great sin. It is likened to harming one's own mother. The cow is also associated with mythological stories that surround several Hindu deities, including Krishna, said to have been raised by the son of a milkman.

Dalit: Term that *outcastes*, formerly known as *Untouchables*, adopted for themselves. It does not refer to a status or condition at all, but rather to their position in the Indian social system. Derived from the ancient Sanskrit, the word means "crushed, broken, or downtrodden."

Dharma: A moral law, or righteousness. This can vary, person to person, caste to caste.

Dowry: Money and/or property required of the family of the bride by the family of the groom in order to secure a marriage. The amount varies, depending on the "value" of the bride (husband, too, but it is the bride's family that pays). This is crippling for many families of girls. Dowry requirement is a major cause of the abandonment and even killing of female children. It is also a major cause of debt bondage.

Ganges River: "Mother Ganges," sacred river of the Hindus, runs for 1,560 miles, from the Himalayas to the Bay of Bengal. It is revered as the source of life and purity, and is itself considered a goddess. Though the river is horribly polluted, people flock to it to bathe, to perform ceremonies, to float their dead, and even to drink from it. The belief is that anyone who touches these purifying waters will be cleansed of all sins.

Ghatam: A type of drum used in South India. It is basically an earthenware pot. The drummer uses his fingers, thumbs, palms, and heels of his hands to strike the outer surface. An airy, low-pitched bass sound comes from hitting the mouth of the pot with an open hand.

Ghee: Butter, boiled and clarified. It is greatly prized, both as a food and as a part of ritual worship and the preparation of food for gods and goddesses.

Gram Panchayats: Local self-governments at the village or small-town level in India. As of 2002, India had about 265,000 *gram panchayats*.

Guduchi: Also known as *Amrit*, *guduchi* is one of India's most valued healing herbs.

Harijan: Mohandas Gandhi used this as a more humane term for *Untouchables*. Considered to mean "Children of God," the term actually meant, "Children of the god Vishnu."

Idli: Savory cakes popular in South India. Usually two to three inches in diameter, they are made by steaming a batter consisting of fermented black lentils and rice.

Jiggery: Also known as *gur*, this is a raw, syrupy juice made from sugar-cane or palm sap. It is used in India as a sweetening agent, and sometimes to give a syrupy texture to medicines.

Kara: A rich strip of edging that decorates a fine and expensive *mundu*.

Karma: The sum total of a person's actions that is believed to lead to his or her present fate. This major tenet of Hinduism easily brings about an atmosphere of fatalism that can lead to hopelessness.

Kerala: A beautiful southwestern Indian state that lies on the Arabian Sea in the shadow of the Western Ghats. The native language of this state is Mayalalam. Kerala is one of India's most populous states, and it boasts the highest level of literacy.

Kohl: This ancient eye cosmetic is a mixture of soot and other ingredients. As far back as the Bronze Age, Egyptian queens wore it to enhance their beauty.

Kshatriya: The second of the *varnas*, or castes, in Indian society. Formerly the kings and soldier-warriors, they, like the *Brahmins*, are respected and privileged. Also like the Brahmins, they may be "twice-born." Many are in the military, and many others are successful business owners and landlords. Kshatriyas make up about five percent of the Indian population.

Kurta: A collarless Indian shirt.

Mahatma: Great Soul. The title was often applied to Mohandas Gandhi.

Malayalam: The language spoken on the Malabar coast of South India, in the state of Kerala.

Mantra: Sacred words and sounds used for rhythmic chanting.

Manusmriti: The writings of Manu (though said to be authored by the god Brahma) that codified the caste system and sanctified it as a religious institution.

Monsoon: The July-to-September season of torrential rain and wind. While the rains bring relief from the suffocating heat that precedes it, it can be a time of treacherous downpours and flooding.

Mundu: A piece of thin cotton, linen, or silk cloth, fifty inches wide and five yards long, worn by men as a lower garment. It can be an ankle-length "skirt" or tied up to more closely resemble shorts.

Neem: A common and appreciated tree in India. Every part of this wonderful tree is used for medicinal purposes—bark, roots, leaves, branches, flowers, fruit.

Nirvana: The Hindu interpretation of heaven: an ideal condition of rest, harmony, stability, or joy. Most of all, it means freedom from the endless cycle of birth and death and rebirth, and all the suffering and fear that go with it.

Outcastes: Now called *Dalits*, these are the people who fall outside and below India's caste system. They are forced to occupy the lowest position in the Indian social order. For many centuries they accepted their miserable lot as their justly deserved *karma*, a result of their own sins in a former life. More recently they have attempted to assert the rights afforded them when India gained independence from Britain. These attempts are often met with strong resistance from the upper castes, and the results can be horrendous: torture, rape, massacres, and other atrocities. The dominant castes have deliberately prevented the *outcastes* from rising to the level of equality by imposing on them impossible limits in every area of life, from occupation to dress to the very right to eat and drink. The social order has been constructed to keep them helpless and subservient. A conservative estimate of the number of *outcastes* is 25 percent of the Indian population, or roughly 300 million people.

Paddy: This can refer to a food, in which case it means rice with the husk still on. More commonly it refers to the rice field itself—the paddy field.

Paise: Indian penny, 100 to a *rupee*. It is worth a small fraction of a U.S. penny. (See *rupee*.)

Pallu: The loose end of a *sari*. In fine *saris*, the pallu is beautifully decorated.

Panch-kos: Sacred road that forms a boundary around the sacred city of Benares.

Payasam: A delicious pudding made by boiling rice with milk and sugar, and flavored with cardamom, raisins, nuts, and sometimes saffron.

Punya: Meritorious or virtuous deeds, done with good thoughts and laudable intentions. These are believed to earn a person better *karma*.

Purification: A ritual washing to remove sin and/or pollution.

Rupee: The most commonly used Indian currency. Its value varies, as do all currencies, but as of this writing it is set at about 40 *rupees* to the U.S. dollar, or 2.5 cents.

Sadhu: An Indian holy man. Often, *sadhus* dress in saffron-colored robes that set them apart as dedicated to sacred matters.

Sari: A thin garment, fifty inches wide and five to six yards long, worn by Indian women, wrapped around the body to form a dress.

Sacred thread: A thin rope of cotton threads worn over the left shoulder by all initiated males of the *Brahmin* caste—and, though less frequently, by those in the second and third castes, too.

Salwar kameez: A more modern Indian outfit that consists of a loosely-fitted pajama-like pant (*salwar*) and a long tunic top that hits anywhere between the middle of the thigh and the top of the knee (*kameez*). The side seams are left open below the waistline, allowing the wearer to move freely and comfortably. The ensemble is completed by draping a loose scarf (*dupatta*) around the shoulders and then over the chest. This type of outfit is worn by both men and women, though the actual garments vary greatly.

Sanskrit: The ancient language of India, and the language of the *Vedas*. Now it is used almost exclusively by the *Brahmin* caste for religious purposes.

Sarpanch: The chairman of a local *Gram Panchayats*.

Scheduled Castes and Scheduled Tribes: The terms "Scheduled castes and scheduled tribes" (SC/ST) are the official terms used in Indian government documents to identify former "Untouchables" and indigenous tribes. But in 2008 the National Commission for Scheduled Castes noticed that the term *Dalit* was used interchangeably with the official term *scheduled castes*. The term *scheduled castes* was called unconstitutional, and the state governments were asked to stop using it.

Shiva: Hindu god of creation and destruction. (See *Brahman*.)

Sudra: The fourth of the *varnas*, or castes, in Indian society, supposedly created from the feet of the creator god, *Brahma*. Although they are still people of caste, they are of much lower status and privilege. They cannot be "twice-born." They are relegated to such jobs as laborers and farmers and servants. In fact, they are believed to have been created for the purpose of serving the higher castes. *Sudras* are not allowed to read, study, recite, or even to listen to the *Vedas*. The stated penalty for doing so is horrific maiming or death.

Svayamuara marriage: A marriage of self-choice as opposed to the usual arranged marriage.

Thag: An Indian word that is the source of the English word *thug*. The meaning is the same.

Untouchable: An *outcaste*, as determined by the laws of Manu. Depending on strata, and on the area of the country in which one lives, this could also mean a person is unseeable (meaning laying eyes on them is polluting). Not long ago, polluting a member of an upper caste, even with a shadow, a footprint, or a drop of spittle that may result from speaking or sneezing, was crime enough to result in drastic punishments.

Vaisya: Member of the third *varna*, or caste, in Indian society. Businessmen and traders, they are also high caste and may be "twice-born," although their status is much less than the two higher *varnas*. *Vaisyas* make up approximately five percent of the Indian population.

Vedas: Ancient Hindu scriptures, written in archaic *Sanskrit* in the form of a collection of mantras and hymns of praise to various gods. *Vedas* means "sacred, revealed knowledge." The four *Vedas* are: the *Rig Veda*, the *Sama Veda*, the *Atharva Veda*, and the *Yajur Veda*. The *Yajur Veda* is considered to be the oldest and most important. The foundation of the philosophy of Hinduism, the *Vedas* set forth the theological basis for the caste system.

Veranda: An external covered platform that sits at ground level of an Indian house. Most of a family's living took place on the veranda.

Vishnu: Hindu preserver god. (See *Brahman*.)